DAMNED IF YOU DON'T

CHAOS OF THE COVENANT, BOOK FIVE

M.R. FORBES

Published by Quirky Algorithms
Seattle, Washington

This novel is a work of fiction and a product of the author's imagination.
Any resemblance to actual persons or events is purely coincidental.

Cover illustration by Tom Edwards
tomedwardsdesign.com

ACKNOWLEDGMENTS

THANK YOU for coming back for more! Your enjoyment of my work makes telling fun stories one of the most rewarding endeavors I can think of.

THANK YOU to my beta readers for helping me make Damned if You Don't the best and cleanest story it can be.

THANK YOU to my wife, who has supported me through the best, worst, and in between, and like Queenie with her Rejects has always had my back.

1

Abbey stood in front of the shuttle, her eyes passing over each of her Rejects. In one sense, she was excited to see them, her heart feeling a sense of relief that they were alive and healthy and that she had been able to get them away from Azure. In another, she regretted that she was back with them. She was concerned for them. Afraid. She knew what came next. The Shard from the alternate universe had given her a hint, and the shard of the Shard that had saved her life only minutes before had made clear to her the rest of that truth.

"You aren't the one I would have chosen," he had said to her, in the fevered alternate reality she had found herself in when the interior of the shuttle had gone dark. "But you're the one who was available."

It hadn't been a glowing report, but after all she had experienced in the Seraphim compound she had come to the conclusion that maybe the race wasn't as angelic as the mythology around them might have implied. The fact that the Shard was a bit of an asshole wasn't a massive shock.

"I'm changing," she had said to him. "Losing all that I am to something violent and evil."

Her Shard was a male, of course, but she knew from the other one that it didn't have to be. He was handsome. Very handsome. Perfect. Too perfect. Golden hair, light brown skin, a perfect jaw and sparkling teeth. He seemed to know it, which had really ticked her off.

"You have the stink of Lucifer in you," he said. "I can see what he's done to my creation. The way he's twisted it is an abomination to me."

"I didn't ask for this. I didn't ask to be given the Gift, and I don't remember asking you to come along for the ride, either."

He had laughed, smiled, turned his head and moved his hands in a way that she supposed was intended to be seductive or sexy. She was too angry to find him sexy, even if he was.

"Fortunately for you, Abigail Cage, Lucifer's Gift is exactly what we both need. I created the seeds that created this galaxy. You were once nothing more than a mote of cosmic dust. A microscopic speck."

"Sounds familiar."

He nodded. "That is what I became. My life force, my blood, was placed into the Focus, but my physical self? It broke down into dust, and as the Shardship traveled I spread across the stars. It has taken long years for a piece of me to connect with someone with whom I am compatible. With you."

"I suppose you think I should feel honored."

"I'm a god."

"I'm not buying that. You died. Lucifer didn't even have to cut off your head to do it."

"I took an oath of non-violence more years ago than you can even conceive."

"That didn't work out very well for you. I'm guessing your oath is still in place, right? You aren't the one being violent. I am."

"I don't understand your anger toward me, Abigail. I'm trying to help you. I can save your life."

"From what I understand, the same uprising that's happening here is happening in other universes the One created. Which makes me wonder - are the Nephilim really the bad guys?"

His face had gone dark at that.

2

"Reconsidering your oath?"

"Don't be foolish. I have existed for countless eternities. I can't expect children to understand all that I understand. They rebel because they question instead of having faith in me when I have been nothing but benevolent."

"And arrogant. Maybe that was why they didn't like you?"

"The truth isn't arrogance."

"It is when you serve it from a high horse. What are you really?"

"I'm a god."

"Fine. Here's the deal then, god. I don't give a flying frag about Lucifer or you or ancient history. What I do care about is the galaxy I live in and the fact that Thraven wants to destroy half of it and enslave the other half so he can go back to Elysium and kill your bigger whole. And by the way, knowing you a little better, I understand why he wants to because you come off as a prick. But, he's a bigger prick than you, and I imagine we both want him dead. So we have common ground."

"I can help you, and by helping you help myself, but you have to allow me to enter."

"Haven't you already?"

"No. I'm on the surface. I won't go beneath the flesh without your permission."

"Another oath?"

"Yes."

"Why?"

"Because once, long ago, I made a mistake. A terrible mistake. I promised I would do better forever after."

"Gods don't make mistakes."

"Gods don't just suddenly appear. They are born as all things are born. I was made from eternities past, out of more failures than can be counted. There is salvation in the stars, Abigail, if we have the patience to attain it."

"Patience isn't my strong suit."

"I know. Will you let me in?"

"Can you stop the change? Can you prevent me from going insane?"

"Yes. That is why I didn't want you to take the second poison."

"The Serum?"

"It will limit you. It will stifle what you can become."

"And what's that? A Shard? I don't want to be a demi-god. I want to finish raising my daughter in peace."

"You can have it in time if we succeed."

"If?"

"I can help you, but I can't fight for you. What I can give you is an enhancement. An upgrade, so to speak."

"If it keeps me from becoming a mindless killing monster, you can do whatever the frag you want to me."

"You have to say yes, Abigail."

She hadn't hesitated. Now that she was back here, looking at her friends, her Rejects, she wondered if she should have given it a little more thought. What had she signed them up for? And were they up to the task?

Her eyes landed on Gant. He looked like he was about to explode, his eyes huge, expressing an adorable mix of excitement and trepidation.

She already knew the answer to that. It was the same answer she had given the Shard.

"Yes."

It had been immediate. The Light of the Shard had entered her, moving from the Hell brand and into her mouth, from her mouth to her lungs, from her lungs to her heart and throughout her body. She had regained her sight. She had regained her self. The demonsuit had broken away, leaving her naked, but she hadn't cared. There was no shame. She was what she was. She had felt the power moving through her, a cold burn against her insides that prickled her skin and made her veins glow with the Light as it made her into something new. Something unique.

"Gant," she said. "It's good to see you again."

"You too, Queenie," Gant replied. "Are you feeling okay?"

"I'm fine. But why are you all just standing there? We have work to do."

"You're sure you're okay, Queenie?" Bastion said. "You look a little. I don't know." He paused, not sure what words to use.

"Electric," Pik said.

"Yeah. Electric. I guess."

Abbey turned her attention back to Jequn. The Ophanim fell to her knees as she did, bowing her head all the way to the floor.

"My Queen," she said.

"I think the crazy may be contagious," Benhil said.

Jequn lifted her head, though she continued to kneel. "You don't know what you're looking at. I do. Have some respect."

"What's she talking about, Queenie?" he asked.

"This," Abbey replied, holding out her arms.

The glow was beginning to fade, though her skin was still a lighter shade of pale and the naniates remained around her, covering her like a lightsuit. A shardsuit. She was controlling them subconsciously, her connection to the Shard giving her a more innate connection to them. He had repaired the alterations that Lucifer had made. He had returned her naniates to their original state. While he couldn't reverse the changes they had already made, he had stopped her from continuing to alter. He had saved her as he promised.

The price was still unclear, but she was certain there would be one. There always was.

"The Shard," Jequn said. "It has joined with you."

"Shard?" Benhil said. "THE Shard? The piece of a god?"

"I wouldn't say joined," Abbey replied. "It gave me an upgrade. I also wouldn't say god. I'm not sure what the Shard or the One are, but I'm pretty sure it's not that. But yeah, he saved me from the change. He purified the Gift." She turned her arms over, showing off the suit she had made. "Do you like it?"

It shimmered at the question, as though it were made of crystal.

"I like it," Pik said. "You can almost see right through it."

Abbey made a face at him and then turned the shardsuit opaque. "Do you have to be an asshole?"

Pik shrugged.

"Queenie, you said we have work to do?" Gant said.

Abbey nodded, silently thankful to him for deflecting their attention away from her appearance. She was the same person she had been before. Mostly. She wouldn't claim her experience on Azure hadn't changed her or her perception of the war between the Seraphim and the Nephilim. It didn't change her goals or her desires, or her intention of stopping Thraven from ruining the galaxy.

"I need a debriefing, and then I want to talk to General Kett. We need to regroup and prioritize our targets." She looked around the hangar, her eyes stopping on the *Faust*. "What happened?"

"Uh. Queenie," Bastion said. "You should know up front. We didn't exactly leave Kett's company on the best of terms."

"What do you mean?"

"Well. We kind of disobeyed orders and took this ship from the Republic to come and get you."

"And crashed the *Faust* in the process," Bastion said.

Abbey raised her eyebrow.

"It's all on the up and up," Gant said. "Kett was being an asshole. He didn't want to let us come back for you."

"I see," Abbey said. "Cherub, I'm assuming since you're here that you agree with Gant's assessment?"

"Yes, Queenie," Jequn said. "My father was being an asshole. And the fact that you've been touched by the Shard proves that he was wrong."

"There's more," Bastion said.

"More?"

"He wiped Ruby."

Abbey felt her jaw clench. Ruby was their connection to Olus, who was the only person on Earth she could trust, and who was their best chance of staying current on events within the Republic.

"Why would he do something like that?"

"He told me he had a good reason," Jequn said. "But he wouldn't tell me what that reason was."

"He'll tell me what it was, and it had better be the best fragging reason I've ever heard, or I'm going to throw his ass out of the nearest airlock."

Gant chittered in reply to the statement. "It's good to have you back, Queenie."

2

Gant led Abbey out of the hangar with the rest of the Rejects trailing behind them. They passed some of the *High Noon's* crew on the way toward the bridge, and she could see how their faces changed at the sight of her, vacillating from fear to confusion to curiosity and back. She didn't blame them. She knew she didn't look normal anymore. Even though the internal Light of the Shard was beginning to fade and her skin was returning to normal, between the shardsuit, her hair, the ridges on her flesh, and her eyes, she definitely didn't blend in with the others. A part of her was bothered by the change. A bigger part was just grateful that it had been stopped. She wasn't going to turn into a complete monster. She still had a chance to stop Thraven. She still had a chance to provide Hayley a stable galaxy to grow up in.

"All hail the Queen," Pik bellowed as they reached the bridge.

Most of the crew didn't know how to react, but Erlan stood and bowed his head beside his station. As Abbey swept onto the deck and the other soldiers got a look at her, they reacted by standing and coming to attention.

All except Captain Davlyn. He was in the command chair, holding his jaw. Abbey could see the bruise on it beneath his fingers.

"Captain," Gant said. "I suggest you stand."

Davlyn glared at him, his anger obvious. "This isn't your ship, you furry little piece of shit. This is a Republic Naval vessel. I sent an emergency beacon out. They know what you did. They're going to come for you. You put the lives of my entire crew at risk."

"Oh, you sent an emergency beacon out?" Gant said mockingly. "Good for you. Too bad I disabled the transmitter while you were still unconscious when we first took the ship. Nobody is going to hear you scream, Captain. Look around. Your crew seems to get it. Why don't you?"

"Gant," Abbey said. "I'll take care of this."

"Okay, Queenie," Gant said.

Abbey moved in front of the Captain. "Captain Davlyn," she said. "My name is Abigail Cage."

Davlyn stared at her, his face turning pale. "You're the reason we came to this planet."

"I'm also the reason we escaped the planet. I disabled the two ships that were attacking you."

"What?" Davlyn said.

"What?" she heard Benhil say further back.

"Has Gant told you what's happening here? About the Nephilim? About Gloritant Thraven?"

"He's told me a lot of things."

"Do you believe them?"

"I don't know what to believe anymore." He glanced over at Gant. "But nothing I've been told has turned out to be untrue so far."

"Which leaves you in an interesting position, doesn't it, Captain?"

"What do you mean?"

"I'm guessing you had orders that brought you within range of the Rejects?"

"Rejects?"

"Gant, you never introduced yourself to the Captain?"

"Not officially," Gant replied.

"I'm sorry for the rudeness of my Gant," Abbey said. "We're Hell's Rejects." She put out her hand. "A pleasure to meet you, Captain."

Davlyn hesitated a moment before taking her hand. His grip was loose. He was afraid to touch her.

"What were your orders, Captain?"

"We located the *Brimstone* through a disterium trace, along with a larger fleet of ships. We were ordered to identify and confront it."

"You were ordered to attack the *Brimstone*?"

"Aye."

"By who?"

"Admiral Kuill."

"Of the Committee?"

"Yes. We launched the attack, and of course, our weapons were useless. We tried to retreat, but our ships wouldn't jump."

"General Kett used the Focus to keep them from escaping," Jequn said. "He sent his Gifted through the teleporters on the Seedships to the largest vessels in the patrol group. I convinced him to let the Rejects take this one, the *High Noon*."

"Thus allowing us to escape," Bastion said.

"And here we are," Abbey said. "You disobeyed the Admiral's orders by calling a retreat before you ever committed treason against the Republic by aiding known criminals."

"Wait a second," Davlyn said. "I didn't aid known criminals. That one was threatening to kill everyone on board." He pointed at Gant. "I made a judgment call. Follow his demands until I could get my crew to safety. That's all. Any good Captain would have done the same to protect their crew."

"Like I said," Abbey replied. "You're in an interesting position. Do you think the Republic is going to buy that story? Even if they do, what about the fact that you tried to run? It doesn't matter if you were successful or not. The logs don't lie. You had orders, Captain, and you didn't follow them."

"I have a duty to protect my crew."

"You have a duty to protect the Republic. You took an oath."

"Don't spit that shit back at me. Without my ship, you would still be stuck on that planet. I did what I thought was best. What is this, a trial?"

"Let's call it an examination of conscience. You understand that going back to the Republic is going to get you charged with treason and sent to Hell, don't you?"

Davlyn didn't look happy, but he nodded. "Yes."

"But you tried to send a beacon anyway? I've been to Hell, Captain. Trust me; it's not someplace you want to be."

"I have a duty to protect my crew. They're good individuals. Loyal soldiers. They followed me here without question, but I wouldn't ask them to follow me to Hell. You helped me get them out alive. I can bring them back to their families. I can take the fall for all of them."

"And that's what you want? To bring them home?"

"That's all I want. This whole mission turned into a complete frag job the moment we traced the disterium."

"And do you realize they aren't safe back in the fold of the RAS? Thraven will have them reassigned to the front lines and sent in for the slaughter a second time."

"The front lines of what? We aren't at war."

"Yes, you are. It hasn't been declared yet, but we're all at war. I thought you understood that? You can't protect your crew, Captain. And even if you could, the best way for them to protect their families is to fight back against the real enemy. To end the war with the Nephilim before the war between the Outworlds and the Republic can start. That's why I'm here. That's why I have skin in this game. I have a daughter of my own to protect."

"What are you suggesting?"

"I want you to join the Rejects," Abbey said. "You're exactly the kind of individual we're looking for."

"I'm loyal to the Republic."

"So am I. The real Republic. Not this bullshit puppet theater Thraven has turned it into. Help me get it back to what it was. Help us stop the Nephilim. No more beacons. No more bullshit. I need good individuals like you and yours."

Davlyn stared at her, their eyes locking. She held his gaze. They needed every ship they could get, and she would earn them one at a time if she had to.

"How do I know you won't be leading us right into disaster?"

"You don't," Abbey said. "I can't tell you where this is all going to lead. I can promise you I'm going to give everything I have to see it through. Look at me, Captain. Look at what I've already given. What this fight has already cost."

"If it's true that you disabled those ships on your own, it doesn't seem like it's cost you anything. You have a power I can't even comprehend."

"Believe me, Captain. There's a price. A heavy price. I can never go back to what I was."

"Would you want to?"

"Hell, yes. My dreams have been scattered to the stars. Now I only dream of my daughter's future."

"And if I refuse? Then what?"

"I'm going to repair the *Faust*. Once that's done, we'll leave, and you'll be free to do whatever it is you feel you need to do."

"Queenie," Gant said.

Abbey put up her hand. "Not your decision."

Davlyn took a moment. He turned his head away, looking at his bridge crew. They made eye contact, and she could sense their subtle nods. She wasn't so far removed from being a soldier that she couldn't remember why they had become soldiers in the first place. To protect what they believed in. To protect what they loved.

"I believe you," Davlyn said at last. "More than that, I've seen it for myself. As long as you're fighting for the Republic, the *High Noon* and her crew are yours."

"Thank you, Captain," Abbey said. "No more beacons?"

He smiled. "No more beacons. Where to, Miss Cage?"

"You can call me Queenie," Abbey said. "Welcome to the Rejects."

"You're going to regret it," Pik said, laughing.

3

"We had set a course for the edge of the Bain system," Captain Davlyn said. "We'll be there in an hour or so, but we can drop out of FTL and redirect now."

"That won't be necessary," Abbey said. "Stay on course. We'll adjust once we reach the original drop point."

"Adjust to where?" Gant asked.

"Back to General Kett," Abbey replied. "I have a few questions for him, and it seems like he owes me a bit of an explanation. Especially about Ruby."

"Ruby?" Davlyn said.

"She's a synth," Bastion offered. "A pleasure synth turned service synth, so probably the hottest thing you'll ever see in a Republic uniform." Bastion paused. "Well, after you, Queenie."

"You suck at flattery," Gant said.

"I do not," Bastion replied.

"Yeah, you do," Gant said. "Queenie, we haven't had much of a chance to talk. I know you're eager to put Kett back in his place, and damned if I'm not eager to see you do it, but Olus sent intel that I think you should be aware of before we decide which way to pivot."

"What kind of intel?"

"Thraven has Tridium Heavy Industries in his pocket, the same way he had Eagan Heavyworks under his control. While Eagan was tasked with perfecting the Nephilim's ancient tech, Tridium was given a more important mission."

Abbey didn't like the sound of that. "What mission?"

"I'll give you a hint," Bastion said. "It rhymes with hate."

"What?"

"That's a dumb hint," Pik said. "Queenie, it rhymes with Pleasium Fate."

"My hint was dumb?" Bastion said. "You might as well have just said what it was outright."

"That would be stupid," Pik said.

"Elysium Gate," Gant said, sighing. "They've been building a Gate."

She definitely didn't like the sound of that. If a Gate was already under construction, that meant Thraven was further along in his plans than she had guessed. "Do we know where?"

"We don't know where the Gate itself is, but there's a ton of materials being sourced through Avalon. It can't be too far from there."

"What else can you tell me about it?"

"Captain Mann got the intel directly from Tridium's secure datastore. They had dumped as much of it as they could before they had to run, but they wound up with bits and pieces. Tridium was still taking deliveries there as of a few weeks ago."

"They?" Abbey said.

"Apparently, Captain Mann hooked up with the Ophanim on Earth. Some woman named Pahaliah. She helped him with the job."

Abbey looked at Jequn. "Do you know her?"

"No, Queenie, but that doesn't mean she isn't legit. My attention has been focused on the Fringe and the Outworlds."

Gant chittered softly. "You're going to love this. They gave Captain Mann the Blood of the Shard."

"What?"

"He has the Gift, though I doubt it's anything like yours."

"It's going to kill him."

14

"He's an old man," Bastion said. "He'd probably croak before it could do him in, anyway."

"He would be dead already without it," Jequn said. "The Nephilim have a strong presence on Earth already. Our Servants are the only thing that have kept them under control."

"Servants?" Abbey said. "I feel like the more I think I know about the Seraphim, the less I do know."

"Plixians," Jequn said. "We've been friends to them for many generations. We saved them from a virus that was ravaging their homeworld, and they've been loyal to us since."

"You left that out of your original story."

"If I were to tell you everything I knew, I would still be speaking about it."

"Good point. I guessed the Plixians were involved in things when I saw the compound beneath the crater on Avalon." She turned toward Jequn, making eye contact with her. "Did you know it was there? Did you know what happened to it?"

"What do you mean?"

"The Infected?"

"Queenie, I helped place the teleporter at Mother's request. I had never been down there before. She told me the structure was like a bomb shelter, to hide in during an emergency. That it hadn't been used for thousands of years. I don't know anything more, and I didn't have time to question. We were being attacked."

"She didn't want you to know, either. I don't know how your mother was connected to Azure, but I do know why the Gift kills Seraphim hosts. They were experimenting on the naniates, trying to alter them to combat the Nephilim. What you saw was only the top level of the complex. It went much deeper. It was filled with Seraphim. Not dead, but not alive. The naniates were in them, controlling them, holding them in stasis or something while they waited for fuel. They seemed to know when I was there, and when Thraven's forces came down after me. They attacked us both."

Jequn shook her head. "I didn't know about any of this."

"I figured you didn't. The odd thing is, the Venerants Thraven sent to kill me did." Abbey looked over to Trin, who had taken up position near the rear of the group. "Did you know?"

"No, Queenie," Trin replied. "But based on that I would guess that planet isn't the only site where such a thing occurred."

"You heard Koy, didn't you? He thought I might have found something else down there. A weapon of some kind."

"Yes. They believed that I could be that thing, so it must be something like I have become. Perhaps a robot of some kind, powered by the Gift?"

"Jequn, have you ever heard of anything like that?" Benhil asked.

"No," Jequn replied. "If there were machines like that, they must have been a failure, like the other experiments."

"It sounds like the Seraphim have kept a lot of secrets," Gant said. "Even from each other."

"It sure does," Bastion said.

"I found something else down there," Abbey said. "A pool filled with crystals. A way for the Seraphim to communicate across universes. I spoke to a Shard. She wasn't the original. Her Shard had been killed as well. She begged me to close the connection. She said without a containment field things could go horribly wrong. So I closed it. That was when the Light of the Shard made itself known to me. It led me to the laboratory where the experiments had taken place. It wanted me to know about them."

"Why?" Gant asked.

"I don't know. I'm going to ask Kett what he knows about it as soon as I see him again. I don't know if Charmeine ever told him what was going on down there. They sealed the whole thing off when they lost control of the complex, and as far as I can tell she was one of the only ones who made it out alive."

"How do you know Charmeine didn't give you the teleporter hoping you would find the complex?" Bastion said.

"What do you mean?" Abbey asked.

"Well, you said the Light of the Shard came to you down there. I remember you told Charmeine you had seen it before. Maybe she was hoping you would wind up in the complex, and that being down there would wake it up."

"She couldn't have known I would find the compound."

"No, but she could have been hopeful. Only you would have been able to survive what she knew was down there."

"We can't rule it out," Gant said. "If she was keeping secrets, she's certainly capable of that sort of deception."

"How many things would have to go right to put me in that situation?"

"That's a logical fallacy, Queenie. How do you know things didn't all go completely wrong to put you in that situation? It only seems preordained because it happened, but maybe there were a thousand other events that would have put us in an even better situation than we are now? A situation where you don't even need the Shard to balance things out?"

"That's another way of looking at it."

"It doesn't matter in the end. Now we know the Seraphim aren't the purists they make themselves out to be. I can't say I blame them. It's hard to be a pacifist when your brothers and sisters are trying to kill you."

"But why cover it up? Why not just admit to abusing the naniates the same way the Nephilim did?"

"If your god gave you a perfect, clean pool, and you went and pissed in it, would you want anyone to know?" Bastion said. "Or would you hide the truth and rewrite history to hide the awfulness of it?"

"How would the Focus be sullied?" Jequn asked. "We drew the Blood from it to give to the others. The same Blood that kills us. How could it be impure?"

"Someone at some time thought they had a better way," Abbey said. "Maybe it made the Focus more powerful? Maybe it was the only thing that allowed the Seraphim to hold back the Nephilim the first time?" Abbey paused, considering. "The Shard told me to find the original Covenant. What if the Seraphim's efforts to stop the Nephilim are the reason the Nephilim haven't been stopped?"

"I'm not following," Bastion said.

"The One promised to protect the Seraphim. That was the Covenant. But when the Shard was killed, the Seraphim took their protection into their own hands. They altered the Blood to defend themselves and the other life the One had created. But what if they had a little more faith? What if they had sat back and waited for the One to intervene? What would have happened then?"

"We would have been enslaved a long time ago," Benhil said. "Sorry, Queenie. I'm not buying it. You can't rely on some vague promise to save you when things go sideways. You have to save yourself."

"Agreed," Pik said.

"Maybe I'm wrong," Abbey said. "And maybe I'm right. I think we'll find out before this is over."

"As long as we win, I don't give a shit how we do it," Bastion said.

"Agreed," Pik said.

"Did Kett know about Avalon?" Abbey asked.

"He did," Jequn replied.

"What was his plan?"

"We were," Gant said. "Gain control of the *High Noon*, scout out Avalon, and then detour to Azure to find you. We decided to find you first."

"Kett isn't going to do anything about Avalon if we can't do it for him," Bastion said. "That's how he works. He's afraid to lose."

"Then that's what we're going to do. Captain Davlyn, change of plans."

"Aye, Queenie?"

"Bring us out of FTL. We can't afford to give Thraven the chance to finish the Gate."

"Ensign Sil, set new coordinates for Avalon," Davlyn said.

"Not so fast," Abbey replied. "You aren't going to Avalon, Captain. This ship is beat up as it is, and we have no idea what's waiting there."

"Captain Mann said Tridium hired an outside agency for security," Gant said. "Mercenaries, most likely."

"Hopefully not the Riders," Abbey said.

"Who?" Bastion asked.

"Never mind. The point is, the *High Noon* won't stand up to another assault without some repairs. Jequn, do you know where General Kett was taking the fleet?"

"I can access his location."

"Good. Nerd."

"Aye, Queenie?" Erlan said, standing again.

"I want you and Dak to ensure the *High Noon* and her crew make it back to Kett. The rest of us will go on to Avalon in the *Faust*, see what there is to see, and then catch up to you."

"Aye, Queenie," Erlan said. He sounded disappointed not to be coming along.

"Sorry, Nerd. I need you back with the *Brimstone*. You're a damn good starship pilot, and I want you flying her."

Erlan smiled proudly. "I don't think General Kett feels the same way, Queenie."

"When you get back to the fleet, I want you to tell General Kett I don't give a flying frag what he feels or thinks. Tell him the fleet is mine, and I'll be coming back for it and him."

"Aye, Queenie."

"Uh, Queenie?" Bastion said. "No offense, but in case you didn't notice earlier, the *Faust* is fragged."

"I did notice," Abbey said. "I heard you were a good pilot? I bet Nerd wouldn't have crashed her."

"If I couldn't get her in undamaged, nobody could."

"I could have," Erlan said.

"I could have," Bastion mimicked. "You could not. You were there, Gant. Tell them."

"I think Nerd could have done it," Gant said, chittering.

"Me, too," Pik said. "I was there, too."

"Fraggers," Bastion said. "Whatever. The *Faust* is still busted."

Abbey smiled. She could feel the Gift of the Shard flowing through her, eager to do her will. "Not for long."

4

Abbey returned to the hangar with the rest of the Rejects still trailing behind her. She was almost amused by the way they followed her, their curiosity and excitement obvious. They knew she was going to do something cool, and they all wanted to bear witness to it.

Even she knew it was going to be cool, and she hadn't even started yet. She could feel the Blood of the Shard within her, the True Gift a familiar and yet altered tingle that ran across her flesh and down into her soul. It was power, clean and fresh and pure. Not the same as before. Maybe not as overtly destructive, but perhaps more useful. She didn't need to be furious to use it. She didn't need to think violent thoughts. It was just there, waiting.

She came to a stop in front of the *Faust*. The star hopper was tilted over, resting on the unbroken wing. The other one was still on the floor, one long main section and a number of broken pieces. They didn't need the long surfaces to fly, but if they wanted to land in any sort of atmosphere with gravity? Some lift would be nice for added maneuvering.

"You really think you can fix her?" Bastion said.

Abbey didn't respond. She noticed there were more individuals entering the hangar. Captain Davlyn and his crew. They had come to see as well.

"Give her a little space, will you?" Pik said, ushering some of them back.

"Queenie, this isn't going to knock you cold is it?" Gant asked.

"I'm not sure what's going to happen. I'll probably just be really hungry."

"There's ice cream in the Mess," Bastion said. "Unless Pik ate it already."

"I did not," Pik said. He paused. "I don't think."

"I tasted of the ice cream," Phlenel said. "It was disgusting."

"Thank you," Gant said.

"You two have no taste," Bastion replied.

"At least you can taste," Trin said. "I miss eating."

"How are you alive in there anyway?" Benhil said. "And are you sure you aren't going to kill us all in our sleep?"

"Distracting," Abbey said. "She's not going to kill you. We're best bitches now."

"Seriously?" Bastion said.

"I wouldn't go that far," Trin said. "But I am on your side in this war."

"Why the change of heart?" Bastion asked.

"Maybe a literal change of heart?" Benhil said, laughing.

"Queenie, I might kill this one," Trinity said, pointing at Benhil.

"Be my guest," Abbey said.

"What?" Benhil replied. "I'm just fragging with you. No harm done, right?"

"That's enough," Gant said. "Let her work."

The Rejects fell silent. Abbey smiled out of the corner of her mouth so they couldn't see. She was damn glad to be back with her family. One part of it, anyway. She was worried about the other part. More worried than before, but she had work to do before she could think about that.

She closed her eyes, taking a few deep breaths before opening them again. Then she put up her hands. One toward the *Faust*, the other toward the debris on the hangar floor.

The sleeves of the shardsuit began to move, freeing the naniates beneath them as the atomic machines penetrated through the cells of her skin. She sent them forward with little instruction other than to "fix it."

The *Faust* began to rise as the Gift wrapped around it, pulling it upright and leveling it off, changing its position in the hangar. The bay door was too narrow for the wings to fit through fully extended, but that didn't seem to matter. The intact wing snapped halfway across as a silver shimmer that matched the shardsuit appeared around it, sealing off the outer edge. Further away, the bits and pieces of the damaged wing were lifted into the air and brought together.

Hundreds of parts that would have taken her weeks to sift through and figure out how to assemble spun around one another, shifting position as the Gift worked out the problem. It was obvious by their actions that the naniates did have some level of intelligence, and by the way they seemed to learn it appeared to be shared. They re-engineered the wing within minutes, altering the form to match the opposite side before carrying it over the heads of the still-gathering crowd and moving it into position beside the *Faust*.

"I don't know whether to be amazed or terrified," she heard Captain Davlyn say to the Rudin beside him.

"I'm both," she clicked in reply, the translation following behind the response by a second.

Abbey was too, in her own way. She couldn't believe what she was doing. She was also afraid it wouldn't be enough. Thraven was immensely powerful, and while she was stronger than she had been the last time they met, she was still nowhere near his level.

She turned her hands over, merging the Gift. The wing came in contact with the side of the *Faust* at the same time, a dense cluster of the naniates circling the junction point and welding the two pieces together. A moment later, the reactor turned on, the inside of the cockpit becoming visible as it lit up. The landing skids extended, and only then did the ship return to the floor, turned to face the hangar doors and ready for action.

Abbey put her hands down. She could feel her energy begin to drain as she did, the naniates feeding on the nutrients in her blood to replenish themselves and begin replication. She was amazed by the innate way in which she could sense the mechanical processes, the power of the Gift demystified from a greater understanding of how it all functioned. Maybe it wasn't magic, but even watching it with an idea of how it worked, it still looked like magic. And felt like it.

"I've never seen anything like it without the use of the Focus," Jequn said as Abbey turned to face them.

Abbey could see the wonder written across the faces of the *High Noon's* crew. The Rejects were impressed too, but less impressed. They had seen the Gift before. Her stomach began to rumble. She was hungry. Very hungry. She had expected as much.

"Okay, Imp, can you go see if there's any ice cream left? If not, I'll take whatever you can find that has a lot of calories."

"On it," Pik said. He had to wade through the crew that had come to see the spectacle, and they scrambled away at his approach. Bastion trailed behind him, using the freshly opened lane.

"Cherub, Joker, head down to the armory and start picking out anything you think we can use. Weapons. Armor. That sort of thing. If there's a chance to get our hands on a more stable copy of Lucifer's Covenant, I want it."

"Yes, Queenie," Jequn said.

"Phenel, you don't have a nick yet, do you?"

"No, Queenie, though Bastion has called me jello mold and pudding a few times. I don't know what those things are."

Damn Bastion. "I know what they aren't. Your nick."

"I kind of like pudding."

"You know it's a human food, right? He's making fun of your physiology."

"The sound of it is pleasing to me."

Abbey hated to give Bastion credit for another of the Reject's names, but she wasn't going to keep arguing. "Pudding it is, then. I guess it's better than Shmoo."

"Shmoo?"

"Nevermind. Can you start running diagnostics on the *Faust*, and make sure everything is functioning the way it should? I have something else I need to take care of."

"Of course, Queenie."

"What would you like me to do, Queenie?" Trinity asked.

"Save your energy. I'm not sure when we'll be able to refuel you."

Trin's head lowered slightly, suggesting her disappointment. Abbey couldn't imagine what it must be like to be a living human brain inside a mechanical body. For all the power the form provided, the drawbacks were unbearable.

"Trinity," she said hesitantly.

"Yes, Queenie?"

"If you ever want me to... end it. I will."

"Not while Thraven is still living," Trinity replied. She hesitated for a moment as well. "Maybe after."

Abbey nodded. "Captain Davlyn," she shouted, getting the Captain's attention.

"Aye, ma'am?" he replied.

"When you rejoin Kett's fleet, do what he says until I return, but don't forget whose side you're on. You won't like me when I'm pissed."

He bowed, mimicking the way Erlan had done it. "Of course. After what I just saw? I'm not going to do anything to get on your bad side."

Abbey turned away from him, climbing into the *Faust* and making the short walk to the ship's Construct room. She slipped inside and closed the door before activating the system.

She had been reluctant to contact Hayley before because she didn't want to break her daughter's heart twice if something happened to her. She realized now she had made a mistake. A big mistake. Maybe Thraven would have left Hayley alone before when he still had hope of bringing her to his side. Now? They had destroyed a good portion of his fleet, and soon enough the Crescent Haulers would know who was really responsible for the attack on the *Devastator*. Not only that, but she had almost succeeded in killing him. It was one thing to be a thorn in his side, but she had grown into a tumor, and she knew from Coli that Thraven knew Hayley existed.

Whether for leverage or revenge, her daughter wasn't safe anymore, and she had to warn her. She just hoped she wasn't too late.

She entered Hayley's Construct ID. Even if she were offline, she would get a notification that she was being contacted through the system. Abbey waited impatiently for the connection to be made and the data to be transferred. The activity was easily traced, but she didn't care. Let Thraven come for her. As long as he didn't go after her child.

She could feel the sense of relief as the VR scene morphed around her, a sign that the connection had been accepted. The small farmhouse room appeared. The old couch. The fireplace. It was comforting. It was even more comforting when Hayley's avatar faded into position, standing opposite her.

"Mother," Hayley said.

Abbey's heart lurched. She knew instantly the person who had joined her in the Construct wasn't her daughter. Mom. Mommy. Mamma. Ma when she had been an infant. Even Abbey when she was really throwing a tantrum. But Hayley had never called her Mother.

"Where is she?" Abbey asked.

"Dead."

5

"HAVE YOU FOUND HIM YET?" OLUS ASKED. "WE'RE RUNNING OUT of time."

Pahaliah nodded. "He'll meet us at the Construct Gym downtown," she replied. "He said he wants double. PD almost nailed him after the tri-towers."

"Frag his double. Does he know what's at stake here?"

"He's a Rudin, Olus."

"Do we have the funds?"

"I'll get them."

Olus checked the time. Lorenti had been delivered back to her condo. The vote was going to happen in three hours.

They still had no idea where Ruche was keeping Hayley. He had spent every available minute hacking at the Galnet in hopes of finding something, anything to give him a clue where the Nephilim had brought her, with no luck. He knew it had to be close. Thraven's plan wouldn't work otherwise.

It wasn't as simple as letting Lorenti vote in favor of the legislation and collecting Hayley wherever they decided to drop her off. Olus knew, and he was sure Ruche knew he knew, that there was no way the Nephilim were simply going to let her go. That part of the equation was a ruse, an obvious ruse that was a win-win for Thraven whichever way Olus played it. If he didn't find Hayley, she was going to be on her way to the Gloritant the second Lorenti cast her ballot. If he did find Hayley?

They wanted him to. Hayley was bait. Ruche would be waiting, no doubt with enough Children and Converts to ensure he wouldn't survive the exchange. And once he failed, then the Evolent would ship her off.

Neither outcome was acceptable. Olus was going to find her, and he was going to save her. He knew Ruche was right. If Abbey found out her daughter was in trouble, not only would she be at risk to losing herself to the control of the Gift, she would probably abandon anything else she was doing to find and kill Thraven whether it was strategically viable or not.

Whether she could defeat him or not.

And if Abbey fell, what would happen to the Rejects? He couldn't imagine that group of misfits staying cohesive without her. Not now. And he didn't have many other allies. Efforts to reach Ruby had failed. Her comm seemed to be permanently offline. Without it, he couldn't talk to Kett. He couldn't talk to Abbey or Gant or any of the others. Without it, he was more on his own than ever.

He was grateful for Pahaliah, and for the Servants. Lurix especially. The Plixian had sacrificed himself back at Nez'pa, both saving him from the Goreshin and taking the fall for the attack. He was likely going to spend the rest of his life in prison as a result; a sacrifice Olus wouldn't waste.

Ruche wanted to be found, and Olus wanted to find him. There was a gray area in there, one that Killshot had every intention of exploiting.

"Xanix?" Olus said.

"He's already waiting for us."

"How did he manage to get what I asked for so quickly?"

"He's a Servant. It's part of the job description. You know, to serve?" She passed him a sarcastic smile.

27

"I didn't request milk and cheese," Olus replied. "Zip-10s are hard to come by, even for the government."

"It's all about who you know. In this case, Xanix knows a collector who's a friend of the Ophanim. He lent it out from his private stock, so try not to lose it. Or break it."

"I can't make any promises. You know what we're going to be up against."

She nodded but didn't speak. He could sense her tension. She had spent years preparing for the war, and she had handled herself well so far. But this? This was going to be the most grueling test yet.

Olus guided the car through the city traffic, using a busier lane to blend in more completely. They had borrowed the vehicle from Pahaliah's parents, though the parents didn't know it yet. He imagined they wouldn't be too happy when they found out. If they found out. He had already disabled all of the tracking services on the vehicle.

A few minutes later he guided the car down to the street, landing on the corner of a busy intersection. They were surrounded by high towers, their reflective panes collecting sunlight for energy and creating a mirrored infinity that would dizzy anyone who wasn't used to it. They weren't headed for the towers though. They were going down.

A loop station sat at the corner, and they descended into it, down to the waiting area where hundreds of individuals were loitering, watching the tracks for their ride across town. Most of them were human, but he spotted a couple of Trovers and a few Plixians, as well as a Curlatin and a group of Skinks that looked like tourists. He didn't notice Xanix in the group.

"He should have been here," Pahaliah said, scanning the platform.

Olus put his hand on her shoulder. "Be patient," he replied. "Let's move toward the back of the crowd."

They did, finding a spot behind the others. Within a minute the group of Skinks had eased their way over. Three of them stood in front of them with their backs turned, while the fourth brushed aside his long coat and held out the Zip-10.

Olus didn't even look at it. He just reached out and grabbed the sniper rifle, tucking it under his jacket. That Skink kept moving, circling to the others. The next in line backed toward them, passing out ammunition. The third handed over a small, wrist-mounted device, while the fourth gave Pahaliah a fancy handbag. It all happened in a matter of seconds, and then they faded back into the crowd without a word.

"Let's go," Olus said.

They made their way back out of the station. Olus slapped the small controller onto his wrist as they ascended, pulling up the projection and activating the transport bot. It was at the top of the steps by the time they arrived, a round, narrow, self-balancing wheel with a storage compartment in the center. He wasn't going to open it in public to see what prizes waited inside. He directed it over to the car, opened the back and lifted it in. He gave a cursory glance before pulling the Zip-10 from beneath his coat and placing it on top of the bot. Then he closed the trunk and regained the front seat.

"Xanix should have told me he was sending someone else," Pahaliah said as they started rising into the traffic lanes.

"Then you would have been too obvious looking for them," Olus replied. "It was a smart move, as long as he can trust those Skinks."

"I'm sure he wouldn't have used them if he couldn't."

Pahaliah opened the small bag. She lifted a smaller container out of it. There were four pills inside. He recognized two of them.

"I-" Pahaliah started to speak, then stopped. She shook her head. "I'm not ready to do this."

"You don't have to," Olus said. "I'm not asking you to."

Dilixix had given him the pills without telling him what they were. At least Pahaliah had a chance to make an informed decision. It was her life, after all.

"I'll keep them close," she said. "If things go really bad, I'll take them."

He nodded. "Do you know what the other two are?"

"Yes," she replied. "Kill-pills. If things go wrong, they'll guarantee a quick, easy death instead of a slow, torturous one."

"That won't work on me."

"It will. They contain a radioactive isotope that will weaken the Gift while the poison kills your body."

"I thought cutting off the head was the only way."

"It's difficult to force someone to swallow a cocktail like this in the middle of a battlefield, and external poisons aren't as effective. They can weaken the Gift but are rarely fatal."

"But we could use something like this to weaken Thraven?"

"If you can touch him with something poisoned, I suppose. You'd have to be able to touch him first."

"The devil is in the details, isn't it?"

"Always."

She dug one of the kill-pills out of the container and handed it to him. It wasn't the first time he had been given the means to take himself out of a situation this way. He shoved the pill into the back of his mouth and then checked the time. A little over two hours.

He started to descend again when the Construct Gym came into sight ahead. It was easy to pick out by the projections that surrounded it, each a stream of some of the action going on inside. Different types of warfare, mostly. Starfighter battles, mech fights, even some historical action using cannons and muskets. You could be anyone, anywhere, in any time real or imagined in the Construct, and some people got so addicted they lost everything to dedicate their lives to the escape.

Not Olus. He had never used it and never intended to. No matter how shitty reality got, at least it was real.

There was no external parking near the Gym. Instead, they were directed to a landing sled. He placed the car on it, and they disembarked. Olus turned back to watch as the car was carried into underground storage, slightly concerned about having left their equipment inside. The Zip-10 was irreplaceable.

As long as they hadn't been tracked or followed, it should be safe enough.

"Is he here already?" Olus asked.

"Yes. In a private booth. Of course, we'll be paying for the booth." She smiled and shook her head.

They entered the Gym. Olus had always found moving around inside of them a surreal, disorienting experience. The entire thing was for all intents one massive construct room, with millions of points providing the proper VR to the hundreds of individuals standing within, each of them wearing goggles and earplugs that provided the visual and auditory immersion into whichever world they were in. The floor was specially designed so that players could move in all directions without actually moving no matter where they stood, while non-players could travel around them without incident.

What made it the most creepy was the sound. Since everyone was in their own little microcosm, they elicited noises that suited their situation, which combined with everyone else to provide a chilling audio track. While this was a public Gym and mature themes were banned, that didn't prevent a strange mixture of screaming, laughter, cursing, joy, and most other vocalizations of emotions from mingling.

"Can I help you?" one of the employees asked. He was a kid, no more than eighteen, wearing special gear that would allow him to peek into the different Construct nodes.

"Room Forty-six?" Pahaliah said.

"Over there," he replied, pointing to a door that nearly vanished against the dark walls.

"Thanks," Olus said.

They approached the room. The door slid open as they neared it. A small Rudin was waiting inside, standing beside a portable terminal. He was wearing a heavy drape over his body with so many pockets Olus couldn't imagine what they were all for, though they seemed to all have something in them.

"Pahaliah?" the Rudin said, the name coming out oddly in clicks and snaps.

"Goillisi?"

"In the flesh," the Rudin replied. "You must be Captain Mann. I'm honored to meet you." He held out a tentacle. Olus took it, shaking it lightly. "Of course, you didn't come to make small words. We're looking for Nephilim."

He used four of his tentacles to access the terminal, using the other four to hold himself up. They made quick, sharp movements in front of it, turning it on and cycling through data faster than Olus could manage to read it.

"I hope you are not offended, but I started without you. The less time we are together, the better it is for me. I barely inked my way out of my setup during the tri-towers job."

"Did you just say inked?" Olus asked.

"Yes," Goillisi replied. "Why?"

Olus shook his head. Every once in awhile someone with a sense of humor would do something like that with the translators. He was sure the Rudin didn't mean the word as it had been presented.

"Nevermind. What have you found so far?"

"I've traced three hundred possible locations within a fifty-mile range of the city back to Nephilim holdings. Shell corporations, off world investors, and the like."

"Three hundred?" Pahaliah said. "We have two hours to find the right location."

"Less than that," Olus said. "Once we have the right place, we need to work out how to approach it. You're charging us an arm and a leg. Or at least two tentacles. You have thirty minutes."

"Captain Mann, I'm an accomplished network infiltrator and data scientist, but I can't work miracles. You should be impressed that I've managed to narrow the field as much as I have this quickly."

"I know how much Pali is paying you. You can do better than that."

"I swear, I can't."

"We'll double the double," Pahaliah said.

The Rudin's tentacles quivered, betraying his excitement. "I'll find a way. There's always a way, isn't there?"

Olus glanced at Pahaliah. It was her money. Or rather, her family's. Still, he knew he could have convinced Goillisi to hurry it up without resorting to more bribery.

The Rudin's tentacles slithered and snapped ahead of the projection, the different views moving rapidly in and out. The logical nature of the Rudin mind made them well-suited for this kind of work, and whenever one was able to break away from the species' overall law-abiding nature, it made them doubly efficient.

Even so, it took nearly forty minutes for Goillisi to settle, his tentacles finally coming to rest beside the terminal. Olus had grown impatient well before then, and while he was experienced enough to keep it to himself, he had been just about ready to panic.

"I have it," Goillisi said. "An abandoned power plant in the Catskills." He lazily waved a tentacle, and the projection changed.

Olus leaned forward. The Rudin had tapped into a feed from the facility. It was the same camera view of Hayley that Ruche had provided hours earlier. It didn't look like they had moved her at all. No food. No water. No bathroom. Her father was dead. Her mother was gone. He would have expected any child to be in tears. To look exhausted.

She didn't. She was asleep, bound in the chair.

"Poor thing," Pahaliah said.

"They don't know you're in there, right?" Olus said.

"Of course not. The tri-towers was different, and they only caught up to me because you tripped the datastore security. The plant's systems are nowhere near as advanced or secure."

"Give me your new identifier so we can communicate over the Galnet," Olus said.

Goillisi transferred the data.

"The price was to find her," he said. "Not to accompany you on the job."

Olus glared at the Rudin. Goillisi was non-plussed.

"How much?" Pahaliah asked.

"You do understand that if that girl dies the entire galaxy could go up in flames?" Olus said.

"Mamma always said that it's a big universe," Goillisi replied. "There's never nowhere to hide. Two million."

"Million?" Olus said. "Mamma Oissi is dead because she thought she could escape this. Do you want to end up like her, too?"

"I won't. I'm low profile. Invisible. A ghost."

Olus stepped toward the Rudin, grabbing the pistol from under his coat. "You will be a ghost."

"Olus," Pahaliah said, getting between them. "I can pay it. But not right now. After."

"Sorry, Pali," Goillisi said. "You know the rules. Up front."

"Half now, half later," Pahaliah argued.

"No exceptions."

Olus gently shoved Pahaliah aside, reaching out and grabbing the Rudin by the top of his head and shoving him back. Goillisi's tentacles flailed, trying to grab him, but a hard squeeze caused enough pain that he lost the will to resist.

"You won't get anything from me if you kill me," Goillisi said.

"I'm not getting anything from you now, so what difference does it make?" Olus asked. "You can't use any of the money you've earned if you're dead."

"Murder is a felony offense."

"Are you joking? I'm already one of the most wanted Terrans on the planet."

Goillisi's eyes shifted to Pahaliah, pleading with her for intervention.

"You'll get paid after," she said.

"If I agree, how do you know I'll stick around once you let me go?"

"If you're invisible and I can't find you, I'm sure I'll be able to find someone that you care about," Olus replied. "And this is too important for me to make idle threats about."

"Okay," Goillisi clacked. "Two million, post-paid. A one-time exception for you, Captain."

Olus let him go. He sank on his tentacles, raising two of them to rub at his tender head.

"Now, give me everything you have on the plant," Olus said. "Blueprints, schematics, camera feeds. I want to know who is there, how many of them there are, how they are armed, everything. We have one hour."

"Yes, Captain," Goillisi said.

Olus glanced back at the projection before it vanished. His eyes narrowed as he noticed the smallest bit of movement from Hayley's wrists.

She wasn't sleeping. She was trying to loosen the bonds.

"Don't worry, Ms. Cage," he said. "I'll get you out, if for no other reason than I don't want to be stuck within one hundred galaxies of your mother if anything happens to you."

6

OLUS CHECKED THE TIME AGAIN. TWELVE THIRTY-NINE. THE VOTE WAS scheduled to happen in twenty-one minutes. That was how long they had to get Hayley out and inform Lorenti that she was safe.

He raised the Zip-10 to his shoulder and put his eye against the sight. The weapon was a throwback to another time, a time when personal skill was the ultimate difference between life and death. When there was no computer augmentation to aim. A time when only one round could be loaded per shot.

It was the weapon of a true craftsman. A master's tool. A paintbrush instead of a camera. It was nearly three centuries old, one of a few hundred left in existence. Killshot had once been infamous for his use of the rifle to take out targets from up to four kilometers away. He was closer than that now, only half a klick, but the power of the weapon combined with the large caliber of its ammunition would be enough to reduce a head to a pulp as long as it hit the right spot.

And he always hit the right spot.

"Pali, I'm in position," he said into his comm. "What's your status?"

"Almost there," she replied. "Standby."

One of their minutes burned away.

"I've reached the rear access gate. Waiting for your mark."

"Roger. Goillisi, give me a feed on the gate."

"Transmitting, Captain," the Rudin replied.

One of the items in the transport bot had been a pair of tactical goggles that connected to his seraphsuit's SoC. While he couldn't use it to aim his shots, he was able to bring up the feed Goillisi was sending in his submissive eye, getting a secondary look at the gate where Pahaliah was waiting. Two guards were stationed near it. Another two a little further back. Olus didn't know if they were Converts or Children, and he didn't care. He wasn't taking chances either way.

"Be ready to switch feeds in order as we discussed," Olus said.

"Roger, Captain."

"Pali," Olus said. "Mark."

He squeezed the trigger as he said the word. Half a second later, the head of the guard on the left vanished. A second after that, the guard on the right fell, too.

Pahaliah used her seraphsuit to leap over the gate, drawing the attention of the secondary guards as they moved toward it, trying to figure out how and from where their companion's deaths had come.

They didn't have much time to think about it. Olus aimed and fired, grabbed the next round from beside him, loaded it into the Zip-10, and fired again.

Both targets lost their heads.

Pahaliah landed cleanly inside the facility.

"Next," Olus said, loading another round.

The feed from Goillisi shifted, showing the camera near the south side of the gate. The guards there had already changed, revealing themselves as Goreshin. They were rushing toward Pahaliah on powerful limbs, nearing the corner of the main plant.

Trigger. Kill. Trigger. Kill.

Both Goreshin died before they could reach the corner. Olus reloaded. "Next."

The camera on the other side. The Goreshin were getting close to

Pahaliah, and she was bouncing back toward the ones he had just killed.

"Captain, Ruche is moving," Goillisi announced.

He shifted his aim, the reticle falling on Pahaliah's head. One of the Children was right behind her. He shifted three millimeters left and squeezed the trigger. The bullet came close enough to cut through some of her hair as it slammed into the Goreshin's mouth and detonated.

"Frag," Pahaliah said, the blood splattering onto her back. "Too close."

He adjusted his aim and fired again, killing the other one.

"Where's Ruche?" Olus asked.

"Tracking. Captain, the feeds are going dead. He's manually killing the cameras."

Olus had figured he would. He shifted his fingers to drop the feed, using both eyes to scan the plant below. He found three more targets, quickly dispatching them before getting to his feet. He was reluctant to leave the Zip behind, but it had done its job. Now he had to reach Hayley before the Evolent did.

"Killshot, I'm inside," Pahaliah reported.

"Roger. Goillisi, give me something."

"The cameras are dead, Captain."

"It's a fusion plant; there are other sensors inside."

The Rudin clattered. "Of course. Standby."

Olus took three steps toward the edge of the nearby bluff he was positioned on and jumped.

It wasn't an ordinary jump, even with the assistive musculature of the suit. It was augmented by the Seraphim Gift, the Blood of the Shard, and it carried him hundreds of meters through the air. It made him more like a bird than a human, a massive leap that brought him over the wall and into the compound. He reached for the weapons on his hips as he neared the ground, bringing a gun to one hand and a Uin to the other. He still wasn't overly confident with the Seraphim blade, but if he could disable his opponents with bullets first removing their heads wouldn't be that difficult.

He hoped.

"Goillisi, what do you have?" he barked, straightening and dashing toward the building.

The Rudin had already figured out where the space they were keeping Hayley was, based on the positioning of the cameras and some other network hackery that he didn't completely understand. It was enough that he had an idea where he was headed.

"There are heat sensors spread along the plant for the fire control systems. They're sensitive, and I am using them to determine target locations. I can't tell you which one is Ruche, though."

"Something is better than nothing."

Olus grunted, throwing himself to the side as a Goreshin pounced down at him from the rooftop. He came up, raising a forearm and blocking the creature with the strength of the Gift, bringing his arm around and firing right into its head. It shuddered and fell back, and he jumped at it, slicing its head off cleanly with the Uin.

He looked up at the concrete side of the structure. Hayley was on the other side of the stone. That was where he needed to be.

"Pali?" he said, asking for her status.

"I've got four Converts closing on me," she replied. "I can handle them, but no sign of Ruche."

"Roger," Olus said. Ruche had gone to grab Hayley. It was the only thing that made sense.

He reached into a tightpack, producing a wad of putty. He rolled it into a ball in his hand and then threw it at the wall above. His aim was slightly off, but he reached out with the Gift, guiding the explosive to a more proper position.

Someone shot him.

He clenched his teeth in pain, diving away as the bullets kept coming, turning toward the source. Soldiers had reached his position. He took three more hits as he returned fire, squeezing off one round after another, each of them well-aimed, striking his targets in the forehead one by one. The soldiers froze momentarily, stumbling but not falling before something else took over. With jerky motions, they renewed their attack.

Olus put up his hands, still amazed when the slugs found purchase in the empty air, freezing and falling to the ground. He held the shield ahead of him while he turned back to the explosive. He moved his fingers, triggering its detonation.

The wall exploded outward, the debris falling around him and obscuring him in a cloud of dust. He dropped the shield, using the seraphsuit to leap the distance to the hole he had made, the hole that should have penetrated directly through to Hayley.

He landed inside. The charge had been shaped to blow outward, leaving the interior undamaged but still grainy with dust. His eyes landed on the chair where Hayley had been bound. The tie that had held her hands was unbroken on the floor. The straps that were holding her feet to the chair were open.

Hayley was gone.

For a moment, he thought he was too late. Then the door slid open.

Evolent Ruche was standing behind it.

7

THEY REACTED TO ONE ANOTHER AT THE SAME TIME. RUCHE RAISED HIS hand, sending his Gift outward toward Olus, intending to knock him back and out of the building. Olus put the Uin up as though it were a shield, his Gift countering, absorbing some of the blow.

Some, but not all. He was still pushed back, left only centimeters from the edge. He fired three times; his bullets stopped by the Evolent, who shifted his attention to deflect them. That split-second break allowed Olus to regain his footing and bounce forward, nearly slamming into Ruche before he was thrown aside by an invisible hand, crashing through the chair and into the wall.

"Olus," Ruche said. "Where is she?"

He didn't know? Olus could have laughed if the blow hadn't broken his ribs.

"Gone," Olus replied. He could feel his body being put back together. "But I'm here. Isn't that what you wanted?"

"You should know by now; we want everything."

The force of the Nephilim Gift slammed him again, shoving him against the wall. He fought against it, the weaker Seraphim Gift giving him enough resistance that he was still able to move. He got the gun in line with Ruche again, forcing the Evolent to release him in order to block or avoid the projectiles.

"You aren't going to get it," Olus said. "Without Hayley, you've got nothing to bargain with. No leverage."

He used Ruche's distraction to bounce in again swinging the Uin, slashing down toward the Evolent's chest. Ruche spun away, catching his wrist, dragging him into his other hand and punching him hard in the face. Olus took the hit, returning a hard kick of his own that slammed into Ruche's leg, breaking the bones.

"We got Lorenti back," he said, trying to back away. Olus didn't let him, knowing that he had the best chance close up. He moved with the Evolent, pressing the attack. "That's all we really needed."

"I wouldn't be so sure," Olus replied. "You're assuming she's going to vote in Thraven's favor." He slashed down with the Uin. When Ruche knocked it aside, he followed it up with a pair of bullets in the same place. They dug into Ruche's gut, knocking him back. "Plus, I'll finally get to kill you, which is a bonus."

He slashed with the Uin again while the Evolent was off-guard. He felt the Nephilim Gift pressing the attack, but he met it with his own, refusing to let it knock him away. Ruche turned, getting his arm ahead of the Uin and taking the hit there, letting the blade sink deep into his arm and cut into the bone. He turned again, quickly enough that he yanked the weapon from Olus' hand, leaving it embedded in his flesh.

Olus stumbled, surprised by the maneuver. That surprise caused his focus to waver, and then he was choking, the Gift wrapping around his throat and squeezing tight.

He tried to fight against it, putting his free hand to his neck, the palm warming from the flow of the Gift. Ruche was regaining his composure, his power increasing as he did. The Gift slammed against Olus again, knocking him back against the wall. He fell to the ground there, still trying to cast off the invisible noose, suddenly pinned.

"You're a fool, Olus," Ruche said. "Did you think the Watcher's Gift would be enough to make us evenly matched? Did you think a pre-emptive attack would keep me from killing you?" He pulled the Uin from his arm and dropped it on the ground.

"No," Olus replied. "But I did think I could get Hayley out, and I have. It doesn't matter if I live or die. Only her. Only Abbey. The vote? You have no idea what is going to happen. But I do."

"What do you mean?" Ruche said. He tightened his grip. "Tell me."

Olus tried to choke out an answer. Ruche relaxed the hold slightly to let him speak again. At the same instant, the fire control system went off, spraying the Evolent with a thick white foam. It was just enough of a distraction to let Olus break free, and he got his gun up, emptying the magazine into the Evolent and knocking him down.

He didn't waste time, jumping to his feet and moving toward the Uin, still barely able to breathe. He would have seconds at best to remove the Evolent's head. He dove toward the weapon, reaching out for it.

It slid away from him, pushed aside by Ruche's Gift. Olus cursed, rolling over and facing Ruche again. He bounced forward, pulling a knife from his seraphsuit and stabbing downward, catching the Evolent in the shoulder. Ruche cried out, punching Olus in the stomach, but he managed to hold on. He twisted the knife, trying to dig it in deeper, using his other hand to grab another. He raised it to strike before being thrown away by the force of Ruche's fury.

He slid across the floor, returning almost to the place he had started. In truth, he had thought the Blood of the Shard might be enough to let him beat Ruche. He couldn't have been more wrong. He was completely outmatched. Hell, he wasn't even in the same league.

He was going to die here.

At least Hayley had escaped.

Ruche got back to his feet, wrenching the knife from his shoulder and throwing it aside. He reached up again, and again Olus started to choke.

"I don't care what you did," Ruche said, his voice a rough growl. "You can't stop us. You can't stop Thraven. The Great Return is coming. The Promise will be kept. Nothing can stop that. Do you understand, Olus?"

"Captain," Goillisi said in his ear. "Pali isn't responding. Captain? Are you there?"

Not responding? Did that mean he had failed? He felt a surge of strength, and for a moment he thought he could break free of his invisible bonds. He took a step toward Ruche, only to be held again before he could do anything meaningful.

How could he have failed?

Hayley was loose. She had escaped her bonds on her own. Could she get out of the building on her own, too? He had a feeling she could. Lorenti was taken care of, that part of their plan secure. Thraven probably thought the Councilwoman was still on his side, but she hadn't turned out to be that selfish in the end. She had agreed to follow his lead even though her odds of survival were slim.

So maybe he hadn't failed. Just because he was going to die didn't mean the war was over. It didn't mean all hope was lost. He had done everything he could to fight the good fight. He had given everything he had and then some.

He looked up at Ruche. The Evolent's face was twisted in fury; his hand curled as though it was physically wrapped around Olus' neck. He increased the pressure, enough that Olus could feel his spine beginning to collapse beneath it. Would the Evolent end him outright?

He was suddenly glad for the pill Pahaliah had given him. There was a finality to it, and a sense of control. He would die on his terms, at his time, not Ruche's. It wasn't much, but it was better than nothing.

"Captain?" Goillisi said again. "Captain? Frag. I haven't gotten paid."

Olus would have laughed if he could have. That truly was all the Rudin cared about. It figured. He shifted his tongue, bringing the pill onto it.

Without warning, the pressure disappeared. He watched Ruche's face change, going from anger to surprise. He drew in a sharp breath, ignoring the pain of it as he tried to make sense of what was happening.

Ruche was doing the same. The Evolent began to turn.

Olus noticed the sound for the first time. Pop. Pop. Pop. Pop. Gunfire. Bullets. One after another after another. Ruche's body contorted, caught unaware, pushed back by the impacts. Olus' eyes shifted to the doorway, expecting Pahaliah to be standing there and finding Hayley Cage instead. She had one of the guard's rifles in her arms and was handling it like she had been doing it all her life.

Ruche stumbled, slowly catching up. The rounds started to fall in front of him, deflected by the Gift.

Olus dove forward, grabbing Ruche around the neck and throwing him down. He leaned over him, biting down on the pill, dipping his head, putting his lips against the Evolent's and spitting the poison into his mouth.

Ruche choked, his hand coming up and pummeling Olus in the ribs, the force knocking him aside. He sputtered, trying to spit out the poison, but it was too late. He had swallowed too much of it already, and the effect was immediate. He managed to get to his knees, but when he put out his hand to use the Gift again, nothing happened.

"Hayley," Olus said, his voice weak. "Kill him. Kill him now."

She didn't hesitate. Not at all. She emptied the magazine into Ruche, a dozen rounds penetrating his body in a spray of blood. Olus crawled over to the Uin, picking it up. The Gift was healing him, fixing his neck and giving him breath. He stood and walked over to the Evolent. Ruche's face was pale, his eyes wide open but unmoving.

Dead, for now.

Olus leaned over him, bringing the Uin across his neck and making it permanent.

Then Olus turned around, his eyes falling on Hayley once more. She had already discarded the spent rifle, replacing it with the knife he had dropped.

"I'm here to rescue you," he said. "I'm a friend of your mom's."

Hayley returned a weak smile, approaching him slowly. Then she collapsed into him, sobbing.

"It's going to be okay," he said, wrapping his arm around her and holding her while she cried. "It's going to be okay."

He only wished he knew whether or not he was telling her the truth.

8

HAYLEY ONLY CRIED FOR A FEW MINUTES. OLUS DIDN'T HAVE THE HEART to stop her, or to tell her they needed to hurry. Not after all she had been through. He held her close, told her it would be okay, and didn't push. He quickly checked the time when she backed away. It was past one o'clock. The vote was happening, with Lorenti's decision to come at any moment.

"Goillisi," he said.

"Captain Mann? You're still alive?" He could hear the relief in the Rudin's clacking. "I thought I was out of my payday."

"Shut up and transfer a feed of the Council proceedings to me," Olus said. He looked at Hayley. "I came with someone else. I think she might be hurt. Did you see anyone?"

Hayley shook her head. "No. What's your name?"

"Mann," Olus said. "Olus Mann."

"The rogue agent," Hayley said, smiling. "That's what I thought. You looked better on the streams."

"I didn't just get my ass kicked on the streams. Thanks for saving my life."

"Thanks for trying to save mine."

The feed came in, overlaying his left eye. He adjusted the transparency so he could see it, and also see past it. The votes were being taken in order. Lorenti was fifteen down.

"I went to Hell to rescue your mother," Olus said. "She ended up rescuing me instead. That seems to be the way it goes with you Cages."

"Why was she in Hell?" Hayley asked.

"It's a long story."

"Is she okay?"

"I don't know. We were separated. Your mom's a real warrior. I wouldn't bet against her."

"I won't. I'm happy that she's still alive. I figured she was, but since I hadn't heard from her..."

"She didn't want you to get involved in this. I'm sorry that didn't happen. Are you hurt at all?"

"Not really. Can we get out of here?"

"Absolutely." He stood up. The Gift had put him back together, leaving him feeling almost as good as new, despite Ruche's best efforts. "That asshole was the one who got your mom sent to Hell," he said, pointing at the Evolent. "She'll be happy when she learns you killed him."

"I don't think my mom will be happy about me killing anyone."

Olus froze for a second. His experiences and perspectives weren't the best suited for children. "Maybe not."

He found his gun on the floor, picked it up, and replaced the magazine. Then he handed it toward her. "Killing innocent individuals is wrong, I agree. Killing individuals who are trying to kill you?"

She took it from him. "I'm not naive," she said. "And I'm not afraid to use this."

"I noticed," he replied. "Come on. Stay behind me. I can take a few rounds and not die."

"How?"

"Another long story. I'll tell you all of it when we get somewhere safe."

"Okay."

Help

They moved out of the room and into the hallway. A long corridor stretched in both directions. Olus turned left, following his memory of the schematics they had reviewed.

"Councilwoman Lorenti," the Head of the Council, Danube Kiliwani said, calling on her.

Olus paused, shifting to the side of the hallway. "Hold on a second," he said to Hayley. "Kick me if there's any sign of trouble." Their situation wasn't optimal, but he didn't want to miss this.

The feed shifted to Councilwoman Lorenti. She was sitting at a long desk. Her hair was up, her makeup perfect. For anyone watching, they would never have guessed her husband had been killed the night before, or that she had been kidnapped and returned. They would have no idea how much had changed inside the woman in the last twenty-four hours, or how much a single event could change someone's perspective.

"My condolences for your loss," Kiliwani said as she got to her feet. "And my apologies for asking you to be here, but as you know, this vote simply cannot wait. There are millions of lives at risk."

Lorenti nodded. "Thank you, Councilman Kiliwani. Of course, I understand the urgency of this session. I took an oath to serve the Republic above all things, including my own mourning."

She paused, her eyes shifting around the room. The Council was arranged in a circle around the central dais where Kiliwani was standing. Individuals from every Republic nation were present. Trovers, Atmos, and the rest. They sat still and silent and patient. Olus wondered how many of them felt patient? There were enough votes in the room to override the Prime and send the Republic to war.

At least, Thraven believed there were. Lorenti was the missing piece. The most vital affirmation or dissension. She had promised to help Olus, but now that she was in front of the Council, now that she had to make the sacrifice, would she go through with it?

"Individuals of the Council," she said, her voice solid and strong. "We called this emergency session because we are concerned about the growing unrest in the Outworlds. The activities on Fringe worlds like Anvil, and the destruction of Eagan Heavyworks on Feru including the theft of the *Fire* and the *Brimstone*. We've heard rumors of Outworld attacks on our patrols, and of fleets massing beyond our sensors, preparing to launch an assault on our freedoms and our way of life. The Outworlders want our planets for their own. They want our resources. They want revenge for pushing them beyond the most fertile system in the galaxy all of those years ago. Those are all valid reasons on the surface. But over the last twenty-four hours I've been forced to start thinking. What lies beneath the surface?"

Olus felt himself start to smile. She was about to sign her death warrant with her words. She knew it when Olus had asked it of her. But she had seen the Goreshin kill her husband. She knew Ruche had taken a child to get to him. Those were signs she couldn't ignore. Actions that had tripped her over the edge of her selfishness and into a rage of righteousness. She couldn't ignore what the Republic would become if Thraven had his way, even if it meant her life. She was going to paint a massive target on her head.

Would he have time to pull her away from it?

"Captain," Hayley said, stealing his attention from the feed.

A pair of Goreshin had turned the corner ahead of them, and they growled as they noticed him, charging fast.

"Stay behind me," Olus said, holding out the Uin. He raised his other hand, feeling the Gift flowing through him and adding its strength to his seraphsuit. "Aim for the head."

Hayley stayed back as the monsters approached. Olus heard the pops of the handgun behind him and saw the rounds sink into the Childrens' thick foreheads. He was impressed with her aim, even if the slugs weren't powerful enough to penetrate.

He bounced forward at the lead monster, brushing aside its claws, using the Uin to cut off one of its hands. Its head came down toward his neck, trying to bite. He shifted his weight, ducking and throwing it up and back, into the second creature. He rolled up, diving back toward them as they tried to untangle themselves.

Hayley fired into the mess, causing them to grunt as bullets dug into their flesh. It was a distraction to them nothing more, but every little bit helped.

Olus could hear Lorenti speaking in the background, in a third channel of his consciousness.

"My husband was a good man," she said. "An honest man. To be frank, I didn't deserve someone like him. He let me be who I was without complaint, without judgment. He let me feel like I could live free without consequence. But there is always a consequence, and true freedom is an illusion. We are bound to morals, to justice, to righteousness. As members of the Council, we have a duty to uphold to all of these things regardless of the circumstances."

"Councilwoman," Kiliwani said. "What is your vote?"

"I'll give you my vote when I damn well please, Councilman," Lorenti snapped. "I have a right to speak. All of us do."

There was no further objection. Olus moved in on the Goreshin. One of them turned to him, while the other broke for Hayley. He cursed himself for letting them get in the middle, leaping toward the closest, breaking his guard and throwing his hand forward into its chest. The strength of the Gift flowed through him, and he sent the Goreshin into the wall with enough force that he could hear its bones shatter, and feel the structure vibrate under the impact. He would have taken a moment to remove its head, but there was no time.

"As I was saying," Lorenti continued. "What lies beneath the surface. Let me put in perspective with myself. On the outside, I'm a respected Councilwoman. Hardworking. Honorable. Beneath the surface?" She paused. "I have an alternative lifestyle that is not compatible with my standing or reputation. I've visited so-called X-clubs on numerous occasions to have consensual sex with members of other species. Not illegal, but also not something the voting public ignores during elections."

The Goreshin closed on Hayley. She crouched into a position Olus recognized as Takega, prepared for the incoming creature. She ducked under its first attack, bouncing lithely back, rolling to the side, and avoiding it. It bent down to snap at her, and she popped up near its head, placing the gun against its skull and firing the remaining two rounds. The bullets made it through the skull at that range, penetrating its brain and leaving it stunned. It stumbled ahead of her, and then Olus was on it, digging the Uin into its neck from behind.

"What does this have to do with the vote?" Councilman Kiliwani asked.

"Half of you in this room know exactly what it has to do with this vote," Lorenti replied. "Someone within the Republic captured video of one of my interactions in an X-club. They were using it to blackmail me and control my vote. For the last year, I've been making decisions based on my embarrassment, not what I believe in. Look beneath the surface. Look at yourselves. What value is there to be gained by engaging in an all-out war with the Outworlds? Why here? Why now? What proof do we have that the Governance was behind the theft of the *Fire* and *Brimstone*? And if they weren't, then how can we blame them for the attacks on our fleets? Why does the Prime not support this measure? Why are we trying so hard to circumvent our own rules by writing new ones? Not enough? What about this?"

Olus rounded back to the first Goreshin. It had recovered from his blow and was stalking toward him, being more careful this time.

"What are they?" Hayley asked.

"Assholes," Olus replied.

Then he burst forward on the power of the Gift, charging the creature. It tried to keep up, but he had been an accomplished assassin long before he had been upgraded with the Blood of the Shard. He moved too fast for it to manage, breaking past its defenses and slashing it with the Uin. Once. Twice. Three times. He cut deep wounds in its arms, disabling it before bringing the blade up and into its neck, shouting as he did.

The creature was static for a moment, and then its body and its head toppled in different directions.

Olus flicked his eye back to the feed. Lorenti had activated the projection on her comm. The conversation that Ruche had with him about Hayley, showing her bound and held. Of course, Olus had been able to save the transmission from the device's memory cache before it was wiped. Ruche was an idiot not to realize it could be done, and that the Director of the OSI would have the tools and knowledge to do it.

"Thraven," Lorenti said. "Half of you know that name or at least the voice of his servant. Beneath the surface of logic, a snake is waiting to strike. Waiting to erode the strength of the Republic and the Outworlds both to complete his agenda. Willing to sacrifice anyone and anything to do it."

The Council erupted, with dozens of members rising at once in defiance and confusion.

"My vote is no, Councilman. And no matter what he has on you, no matter what you've been promised, if you know Thraven I suggest you vote the same. Uphold your promises. Sacrifice yourself for the-"

Something hit Lorenti, forcing her head to snap back sharply. Her body collapsed, the stream breaking away from her in an instant.

"Frag," Olus said.

A bullet? The Gift? He didn't know. Either way, someone had shut her up before she could further incite the Council. Before she could reveal Tridium's participation in Thraven's Great Return.

The feed went dark, the public stream shut down before any more violence was shown. He could imagine what kind of chaos was occurring.

Or maybe he couldn't. If there was a Venerant or Evolent on the Council, who knew what could be happening?

Either way, his plan to try to get Lorenti out of the crosshairs was never going to materialize. They had dealt with her more swiftly and more publicly than he had imagined.

If Thraven was watching, he was surely going to be beside himself with rage.

Olus loved that thought.

"Goillisi, are you still with me?" Olus asked.

"Yes, Captain."

"I need anonymous passage off Earth. Can you arrange it?"

"For a price."

"The price is your life, you wormy piece of shit," Olus snapped.

"Fine. I'll include it in your original fee as a thank you for your business."

"Whatever. Standby."

"Yes, Captain."

Olus killed the overlay, lifting the goggles off his head so Hayley could see his eyes.

"We're going to get out of here, okay? If I can, I'll get you to your mom."

"I like that plan," Hayley replied.

"Good. Let's go."

9

OLUS AND HAYLEY KEPT MOVING THROUGH THE PLANT, TRACING THE corridors back toward the entrance. He kept hoping he would find Pahaliah out there. He kept hoping she was still fighting, and that maybe her TCU had been damaged, or the comm link had somehow short-circuited. It was a rare occurrence, but it wasn't impossible, and after what had happened with Zoey and Gyo he was reluctant to leave someone else behind.

They found a few dead Converts further into the plant, their heads cleanly removed by a Uin, a path of destruction that he decided to try to follow. They claimed the Converts' rifles first, reloading them with fresh magazines and continuing together. Olus remained impressed with Abbey's daughter. Hayley had her mother's courage and will. He knew she was hurting on the inside, but other than the short window during which she'd been unable to contain her emotions, she was carrying on like a real soldier.

Their search brought them to the plant's main control room, a box that didn't look all that much different than the bridge of a star-ship. Different terminals controlled different aspects of the power station's functions, and while the ones directly related to the fusion reactors were offline the terminal that managed interior functions wasn't.

Its projection was visible, a multi-layered view of all of the cameras in the facility that Ruche hadn't destroyed. Through it, Olus could see the organization of the remaining enemy forces. They were mostly covering the exits, waiting outside for him to emerge, no doubt aware that their leader was dead.

Pahaliah wasn't in the room, which gave him an equal of measure of comfort and concern. Had she left the terminal active in case he showed up? Or had the enemy set it up, hoping to lure him into a trap? Was her body gone because she was still alive and had left the area, or had they removed it so as not to give their intentions away?

"We'll go out that way," Olus said, pointing to the entrance where Pahaliah had entered. The bodies had been removed, replaced with three squads of soldiers in blacksuits.

"There are fewer of them there," Hayley said, pointing at a smaller service entrance. Only three soldiers waited.

"If it's a trap, they'll be trying to get us to go that way," Olus replied.

"Unless they know you'll do the opposite of what you think they want?"

"But then they'll know I know that and will do the opposite again, which puts us back at the beginning," Olus said, smiling. "We'll go that way."

"Roger."

They left the control room, moving back into the plant. They crossed the corridors, heading for the exit. Olus stopped when he caught sight of Pahaliah's Uin resting on the ground, discarded. He leaned over it, picking it up and scanning the area. There was blood on the wall, a smear that looked like it could have come from her arm. She was wounded, at least. He remembered she had one of the Blood capsules. Had she taken it?

He kept the Uin, folding it and putting it into a tightpack. They kept moving until they reached the end of the corridor.

They were on the upper floor of the facility, above the open space that led to the outside. Another two squads of soldiers were waiting there, taking cover behind abandoned supply crates but visible from their raised position. The terminal hadn't shown them this area, and when Olus glanced over at the walls he could see the burn marks around the camera positions.

"I think we should have gone the other way," Hayley whispered.

Olus glanced over at her. Maybe she had been right. "We still can. Follow-"

He stopped talking when he heard a buzz growing in pitch outside. Something was dropping toward the facility in a hurry. The soldiers below them froze momentarily and then began to rush outside. What the hell?

Gunfire followed. Lots of it. Shouting and screaming came next.

"Hold on," Olus said, turning and scooping Hayley into his arms.

He lifted her easily, holding her tight as he vaulted the railing, dropping to the floor below. He flexed his legs on the landing, the seraphsuit and the Gift helping him manage the stress without issue. He put Hayley down, leading her forward behind one of the crates.

He brought his rifle into his hands and raised himself over the cover so he could see outside. The enemy soldiers were backing toward the inside of the structure, firing at something. The buzz had remained over the plant. It sounded like an older model atmospheric dropship. But who would have come to his aid? Nobody knew he was here except...

One of the enemy soldiers fell as their head was pulverized. Two seconds later, a soft crack followed.

Pahaliah.

Another soldier fell. Then a third. The ones that weren't getting hit by the Zip-10 were getting back up. Converts.

"Cover me," Olus said.

"Roger," Hayley replied.

He leaped over the crates, running toward the rear of the enemy line. One of the soldiers turned to face him and was promptly shot by the younger Cage. He spread the Uin and sliced through the target's head, then moved to the next, cutting that one down as well.

He neared the outside. He could see the full scale of the fighting now, a dozen armed Plixians facing off against Thraven's soldiers, while Pahaliah picked them off from a distance. At least, he assumed it was her. Who else would have known the weapon was up there?

He joined the battle, coming at the enemy from the rear, getting into the mix and taking them down one by one. It was over within seconds, the blacksuits quickly defeated by the Servants.

Olus hurried back inside, finding Hayley already on the move toward him. They reconnected and went moved to the group that was assembling nearby.

"Captain Mann," Xanix said as he approached.

"Xanix," Olus replied. "Pahaliah contacted you?"

"Yes. There is no time to speak, Captain. Now that you are out, we must get away from the area."

Olus didn't argue. One of the other Plixians ducked down beside Hayley. "May I carry you?"

Hayley looked at Olus, who nodded. She nodded in turn, and the Plixian picked her up. Then they all began to run, back toward the small dropship hovering near the slope of the hill where the sniper was positioned.

A sharp whistle began to grow in volume as they ran.

"What the frag is going on out there?" Olus said, recognizing the sound.

"War, Captain," Xanix said. "War like you've never seen it."

They reached the dropship. It was still hovering, and the Plixians had to jump ten meters to reach the open hatch, gaining the ship one after another. Olus made sure Hayley was on board before he joined them, his bounce carrying him in last.

"Go, go, go," Xanix shouted to the pilot.

The whistle had grown so loud the noise penetrated the armor of the dropship, which began lifting up and away.

"I don't understand," Olus said as they gained thrust and altitude.

The whistle vanished. He closed his eyes, waiting for the deep rumble and thump he knew would follow. Had they gotten far enough away?

The dropship began to shake as the blast wave caught up to them, knocking them around. Warning tones sounded throughout the craft, and his stomach dropped as they lurched.

A moment later, it was over. The dropship straightened out, still airborne.

He had said he didn't understand, but that wasn't the truth. Not at all. He did understand.

Gloritant Thraven wasn't taking no for an answer.

10

COMMANDER KYLE NG TURNED OFF HIS TERMINAL, LEANING BACK IN his chair and closing his eyes. The feed to the Republic Council meeting on Earth had gone dead, blacked out after Councilwoman Lorenti had been assassinated before she could say too much.

He had known the vote was coming. He knew what the outcome was supposed to be. He also knew things hadn't gone according to plan.

Not at all.

He had made promises. So many promises. They didn't always align with one another. He had promised his partner he would love him forever. He had promised their son he would be on leave for his fifth birthday. He had promised to protect them and take care of them. He had made the same promise to the Admiral, in relation to the rest of the Republic.

But then, he had also promised Gloritant Thraven his loyalty and devotion, in exchange for the comfort of his family once the galaxy was subdued. How could he not? He had seen what the Gloritant was capable of doing. He had seen the power the Gloritant and his followers controlled. The Republic had no chance against a force like that. No chance at all. And he had promises to keep. A lot of promises. He had to prioritize them somehow.

Things were going wrong. It had started when Ruche had taken delivery of Cage and had only continued from there. Kyle didn't know all of the details. He didn't need to know. He understood that the fleet on Kell had been lost. He knew the *Brimstone* was lost. He knew Cage was a big reason why. He had only served with her briefly, but he couldn't say he was completely surprised.

And now the vote had failed. The one that would have seen those loyal to Thraven positioned as defensive patrols in the rear lines of the war with the Outworlds while the rest were sent forward to face off against the Shrikes. It hadn't failed simply or quietly, either. It had failed big, with Thraven's name cast out for all of the galaxy to hear, along with clear evidence that he had taken Cage's daughter to use as leverage. Blackmail was one thing. Abduction was another. Either way, the Republic was going to know they had been infiltrated and tricked. Or as Lorenti had put it, they were going to be forced to start looking below the surface.

He knew what they were going to find.

One storm was going to be traded for another. He had been a soldier long enough to understand how these things worked.

The question then was whose side would he be on?

He already knew the answer. He had gone too far to turn back. He was past the point of no return. He wasn't the only soldier on the *Nova* who had pledged loyalty to Thraven. The compromised Committee had seen to it that the right people had been reassigned to the right places. A change of heart would likely lead to death, and dying was the last thing on his agenda.

The minutes passed. Kyle soaked them up, trying to drag as much peaceful enjoyment out of them as he could. He had a feeling there would be no peace for a while. Maybe not for the rest of his life.

When his comm sounded in a special, reserved tone, he knew his time was up.

He opened his eyes, leaning forward and tapping his terminal. The projection turned on. He felt a chill at the sight of Gloritant Thraven, resplendent in his uniform, crisp and composed and fully in control. The vote was a setback, not a defeat. A blip of unfortunate circumstance, not the end. There was always a contingency.

"My Warriors. My Army. My Children. The time has come."

The words sent a shiver down Kyle's spine. There was such power to Gloritant Thraven. Such dignity. Such strength.

"We have done our best to lead the Republic into our future, but like a stubborn animal they refuse to be moved. They pull back and resist because they do not know the glory of what they are resisting. They do not know the beautiful future of His Promise or the honor of the Great Return. We no longer have the time to explain it to them. What will not be given must be taken if the new order of the universe is to take a firm hold.

"This will not be an easy time, but it will be our time, our opportunity to cast aside the shackles of the past and move forward into a glorious future. I demand nothing of any of you. But I do ask that you remember the promises you have made to me and your Honorants. I ask that you keep your oath, your pledge, even as the days ahead grow dark and violent and chaos grips all that we know. The dark precedes the dawn, and only we can ensure the brightness of salvation comes to all who believe."

Thraven paused, his face stoic, his posture proud and confident. Kyle couldn't help himself. He stood and raised his hand in an act of solidarity and union with the Gloritant. He believed in the future of a unified galaxy. He believed in the promise of salvation and glory. He believed that the universe would be better when Gloritant Thraven was controlling it, not from the shadows, but in front of all the nations where his Gift would be on full display.

"You will each be receiving orders shortly from your Honorants," Thraven said. "I have complete faith in you. Go forward with my blessing, and the blessing of His Promise upon you. Go forward, and do not look back. The time for secrecy is over.

"The time for war has begun."

11

CAPTAIN GOLT SHOOK HIS HEAD IN DISBELIEF. WHAT THE HELL WAS happening back on Earth? What the hell was happening to the Republic? The Council had always been a bastion of faith and security across the nations of the interplanetary government, but now it had been turned into a scene of absolute and utter chaos.

Council members under the control of an outside influence? Children being taken and held prisoner to force compliance? He had felt anxious and uncertain since the Committee had repositioned his fleet nearer to the Fringe, not many light years from where the patrol had been assaulted by the *Fire* near Anvil. The Committee had been making a lot of decisions he didn't agree with lately, showing a change in tactics that he recognized as a more aggressive stance toward the Outworlds while remaining within the guidelines of the Prime.

But now? After what he had just seen occur in the Council Chambers? Councilwoman Lorenti had brought a dark wound into the open and had been murdered for it. The feed had gone dark, leaving him and all of the other Republic Officers around the galaxy to wonder where their next order would come from, and what kind of order it would be.

He was beyond anxious and uncertain.

He was afraid.

"Sir?" Ensign Grool, a fellow Curlatin, said. "What do we do now?"

"Nothing, Ensign," Golt replied. "We continue on our mission until we are ordered otherwise."

"Aye, sir."

They were patrolling the Fringe fifty light-years from Anvil, ordered to run interference should the Outworlds make any sudden moves toward the Republic, and be prepared for orders to launch an assault on the nearby planet. A second battle group was stationed ten light years distant under the same commands, sweeping back and forth and waiting for action from one side or the other.

"Sir?" Grool said. "Do you think there will be a coup?"

"No," Golt said. "The Republic is too resolved to fall in that way. Her soldiers are loyal."

"Aye, sir."

Golt rubbed at the fur beneath his chin. It was a reflexive action intended to soothe his fraying nerves. He had said the words, and now he needed to try to believe them.

"Sir." Lieutenant Roskov approached him from the left side of the command station, holding a thin tablet. "The procurement documents require your signature."

Golt took the tablet and quickly scanned the form. It was a typical request for resupply. He moved his large finger along the bottom of it to sign it.

"Thank you, sir."

Roskov headed off to transfer the form back to Central Command. Golt looked out of his battleship's forward viewport, at the sea of stars around them, split by the other ships in his group. Half of them were the newer Kirsten class battlecruisers from Tridium Industries, fast and powerful attack vessels that in conjunction with the Apocalypse fighters were intended to help the stand up more confidently against the Shrikes.

He sighed out some of his tension, returning his attention to his terminal. He scanned through the Milnet streams, searching for incoming news from the Council Chambers. He needed to know what was happening down there. If he was going to be uneasy, he at least wanted to be informed.

Nothing. There was nothing. It was as if the entire Milnet had gone dark. The existing streams were all dead. The wider channels that were normally filled with chatter were silent. There was no data flowing through his identifier. No positioning updates. Nothing.

"Sir," Roskov's voice came over his terminal.

"Yes, Lieutenant?" he replied.

"I'm trying to send the procurement request. The transfer is failing."

Had something happened to their communications equipment?

"Chief Petty Officer Roils," Golt said, contacting the Communications Chief.

"Yes, Captain?" Roils said.

"Is there a problem with the comm gear? Our Milnet connection is dead."

"Sir, I haven't registered any discrepancies."

"Can you double-check it for me?"

"Aye, sir."

Something was wrong. Very wrong. The Milnet didn't just disappear like that.

"Sir," Grool said. "We're picking up a disterium plume."

What? "Put it on projection."

The front of the bridge updated with the projection, showing the cloud of gas on the starboard side of the battleship.

"It's the Nova Battlegroup, sir," Grool said.

Golt remembered to breathe. He was so on edge that for a moment he had been afraid of his own ships.

"Open a channel," Golt said.

"Aye, sir. Channel open."

"Commander Ng," Golt said. "What brings you to our part of the galaxy?"

He waited a few seconds. There was no reply.

"Commander?" he repeated.

"Sir, incoming torpedoes detected!" Ensign Bashir cried.

"Raise shields," Golt said.

The flare of light from the torpedoes' thrusters became visible a half-second later. They had been fired by the *Nova*! He tapped the commands on his terminal, putting the entire fleet into an immediate red alert.

"All hands to battle stations," he said. "We're under attack."

The other ships in the Nova Battlegroup began to move out from behind the battleship, firing their munitions at the Dain Battlegroup's assets. Two ships were hit before they could get their shields up, the torpedoes blowing out the sides, destroying the reactors, and venting life from the vessels.

"Treason!" Golt shouted in anger. "Scramble the fighters. Fire back. Target the *Nova*."

"Aye, sir."

"Solstice, Moonlight, Calaban," Golt said, calling out the names of the battlecruisers. "Move around to the left flank and open fire. Hit them hard and fast."

"Aye, sir," the ships' commanders replied.

"Sir, fighter groups are launching from the *Nova*."

Golt watched the projection. Four squadrons of fighters had already been dispatched, too quickly for them to counter. They were taking heavy damage, the surprise assault catching them with unaware. How could an entire Battlegroup be part of this? How could they be turning on the Republic in this way? It didn't make any sense.

"Sir, another disterium plume," Grool said.

A second plume? There were no other Republic ships in the area. He tapped the commands to switch the projection to the new targets, confused by the sudden appearance of the long and angled Outworld battleships. What were they doing here?

A moment later, a stream of black shapes began to pour from the new vessels, a hundred or more of them spreading out and heading for their position.

"Shrikes!" Grool said, the fear obvious in his voice.

"Sir, this is Commander Fifel on the Solstice. Our systems have gone offline. Our terminals are locked, our engines powered down."

"This is Commander Huggins on the Calaban. We're having technical difficulties, sir. Our weapons systems are offline. We're sitting ducks out here!"

"We need to retreat, sir," Grool said.

"Captain, Red Leader reporting. Fighters are disabled. I repeat. Our fighters are disabled. They all shut down at once."

Golt stared at the viewport, and then at the projection. They were surrounded, and everything was going wrong. He watched as the *Logan*, one of his battleships, crossed ahead of him, firing everything it had at the *Nova*. A moment later, the Shrikes joined the fray, circling the ship and unleashing one hundred small stings on it that quickly destroyed the shields. Three torpedoes from the *Nova* tore into the *Logan*, ripping three gaping holes in the superstructure.

"Call the retreat," Golt said. "Get us out of here. We need to warn the others."

"Aye, Cap-"

A sharp report sounded, and Grool slumped forward at his station, blood spraying onto his terminal. Golt reached for the sidearm at the side of his chair as two more of the bridge crew were executed.

He never got to use it. A barrel was pressed against his skull, right behind his large left eye.

"I'm sorry, Captain," Lieutenant Roskov said from the other end of the weapon. "For the glory of the Great Return."

Golt was dead before he could make any sense of why.

12

"Bullshit," Abbey said, staring at the avatar of her daughter. "I don't believe you."

"I don't care if you believe me. Gavin is dead. So is Hayley. Maybe Liv will be next?"

"Who the frag are you?"

"Venerant Holst. It's a pleasure to meet you, especially under these circumstances."

Abbey could feel her heart thumping, her soul preparing to scream out in agony. She had no reason to believe the Venerant, other than the fact that they had access to Hayley's Construct ID. Any decent Breaker could hack the Construct though. That didn't prove a damn thing. She had to stay calm, and not let Thraven and his goons get the best of her.

"If you don't care what I believe, then why are you here? Why did you answer me?"

"To give you the news. I know you've been out of touch with current events lately."

"I've got some news for your boss, too," Abbey said. "Elivee and Koy are dead, and the Haulers know it was his fragging Curlatin that killed the crew of the *Devastator*, not me. I imagine the Don won't be too happy when he finds out about that."

"It's already happened," Holst said. "A hand well-played, Abigail. The Haulers are nothing compared to the glory and might of the Gloritant and the Nephilim. They will fall as the Republic will fall. As the galaxy will fall."

"Not if I can do anything about it."

"Which you can't. Or won't. You're nothing, Cage. Too little. Too late. Why bother, anyway? Your daughter is dead."

Abbey shuddered. She couldn't let this asshole get under her skin. They were trying to make her angry. Why? To accelerate her change? She almost laughed at the idea of it. They didn't know she wasn't going to change. How could they? Thraven didn't know about the Shard either. She sure as hell wasn't going to tell him.

"She and Gavin aren't the only ones," Holst continued. "Do you remember Captain Mann?"

"Just keep throwing names out there. Forget it. I'm done here. If Thraven sent you to frag with my head, you're doing a lousy job. And you're just proving how desperate he's getting. He thought I was going to die on Azure, and I didn't. Just like I didn't die on Anvil. Just like I didn't die on Hell. I'm sure we'll meet at some point. You'll probably be stuck to the edge of my Uin."

Abbey reached out to disconnect from the Construct.

"One second, Abigail," the Venerant said. "I want to show you something."

Abbey knew she shouldn't hesitate, but she did.

An image appeared beside Hayley's avatar, floating in the center of the room. Abbey felt her stomach turn at it.

Gavin. He was bloody and broken; his throat ripped away.

"Anyone can fake a photograph," Abbey said.

"I thought you might require more."

The image changed to a video of the Goreshin ravaging her ex-husband. She only caught the first seconds before disconnecting her link to the Construct.

She leaned over in the module, bracing herself on the wall, her stomach sick. If the Venerant wasn't lying about Gavin, did that mean he wasn't lying about Hayley? She could barely handle the thought.

She felt the tears spring to her eyes. She should have warned her. She should have told her that trouble might be coming her way. Hayley was smart. She was strong. She could have handled it.

She threw her fist into the wall, the power of the shardsuit allowing her to dent the metal. She was falling into the Venerant's trap. She was allowing herself to get angry. So what? She wouldn't become a monster. Not now.

At least, not the kind of monster Thraven was expecting.

"Queenie?"

Gant was outside the module, knocking on the door.

"Queenie, are you in there?"

Abbey wiped her eyes. Hayley wasn't dead. She couldn't be. She would have known. The Shard would have told her somehow.

"Am I right? Is she alive?"

She said it out loud, hoping for resolution. The Shard couldn't speak to her. It had used itself up to repair her.

"Queenie?" Gant said again.

Abbey opened the door. Gant was looking up at her, concerned.

"Queenie, what were you doing? What happened?"

Abbey fell to her knees. "I tried to contact Hayley. To warn her." She could feel fresh tears coming. "Some asshole Venerant named Holst answered using Hayley's identifier and avatar. He said she was dead."

"Oh, Queenie," Gant said, reaching out and putting a hand on her shoulder. "You don't believe it, do you? Thraven is trying to get to you. He knows you made it off Azure, and he's afraid of you."

"I told myself that. But Holst had video of a Goreshin killing Gavin, my ex-husband."

"It could be fake."

"It wasn't. I'm sure it wasn't. Gavin was a good man. We didn't work out, but he was a good father. If they got to him, then they were close to Hayley. How would she escape from them? How could she still be alive?"

"You told me she wanted to be like you. That she was preparing to be a Breaker when she got older. Queenie, I'm sorry for your former mate, but that doesn't mean your child is lost. You can't believe what Thraven tells you. He expects the Gift to drive you mad. He wants it to do his dirty work for him and take you out of the equation."

"I know he does. I know I shouldn't believe this. But this is my daughter, Gant. I was so close to going home to her, and it was all ripped away."

"Queenie, I." Gant paused. "I don't know what to say. This is where we are, here and now. The Rejects need you. Like you said, we have a lot of work to do. We can't let Thraven beat us. You can't let him beat you. Too many lives are at stake. Too many mothers who might lose their children. Too many children who could lose their mothers."

"I can't do this knowing I let her down. I failed her."

"You can, and you will," Gant said, his barks becoming deeper and more forceful. "This has blown up beyond any one of us, and especially beyond you. The Light of the Shard came to you. It gave you power no one else has."

"Not because it wanted to. I was the only one around that it was compatible with."

"Whatever that means. That isn't the point. You're special. How? Why? It doesn't matter. It just is. The entire galaxy is at stake, Queenie. You know what we need to do. You know what you need to do. If your child is dead, then we'll avenge her. If she isn't, then we'll save her."

Abbey looked into Gant's furry face. The way his nose was wrinkled and his eyes were lowered was the most pathetic, adorable thing she had ever seen. She swallowed her fear and nodded.

"You're right. Whatever Thraven's goal is to hit me below the belt like this, I'm not going to give him the fragging satisfaction. He wants to turn me into a rage monster? I'll give him a fragging monster all right."

She leaned forward, embracing Gant and letting herself smile when he started to purr.

"Damn it, Queenie," Gant said, trying to wriggle free.

"Relax, Gant. There's nobody else around, and I could use a hug right now."

Gant stopped fighting it, wrapping his long arms around her. "For what it's worth, I don't believe she's dead," he said. "It's strategically short-sighted, and while Thraven is many words that translate to four letters in your language, the one thing he isn't is short-sighted. She's leverage he'll want to keep on hand to control you."

Abbey relaxed slightly, realizing he had a point. Thraven was hoping for a visceral, emotional reaction, not a logical one. Besides, she knew deep down that Hayley was still alive. She didn't know how, but she was sure of it. "How did you get so insightful?"

Gant's embrace softened as he froze. "A lot of pain," he replied.

Abbey was going to ask him what he meant, but Bastion appeared in the doorway ahead of her. He made a face when he saw how she and Gant were holding one another.

"Whoa," he said. "I don't mean to interrupt, err, whatever this is, but Queenie, the shit is going up big-time."

Abbey pulled away from Gant, getting to her feet. "What do you mean?"

"Captain Davlyn had Nerd send word down to us. One of the Council members was just murdered after she refused to vote for the Crisis Consolidation Bill."

"Crisis Consolidation Bill?"

"Yeah. I don't know; Nerd doesn't always speak in words that any human being can understand even though they're in Terran. Something like control of the RAS blah blah, Thraven has power over the military blah blah."

"You're saying it failed?"

"Yeah. That's what I think Nerd said. That's not the juicy part, though."

"Can you get to the point?" Gant said.

"Is that a wrench in your tightpack, or are you just happy to see me?" Bastion replied, glancing down.

Gant growled softly. "You aren't funny."

"What's the juicy part?" Abbey asked.

"The Milnet is down."

"Down?" Gant said. "You mean offline?"

"Completely. Davlyn says there's nothing moving on it."

"Queenie, this is bad," Gant said.

"What do you think? Abbey asked.

"Captain Mann's message to Ruby. He said something about an alternate network, but it was only supposed to be on Tridium-built ships."

"You're saying Tridium is in bed with Thraven?"

"In bed and making the beast with two backs," Gant replied.

Abbey wasn't familiar with the term, but she could guess what it meant. "The Republic sources hundreds of components from Tridium. Not just ships. They have contracts for everything from laser batteries to refrigeration."

"A lot of those components don't interface directly with critical systems," Gant said.

"No, but they're all on the network, aren't they?"

"Of course. Everything is. Oh. Yeah. You're right. This is worse than bad."

"What are you two getting at?" Bastion said.

"Security protocols won't allow a refrigerator to have the same access level as a main control system," Gant said. "But if you embed an undiscovered alternate network protocol in a refrigerator, and then take down the standard private communications platform also known as Milnet -"

"You can bring up your proprietary communications network and still talk to the individuals who are loyal while destroying the opposition's ability to effectively coordinate a defense," Abbey finished.

"So you're saying what, exactly?"

"Losing the vote forced Thraven's hand. He's moved up his timetable and started his war. A war the Republic has no chance of winning on their own."

"Oh," Bastion said. "You're right. That is bad. So what do we do?"

"You're going to head to the cockpit and get the *Faust* on the way to Avalon. Call back the others, whatever they've gathered is all we're taking. We don't have time to frag around. Tell Davlyn to get his ass back to Kett. I'm sure the General will understand what's happening. I don't know how he's going to react to it, but his forces are the best hope of slowing Thraven down."

"What if that asshole won't fight?" Gant said.

"Avalon first," Abbey replied.

"Isn't Thraven's attack more important?" Bastion asked.

"We can't win with what we have right now. If there's a Gate out there and we have a chance to destroy it, we need to destroy it. That will force Thraven to slow down and give us an opportunity to even the odds."

"Even the odds how?" Gant said.

"I'm saving that surprise for later," Abbey replied. "You're not going to like it."

Bastion laughed. "I can't fragging wait."

13

"EVERYBODY BUCKLED IN BACK THERE?" BASTION SAID, FLIPPING THE switches in the *Faust's* cockpit to get the old star hopper back in business.

"If they're not buckled in by now, they deserve the bruises," Abbey replied from the seat beside him.

It was the seat Ruby normally occupied, and she was determined that the synth would again. She had no idea what Sylvan Kett wanted with her or had done to her, but he was going to put her back the way he found her, or there was going to be hell to pay.

"Captain Davlyn, Dak, you know what to do."

"Aye, Queenie," Davlyn replied.

The Captain had been even more agreeable after Councilwoman Lorenti had been killed and the Milnet had gone down. It was pretty easy for him to understand what was happening, and it was validation that the Rejects weren't full of shit. He had been almost grateful to be out in the Fringe with them instead of in the middle of a Republic fleet whose loyalties were questionable.

When Gant had turned over a handwritten schematic for updating the *High Noon's* comm systems to route privately through the Galnet,

Davlyn was even more impressed. It was a system Gant had only just finished integrating with the *Brimstone* before the Rejects had left, and would hopefully allow them to stay in touch.

Not that Abbey wanted them to reach out just yet. She wanted to take the General by surprise. She wanted the *High Noon* to show up out of nowhere with the now fully-loyal Captain and the former mercenary in tow to plant the flag in Abbey's name, carrying a method for their fleet to stay in contact with one another when all of the military assets were down. That was all she wanted them to do for now.

She would deal with Kett herself.

"Let's go," she said.

"Roger," Bastion replied.

He took hold of the *Faust's* control yoke and started adding thrust. The ship slid along the floor of the hangar on its skids, building speed while it moved toward the open bay.

"You know," Bastion said as they approached the black beyond. "Davlyn could frag us the minute you're off this ride. He's been on his best behavior because he's terrified of you."

"He won't. He's more afraid of the Republic falling to Thraven. Do you think I'm frightening?"

Bastion glanced over. "Nah. I think you're perfect."

"Even with this?" she held up her hands. The small ridges were obvious on the back, running up toward her wrists.

"Especially with that. It makes you unique. Exotic."

"You're lying."

"Not this time."

The *Faust* reached the edge of the battleship, slipping through the momentary lapse in shields and blasting out into space. Bastion guided her around, shooting her past the bridge before tapping on the FTL controls.

"Good hunting, Queenie," Davlyn said.

"Roger," Abbey replied. "We'll see you soon."

The *Faust* continued to drift perpendicular to the *High Noon* while the computer calculated the FTL positioning. A green light on the dashboard indicated it was ready, and Bastion leaned over and tapped the control. The disterium cloud expanded around them, sending them on their way.

Abbey unbuckled herself and stood, circling toward the back. "How long to Avalon?" she asked.

"About six hours," Bastion replied.

"Call an all-hands in the CIC."

"Aye, Queenie."

"Thank you."

"No problemo."

Abbey left the cockpit. The CIC was immediately behind it, the main open area in the center of the ship. None of the Rejects were currently present, each of them busy finishing up the preparations for the journey. Pik and Benhil were loading up the weapons and equipment they had taken from the *High Noon*, while Gant was in the Construct module, using the server to integrate his subnet design. Phlenel and her bot were down in the medical module, doing something to the bot there, Jequn was in the living quarters stocking the kitchen, and Trin was... Where was Trin?

"Attention all you losers," Bastion said. "Queenie wants an all-hands in five minutes. Last one there has to kiss Gant."

"Like that's such a bad thing," she heard Gant shout from below.

She couldn't help but smile. It was good to be back with her family. It was good to have their support in this. She was doing her best to stay focused and not worry about Hayley, and she didn't know if she could have without their presence.

"She's okay," she told herself.

She had heard that mothers always seemed to know when something bad happened to their children, even when they weren't with them, and she had never had that feeling. What good was the Light of the Shard? What good was the Shard's Gift if it couldn't do the same?

Of course, that didn't mean she wasn't in Thraven's hands, ready to be used against her. She had to be prepared for that possibility. She had to be prepared to make the impossible choice. Would she let the entire galaxy burn to save her child?

If it came to it, she knew she would. But she would be damned if it would come to that. She would save them both, and that was the end of it.

"Queenie," Jequn said, coming down the ladder into the CIC. Bastion arrived at the same time, moving in from the cockpit. "I've got about three boxes of food bars left to unpack and then we're all set.

"Queenie," Benhil said, his head peeking up from the ladder as he ascended. He scanned the room. "I'm not last."

"Me neither," Pik said, following Benhil. "Gant is behind me."

"It doesn't matter if I'm last," Gant said. "I can't kiss myself."

"I'd like to see you try," Abbey said.

They spread out inside the CIC.

"We're missing Phlenel and Trin," Benhil said.

Phlenel's bot climbed the ladder. "Does it count if I'm not physically present?" it asked.

"Debatable," Bastion said.

"I'll give it to you," Abbey said.

"Thank you, Queenie."

"Where is Trin?" Pik asked.

"Probably planting a bomb or something," Bastion said. "Did you check the engine room?"

"She can't kiss Gant either," Pik said. "She doesn't have a mouth."

"She can hear you," Trin said, her feet appearing on the ladder, leading down from the upper level. "And she doesn't appreciate the comments."

She dropped to the floor, turning to face Abbey.

"My apologies, Queenie. I just wanted some time alone. I am not fully adjusted to this yet. My mind has the capability of feeling sadness, but the lack of a physical response is unsettling."

"Now I feel like an ass," Pik said. "I'm sorry, Trin. Well, not completely sorry because you were working for Thraven and you did try to kill us, but maybe we can call it even?"

"I'm glad you mentioned that," Abbey said. "It's one of the reasons I wanted you all together. Most of us here know who Trinity was and our history with one another. If any of you have any grievances to air or any hard feelings to get out, I want you to do it now. I don't need any bullshit when things get serious."

"Things aren't serious yet?" Benhil asked.

"You know what I mean."

"Do you trust her, Queenie?" Bastion said.

"Yes," Abbey replied without hesitation.

"Good enough for me," Benhil said.

"Me, too," Pik agreed.

"Welcome to the Rejects," Bastion said. "Any shit we give you from here on out is because you're one of us."

"Thank you," Trin said. "For what it's worth, I'm sorry I tried to kill you all. I'm not the same person I was before."

"You need a nick," Bastion said. "So does Phlenel."

"Phlenel has one," Abbey said.

"Pudding," Phlenel said.

"Hah! That's mine," Bastion replied. "Let me think." He put his hand on his chin. "Ironwoman? No. Terminator? No. That's stupid. Robotrin? Ugh. Knight? No."

"Brain-in-the-box?" Pik offered.

"That's worse than mine," Bastion said.

"How about Void?" Benhil suggested. "Since you can't show emotions, and because it's fragging cool and frightening at the same time."

"I like it," Pik said.

"Me, too," Abbey agreed.

"It will do," Trin said.

"Deposit it," Bastion said.

"Deposited," Abbey said. "Void it is. Now let's move on to more important business. I would normally turn to Ruby for this, but she isn't here. So, who can tell us about Avalon?"

"I can," Benhil said. "It's your fairly standard Republic world. Terraformed about two hundred years ago, population of a few million. If Tridium has a factory there, I never heard about it."

"I don't expect their skunkworks to be orbiting the planet itself," Abbey said. "But it's probably somewhere nearby, within a few thousand AU. Close enough to use the planet as a drop point, far enough that they can keep it somewhat secret."

"The Gate would have to be further out than that," Gant said. "If they want to keep it completely secret."

"There's a huge gas nebula a couple of light years from the planet," Benhil said. "I'd be willing to bet the factory is hiding there."

"It could be in any direction," Gant said. "Without coordinates, it'll take weeks to find it."

"If someone is making deliveries to it from Avalon, then someone on Avalon knows where it is," Abbey said.

"We just need to find that special someone," Bastion said.

"Sounds romantic," Benhil said.

"Odds that the someone in question is a Tridium employee?" Jequn asked.

"Too obvious," Gant said. "But I'm sure we'll be able to connect them to Tridium one way or another."

"How are recent developments going to be affecting the planet?" Phlenel asked.

"You mean the potential civil war?" Abbey said.

"Yes."

"Avalon is pretty far removed. Hopefully, it won't be a problem."

"This is us, Queenie," Bastion said. "I'm willing to take bets that there will be some kind of problem."

"And not the one we're expecting," Pik said. "Deposit that."

"Personally, I think we can handle any complications that come our way," Trin said.

"I like your attitude," Abbey said. "Let's go with that. We'll gear up for a civilian excursion in the planet's capital. Cherub, Okay, Joker, you're with me. The rest of you will provide backup."

"Queenie, you don't want me to come?" Gant asked.

"Gant are still relatively rare outside of Ganemant," Abbey said. "Thraven is bound to have a heavy presence on a world so close to his pet project, and I don't want your existence making them suspicious."

"Like you won't?" Bastion said. "You're going to have to do something about your hair, at least."

Abbey put her hand to the thick, sharp locks. "I think I can get away with it as a neo-classical-chic-post-modern cut."

"Whatever the frag you just said. What about your hands? I think it's exotic, but that's not always a good thing."

Abbey looked at her hands. She spread her fingers, feeling a sense of calm as she directed the naniates to cover them over. At first, they were the same color as the shardsuit, but they adjusted to refract the light so that they blended in with her skin, smoothing her out.

"Nice," Pik said. "I bet you could make yourself invisible like that."

Abbey glanced over at him and smiled. "You know, I probably could. We've got six hours until we reach Avalon. Gant, I need you to finish your work on the subnet and then figure out how to change the *Faust's* identifier to something that doesn't make us easy to pick out in a crowd. The rest of you, when you're finished with whatever you're doing, the rest of the time is yours."

"Aye, Queenie," Gant said.

"Good. I'm going to get something to eat. I'm fragging starving. Dismissed."

14

"We've got clearance to land, Queenie," Bastion said, "Seems like it's still business as usual out here, at least for the time being."

"I figured as much when we weren't attacked the moment we came out of FTL," Abbey replied.

She checked the fit of her clothes before sliding a long overcoat above them, making sure the edges of the shardsuit remained hidden beneath the sleeves. She didn't need the individuals on the surface staring at her because she had dressed like a soldier.

She supposed she could have withdrawn the naniates back into her body, but that would have left her naked, and she was so accustomed to the feeling of the pressure on her flesh that she felt like she would be less confident without it. When you were entering hostile territory undercover, confidence was paramount.

They had arrived ten minutes earlier, dropping from FTL in a travel lane a few AU from Avalon's orbit. The planet had seemed busy from the position, with a number of shuttles and transports making their way in and out of the atmosphere, and a smaller ring station providing a rest and refuel for the ships and their crews that didn't want to make landfall. Bringing a loaded cargo vessel to the surface was a massive drain on reactor power that most captains avoided whenever they could.

While there was plenty of shipping activity, there wasn't any sense of a galaxy ready to fall apart and fall to war. Either word hadn't reached Avalon, which Abbey doubted, or the government managing the planet had decided to keep it quiet, and was handling it internally. While the Council's vote was big news to those interested in politics, the number of civilians glued to the streams to see the outcome was likely minuscule. That included freighter captains and merchant vessels.

The fact that there were no Republic fleet assets in the area didn't hurt either. Avalon was close to the Fringe, but far enough from any of the hotspots that it was protected by standard Planetary Defense, most of it ground-based except when under attack. Those were local governmental forces, not national military, who were probably too damn loyal to their world for Thraven to get to turn against it.

Of course, that hadn't meant they were inherently safe. The *Faust* was an older model star hopper, a kind not that common anywhere in the galaxy. One that had been tagged and listed, her supposedly unchangeable identifier placed into a database of ships to be on the lookout for. Abbey was certain that if they had come out of FTL under their original identification, they would have been met with a much harsher greeting.

"I wish we had more time to grab stuff," Pik said, looking down at himself.

While Olus had left them a wardrobe to use for these kinds of missions, the Trover selection had been relatively slim, forcing Pik to cobble stuff together and hope he could make it work. A pair of tight pants, a surprisingly too-big shirt, and a dark jacket gave him the look of a cheap pusher or a pimp.

"There's no planet in the universe where that looks good," Benhil agreed, laughing.

"Queenie, do we have time to stop and do some shopping?" Pik asked.

"What do you think?" Abbey replied.

Pik shrugged. "You never know unless you ask."

"No shopping. We're here on business. Gant, do you have anything for me?"

"Aye, Queenie," Gant replied. "Tridium has an office on the planet. I'm passing the coordinates to you now."

"Roger."

"I still want to come along, you know," he continued. "I could hang behind you, stay out of sight."

"I appreciate the sentiment, but it's too risky. You don't need to worry about me, Gant. I've got the Gift to protect me."

"The Gift has conditions. I don't."

Abbey shivered at the thought. He was right, of course. Even after being cleansed by the Shard, the Gift still didn't work for free. Nothing that powerful did.

"Just follow the orders, okay?"

"You're the Queen."

"Imp, how long to touch down?"

"Five minutes."

The *Faust* began to shake softly the moment he said it, the ship entering the planet's atmosphere.

"Cherub, are you geared up and ready to go?"

"Affirmative, Queenie," Jequn replied. "I'll be down in a minute."

The rest of the ride was uneventful. Jequn had joined them by the time the ship made its landing, touching down onto the spaceport's tarmac.

"Yeah, I can do easy landings too," Bastion said. "It's nice to have a chance every once in a while."

"Don't get too comfortable," Abbey replied. "Keep your eyes and ears open. We don't have Ruby to watch our asses for us."

"Roger. I'll be here. Sitting in the cockpit. Watching the sensors. Trying to stay awake."

"Imp."

"I'm just fragging with you, Queenie. I've got it."

"Open her up."

The hatch on the side of the *Faust* slid open, the short ramp extending to the surface. They made their way to the ground. The air was thick and humid, and the nearby suns were beating down through cloudless skies. They had been directed to the personal landing section, leaving them surrounded by other smaller, privately-owned spacecraft. She could see a cargo ship coming down in the distance, dropping slowly, its reactors pushing out massive amounts of power to the anti-gravity generators that enabled the descent. It would reach the nearby loading station in a few minutes, one of a dozen she could see to the east. Most of the stations were already occupied, suggesting a lot of goods were coming and going today. More than usual? Knowing Thraven was building a Gate nearby made her more curious about the movements.

"The worst thing about ala carte parking is having to walk to the transfer terminal," Benhil said, wiping at his head. "It feels like Hell out here."

"High summer," Abbey said. "It gets equally cold in the winter. You can't say that about Hell."

"At least we're outside," Pik said. "Maybe you'll get a tan."

"Do I look like I need a tan?" Benhil replied, holding up his already dark hand.

Pik laughed.

Abbey blinked a few times, feeling the Gift shifting around and within her. Naniates flooded over her eyes, creating an invisible sheath above them, which became an augmented overlay a moment later. When the Shard had upgraded and cleansed her, it had integrated the technology of the demonsuit into the network of the machines, giving the aggregated instance of them all of the informational capabilities of the hardware embedded into it. In essence, the symbiotes had become an alternate version of the system on a chip, albeit with a massively improved level of responsiveness and redundancy.

The coordinates Gant had transferred to her appeared in the left corner of her eyes. As she looked at the city skyline in the distance, the building in question became outlined in red.

"It isn't that bad out here," she said. "And you should be more accustomed to the heat."

"Are you kidding? I lost my tolerance about three seconds after Captain Mann brought us to the *Faust*. Give me climate control any day."

"Suck it up, soldier," Abbey replied, smiling. "Tridium's office is that way. Considering the location of the factory was being held in an unnetworked data vault, I'm willing to bet that the existence of it isn't common company knowledge, and isn't mentioned anywhere on their networks, either."

"So then what are we doing here?" Benhil asked.

"Didn't you used to be a spy?"

"More like a saboteur. Those were the days."

"What's the weakest link in any secure operation?"

Benhil grinned. "The idiots running it. Okay, I get you. But how do we figure out which idiot it is?"

"You can't run an entire factory completely hush-hush. There are too many moving parts to manage quietly, even if it's all been anonymized or misdirected to throw off the scent. There might not be specific information moving through Tridium's office, but there will be a number of pieces that we could try to tie together."

"Except?" Pik said.

"Except that will be too slow. The point is, someone in Tridium knows about the factory. Maybe they even know what Thraven's building out there, but I doubt it. It won't be one of the executives, that'll be too damn obvious. Someone lower down on the food chain who has enough access to the network to make those types of transactions look innocuous."

"Systems Admin?" Benhil said.

"Could be. Or an accountant. Or Individual Resources."

"Well, that narrows it down."

"Not enough. That's where individual nature comes in."

"What do you mean?"

"If you're secretly in control of one of the Nephilim's most important projects and you know the war has just started, how do you think you might be feeling right about now?"

"That would depend on the status of the project," Jequn said. "If everything was going well, I would be feeling very proud of myself."

"And if it weren't, I would be nervous as hell," Benhil said.

"What about the other Tridium employees who don't know frag all about any of it?" Abbey asked.

"Business as usual," Benhil said. "Smart thinking."

"I learned to think that way in Breaker training. I didn't come prepackaged."

"Queenie-in-a-box," Pik said. "That could come in handy."

"You'll have to settle for Queenie out of the box," Abbey said.

Pik laughed. "Even better."

15

"WHAT MADE YOU DECIDE TO BECOME A BREAKER ANYWAY, QUEENIE?" Benhil asked.

They were sitting together at a table outside of a restaurant across from the Tridium building. They had a spread of dishes across the table, ranging from simple Terran delicacies like curry to more exotic fare, including Atmosian Silbrach. Nobody who saw them would take them for residents of the planet, not with their long overcoats and pants, but that didn't make them stand out. There were plenty of other traders around, many in uniforms that included heavy formal jackets, and the establishment had weak shields surrounding the patio to keep their conditioned air from escaping.

"I was bored," Abbey replied.

She had her eyes on the lobby of the offices, tracking every individual that came and went, surveying their body language for signs of stress or elation the way she had been taught. Being a Breaker was about more than hacking networks. It was about getting into things you weren't supposed to get into, whether it was a locked terminal, a locked door, or a locked head. It was about finding a way past any security measures that stood in the way. Sometimes that also meant hacking people. Social engineering.

Sometimes that also meant killing them.

"That's it?" Jequn said. "You were bored?"

"Why do any of us decide to do anything?" Pik said. "I joined the RAS to get away from my girlfriend."

"You did not," Benhil said.

"I did. She was a brute, that one. It's tradition on Tro for the mother of the son to choose the spouse. Mainly because no Trover male would take a Trover female any other way." He laughed. "I was ready to join Planetary Defense, get paired, have a few little Trovers. But the choice? Ugh."

"What makes Trover women so bad?" Jequn asked.

"Have you ever met one?" Pik asked.

"No."

"Well, there you go."

"I'm still not accepting that you were just bored," Benhil said. "There has to be more to the story than that."

"Not really," Abbey replied. "My parents were regular blue-collars. They owned a small clothing store on Earth, in Chicago. My sister Liv and I had a pretty normal life. Nothing outside of the usual childhood drama. Except Liv was satisfied to stay and settle down, and I wanted to be challenged. Mentally. Physically. I have a strong competitive streak."

"No shit?" Pik said sarcastically.

"I figured the armed services would be the challenge I was looking for. When I heard about the Breaker program, I was all in."

"I heard you have a kid," Benhil said. "HSOCs don't usually have time to have kids."

"I was young and still a little immature. He was older and really good looking. To be honest, we didn't really fit. I should have seen then that it was never going to work long-term, but love is blind. We made the distance work, and in some ways, it made things better. When we got together, things were incredible. He told me he was off prevention when Hayley was conceived. I didn't care. I thought the odds of getting pregnant from one time weren't that high, right? It was stupid. The best kind of stupid."

She could feel the emotions flooding in, threatening to distract her. She had to swallow them. To force them back. They were eating and talking to keep their cover while they waited. She was still working.

"Liv has been more of a mother to Hayley than I have. She's been there when I couldn't. The amazing thing is, for all of that, Hayley still wants to be just like me. She tells me I make a difference in individual's lives, even if they'll probably never know it. That the work I do has a value that goes way beyond me. There was a time when my motivations were selfish. I wanted to be the best for me. Then I wanted to be the best for her. Now? I want to be the best for everyone. Somebody has to."

"I think you're the best, Queenie," Pik said. "With or without the Gift."

"Sounds like a great kid, DQ," Benhil said. "I hope we get to meet her when all of this shit is over."

"Me, too," Abbey replied.

They fell into a momentary silence. Abbey continued watching the individuals moving in and out of the building. Somebody in there knew about the factory, and about the Gate. She hoped they would make an appearance soon. Every minute they wasted on Avalon was another minute Thraven was spending tearing her galaxy apart.

"I joined the RAS to get away from my parents," Benhil said. "My old man was addicted to Lrug Flower."

"Your father was rich?" Pik said.

"Too rich for his own damn good," Benhil replied. "He spent six out of eight days hallucinating, and when he came back to reality, he would get belligerent as hell for having to do a couple of days work to pay for his habit. He took it out on me, from the time I was eight years old until I made it to seventeen and joined up."

"What about your mother?" Jequn asked.

"She would disappear when he would get enraged. She seemed to know hours ahead of time when he would be in a mood. The bitch used me as a shield and let me get beat instead. Thanks, mom." He shook his head. "It's ancient history now. I haven't seen them since I left, and if I ever see them again, it'll be too soon."

"You've got a better family now," Pik said.

"You mean you assholes?" Benhil said. "Marginally." He smiled.

"Queenie." Bastion's voice cut into Abbey's ear.

"Imp," she whispered. "What's up?"

"It may be nothing, but I've been watching the traffic around here for the last two hours. An old jumper detached from the ring station and is headed down to the surface."

"So?"

"Ships dock at the station to avoid the surface, not because they have better brothels. Mostly. Why would a jumper suddenly decide to come down? Like I said, it may be nothing, but you wanted me to keep an eye out."

"Right. Keep tracking it. Gant."

"Yes, Queenie?" Gant said.

"Scout whoever comes out of it when it lands. If they look suspicious, follow them."

"Roger."

Abbey glanced over at the others. The interruption from Bastion had silenced them again.

"Nothing we can't handle," she said.

"Right," Benhil agreed. "As I was saying, I joined up, made it into HSOC training, and angled for work as far away from home as I could get it. That's what got me into the Outworlds. In the meantime, I..."

Benhil's voice trailed off when he noticed Abbey's eyes had locked onto someone.

"I think we've got him," Abbey said, slowly getting to her feet.

"Which one?" Pik asked.

"Just follow me, but not too close."

"Okay."

Abbey left the table, pushing through the shields and into the humid air. She kept her eyes on the target, an older man in simple pants and a stylish blue shirt who looked just a little too pleased with himself. He was wearing an ear-to-ear smirk, as though he knew the punchline to the galaxy's funniest joke.

And maybe he did.

She stayed across the street, walking parallel as he headed away from the building on foot. She could tell by the tension in his jaw that he was fighting to control his emotions and stay at least somewhat reserved. Who was he, and what did he know?

She was going to find out.

Was there a chance she had the wrong individual? Of course. But her experience told her this was the mark, and she had to trust in her training.

"Queenie," Bastion said. "The jumper just touched down."

"I'm headed out to meet it," Gant said.

"Roger. I'm tailing our idiot. Maintain comm silence unless it's an emergency."

"Roger," Gant said.

Abbey continued trailing the man, crossing the street and increasing her pace as he descended into one of the city's many transport hubs. If Abbey lost him in the endless maze of computer-controlled tunnels and pods that ran beneath the city, she would never locate him again.

She picked up the pace as she lost sight of him, slipping between other individuals as they rode the belt down. "Excuse me," she said, ducking under a Plixian and easing her way around a Terran woman.

"Watch where you're going," the woman said.

"Sorry," Abbey replied. She looked at the bottom of the belt. The mark was off already, closing in on the queue. Only a few individuals were waiting for a pod.

She was too far behind. Damn it. A Trover was on the belt in front of her.

"Excuse me," she said. "Can I get past."

"What's your rush?" the Trover asked, turning his head and looking down at her. "It'll get there."

"I'm late for an appointment," she said.

"Not my problem," he replied.

Abbey considered shoving him out of the way but didn't. It wouldn't help to draw that kind of attention. She leaned over to see past him. The target was third in line for a pod.

The belt reached the bottom, and the Trover stepped off.

"Asshole," Abbey said as she finally got by, walking briskly toward the queue.

He was next up, and a pod was already incoming, running along the track to meet him. She started reaching out with the Gift, ready to use it to disable the pod. Too much attention. What if the mark knew about the Gift? What if he was a Venerant or an Evolent?

The pod came to a stop, the door sliding open. Abbey didn't get on the line. She walked past it, running alongside to the edge of the track. The pod door closed and it accelerated into the tunnel. She got a look at its identifier as it did.

"Queenie, where are you?" Benhil asked.

"Pod station," she replied. "He got away."

"Are we fragged?"

"Not yet."

16

"I HAVE THE POD ID," ABBEY SAID. "I'M QUEUING UP. I'LL CONTACT YOU once I have an updated position."

"How are you going to find him? There are at least a thousand tunnels down there."

"Why do seem to keep forgetting that I was a Breaker before I went to Hell?"

"It's the hair, I guess. What are you going to do?"

"All of the pods have to communicate with one another, so they don't crash in the interchanges. I just need to break into the onboard system of one of them and track the identifier. I should be able to get its destination."

"Piece of cake," Benhil said.

"Try to stay somewhat inconspicuous while I do all the work," Abbey said.

"Haha. It's good to be the Queen, isn't it?"

"Yeah, it's fragging great."

It didn't take long for her to move to the front of the queue. She hopped into a pod, leaning back into one of the three seats in the small sled.

"Destination?" a synth voice asked.

"Spaceport," Abbey replied.

The pod began to move forward, quickly gaining speed. She didn't need to go to the spaceport, but it was a two-minute ride away; a fairly long trip relative to the other stations in the system.

She leaned forward, putting her hand on the dashboard and reaching out with the Gift. She could feel a gossamer thread stretch out from the shardsuit, sinking through the material to the electronics hidden behind it and connecting like a built-in extender. She waited a few seconds for the secured terminal to appear behind her eyes, open for instructions.

There was no need to tap a keypad or wiggle her fingers. She thought the commands and the naniates captured them, passing them along to the pod's computer.

She ran through a basic password cracking algorithm first, increasing the complexity as her efforts at gaining entry failed. She ran through her top three algorithms, amazed at how quickly the naniates processed the instructions and executed them against the pod. She was aware of every second that passed as she did. Once the pod reached its destination, she would have to disembark and re-queue for another one, losing whatever gains she made and starting from scratch. She had to stay focused.

She closed her eyes, removing the distraction of her peripheral vision as she dug deeper into her memory banks for the more advanced programming filters. Code spewed out onto the pod's terminal, appearing almost instantly in full as it escaped her mind. Nearly a minute had passed. She was halfway there and still hadn't gotten in.

"Damn it," she whispered, starting to feel the pressure.

She had to remind herself of the same thing she reminded Benhil. She was a fragging Breaker. Cool and confident. She spit out another algorithm, trying a vulnerability that she had skipped, figuring it would have been patched already.

It wasn't. The terminal unlocked, giving her open access to the pod controls and read-only access to the entire transport system. She looked up the identifier of the target's pod, saving the coordinates. Then she entered the new destination. She was jostled as the transport came to a jarring halt, beeping loudly. The lights went off, leaving her stranded in the dark. Had she crashed the system?

She opened her eyes and looked out at the black. A few seconds passed in absolute stillness. The tunnel was small, and there was no easy way out of the pod. She could break the forward viewport if she had to but then what? Walk all the way back?

"Joker, can you hear me?" She waited a few seconds. "Joker?"

Nothing. The fragging comm signals could reach from space, but not through a damned tunnel. She knew better than that. Different tech. It was still frustrating.

She leaned forward, putting her hands on the viewport, ready to push it out. At the same time, the lights turned back on in the tunnel and the pod, and a soft hum indicated the system was coming back to life. Her alterations had forced it to reboot and recalibrate, nothing more.

The pod started moving again, reversing course and adjusting for the thousands of other pods moving around it simultaneously. A minute later, she was at the transfer station, exiting the pod and ascending back to the surface. The individuals she passed were all whispering about how odd it was for the transport system to go offline like that, but there was little sense of panic. Maybe it wasn't as odd an occurrence as she might have guessed? At least she was out of there.

She reached the surface, involuntarily raising an eyebrow when she did. It was as though she had been transported to another planet, not just another place in the city. The suns were almost down, the daylight fading. Everything around her was lit up in bright patterns and colors. Everything, including a large portion of the individuals wandering the area. It was the only thing consistent about their clothing. Some wore cloaks. Some wore skinsuits, some wore almost nothing at all, reducing to skimpy bikinis and thongs that were lined with lights that flashed and vibrated in a rhythm all their own. She had never seen anything like it, and she turned her head, watching in fascination for a moment before regaining her focus.

The target was here somewhere. Now she just had to find him.

"Queenie, do you copy?" Joker said.

"Affirmative," she replied.

"Where are you?"

"I'm not sure. Everything is covered in lights."

Benhil laughed. "Oh, man. I've always wanted to check out Brighton."

"Brighton?"

"What do you think they'd call a neighborhood like that? Light City? Bulby Place? Laser Street?"

"Shut up and make your way over here."

"Sure thing, Queenie, but we're going to need to do a little shopping if we're going to fit in over there."

"Did someone say shopping?" Pik said.

She couldn't argue. The others who didn't have illuminated outfits drew the wrong kind of attention. She looked down at herself and smiled. She didn't need to do any shopping.

She reached out to the Gift that composed the shardsuit at the same time she let her overcoat hang open. The naniates flared with light, sending waves of alternating color patterns running along her entire body.

"Better," she said.

"What's better?" Benhil asked.

"That is fragging awesome," a passing woman said, eyes watching her shardsuit. "You should head over to Taggers. You'll win the Light-show for sure."

"Thanks. Where's Taggers?"

The woman laughed. "It figures a visitor would have the best display. Head that way about four blocks, turn left, look for the building that's lighting up the entire city." She smiled again and went on her way.

"Joker, I"m going to head over to some place called Taggers to look for our mark. Let me know once you've made it into Brighton."

"Aye, Queenie," Benhil replied. "We're dropping at a fashion station now. ETA thirty minutes."

"Roger. Queenie out."

17

THE OUTSIDE OF BRIGHTON WAS A DAZZLING SPECTACLE.

The inside of Taggers was nothing short of insane.

Loud, thumping music. Individuals of all races and nations everywhere, each of them coated in their own array of flashing lights. Multiple bars and stages, bots floating around offering some concoction that spewed smoke, and a chaotic blend of excitement and relaxation threatened to permeate her focus.

She might have enjoyed the place if she were there as a civilian, though there were some elements that didn't sit well. The music was one thing. The lights, something else. But there were other things going on inside Taggers. Pleasure synths, prostitution, drug use. It wasn't obvious just walking through the place, but Abbey could see the signs of it. Dark corners in a place like this? Specially marked doors? Then there were the visitors who had embedded lights directly into their flesh, walking around unclothed for all of the galaxy to see. And it wasn't only humans. Atmos, Trovers, even a couple of Skinks. Taggers was a place where anything seemed to go, and hardly anyone seemed to notice.

But was her target in here?

He would be tough to find in Brighton no matter what she did. He would be harder to find in here, where the density was tight enough that she could barely make it two steps without bumping into someone, or having someone bump into her.

"Joker," she said softly into her comm. "What the frag is taking you so long?"

"Queenie," Benhil replied. "Sorry, Queenie. Pik's being a pain in the ass."

"Nothing fits me," Pik said.

"Too small?" Abbey asked.

"Too big. It's embarrassing. They're sold out of all of the most common Trover sizes. I don't want to be common."

"There's nothing common about you," Benhil said.

"How do you mean that?"

"Do you all have lights on your clothes?" Abbey said.

"Yeah."

"Then get the frag over here. I can't do this by myself. There are at least a thousand individuals in Taggers alone."

"We're on our way. Give us a few."

Abbey dropped the comm link and continued making her way through Taggers. She was drawing a lot of looks from the other partiers, a lot of them making comments on her outfit on the way past. She was having fun with that part of the work, alternating the patterns and colors and impressing anyone nearby. It didn't have to be all business, and it fit with her cover.

She made up to one of the multiple bars in the building, reaching the counter and turning her head to see along the line of patrons. She would never be able to find her target from this angle. She needed to get up higher.

"What are you doing down here?" the bartender asked. He was a Fizzig, and he waddled slowly to her, picking up a glass in a meaty hand.

"What do you mean?" Abbey asked. It was a strange way to approach someone.

He pointed past her overcoat. "You could win the Lightshow with that." He pointed to her left, and she looked to a currently empty stage. "It's starting in two minutes. Just enough time to get over there and win."

Abbey didn't have any interest in winning any contests. She did have an interest in getting her eyes above the crowd. She shrugged off her coat, glancing at the bartender, who was staring at the guns on her hips.

"A girl can't be too safe," she said, before removing the guns and putting them with her coat. She handed the whole thing out toward him. "Watch this for me, will you?"

His eyes traveled the length of her body, mesmerized by the lights. He couldn't figure out how she was producing them. Good. He took her coat and the guns, putting them behind the counter.

"What do I win, anyway?" she asked.

"You don't know? An outfit like that and you didn't wear it specifically to win the Lightshow?"

"No. I didn't think this was that big of a deal."

He laughed. "Trust me, your highness. It's a big deal."

Abbey's eyes narrowed at the reference. "Why did you call me that?" she asked, leaning over the bar.

He put up his hands. "What? Because you're going to be the Queen of the Show. That's all. I didn't mean any harm."

She backed off. "Right. So what do I win again?"

"Fifty-thousand."

"If I win, half of it is yours."

He grunted. "You aren't the first Terran female to make that promise."

"I'll be the first to keep it."

"Yeah, right. I'd wish you luck, but you don't need it." He huffed and turned away.

She shrugged and headed in the direction he had pointed, finding a group of individuals waiting near a set of steps up to the stage. They were all decked out in different attire that flashed and blinked and streamed and glowed, giving them an almost unreal ethereal appearance. They were all talking to one another, clearly accustomed to the friendly competition of the Lightshow, but they slowly fell silent as each of them noticed her approaching.

"Wow," a narrow Atmo female said. She had a complex illuminated contraption circling her naked body, casting her gray skin in a colorful hue. "I might as well not even bother going up there."

"Awesome work," another contestant said. He was a human in baggy clothes, the lights and folds in the cloth working together to create a moving image as he shifted.

"This is not better than that," Abbey said, impressed by the work.

"It is, sister," the Atmo said. "It looks like the light is coming from your skin. All of your skin."

In a sense, it was.

Another Fizzig trundled up to her. "You entering the Show?" he asked.

"The bartender suggested I should."

He smiled. "My brother. Yeah, you should. We're lining up right now. I'm going to put you at the end, let everyone else build up to you."

Abbey shrugged. She didn't care. She just wanted the better perspective. "Okay."

"Queenie," Benhil said as the Fizzig positioned them. "We just reached Brighton."

"Good. Spread out and keep your eyes peeled for the target."

"Okay, but it's going to be like trying to find a cow in a snowstorm."

"What?"

"Cow in a snowstorm. You know, cows are white. Snow is white."

"I grew up on Earth, and I don't know what you're talking about."

"Never mind. It's going to be tough."

"So don't waste time."

"Okay, Creatures of the Light," the Fizzig shouted as the music came to an abrupt stop. "It's time to put on a show."

He started laughing as he tapped the communicator on his thick chest.

"The razzle. The dazzle. The Lightshow is about to begin!" He looked back at Abbey as the crowd in Taggers cheered. "They're going to go wild."

The line of contestants began making their way up the ramp, handled by a Terran at the top of the steps who told them when to start strutting across the stage. Abbey thought the whole thing was stupid, but at least she would get a quick scan of the entire field and then she could get the frag out.

The crowd continued to cheer as each of the contestants made their way up to the stage, vanishing from her sight one by one until she was the only one left. It seemed to her that they held her back a little longer than the others, giving her a grand entrance she didn't want or think she deserved.

"You're up, your highness," the Fizzig said, smiling and ushering her toward the steps.

"Queenie."

Abbey stopped and turned. Gant was pushing through the legs of the closest spectators, and he vaulted the divider and ran up to her.

"Gant? What's going on?"

"I followed the goons in here. Then I saw you. Coincidence?"

"Come on; we don't have all night," the Fizzig said.

Abbey looked at him, and then at Gant. Then she grabbed Gant's hand, pulling him along.

"What's this?" the Fizzig asked.

"He's my Gant," Abbey replied. "He goes with the outfit."

Gant groaned as they started ascending the steps.

"Joker, Okay, Cherub, make your way to Taggers asap. I think we have a situation developing."

"Of course we do," Benhil replied.

"On my way," Jequn said.

"Me, too," Pik said.

"Your Gant?" Gant said. "What are you doing anyway, Queenie? Or should I ask, what are you about to make me do?"

"Do you know how to dance?" Abbey asked.

"No."

"You do now."

They reached the top of the stage. Immediately, all of the lights near them went out, and the crowd hushed as they watched the light show that the naniates were producing. Abbey held onto Gant's hands, tossing him out, pulling him back, and twirling around him. He was stiff. Uncomfortable. Dance lessons had been part of her Breaker training, along with etiquette and protocol. She put it to good use now.

She moved her hips, rocking toward the front of the stage. The crowd was cheering loudly, but she didn't care. She looked out at them, searching every face she could find in the sea of color below. She brought Gant in close, lifting him up, so their faces were close together.

"What do the goons look like?" she asked, flipping him up and over her shoulders and down.

He was stiff. Nervous in a way she hadn't seen him before. He could fix a starship reactor with a wire and some snot, but he couldn't dance?

He stepped back and away from her, scanning the crowd. Then he surprised her, taking a totally different stance, his hips moving, his legs loose and shifting in rhythm to the music. He bounced toward her, climbing her arm and sliding around her torso, pausing halfway.

"About ten rows back," he said. "Black masks. No lights."

She spun him around again, lifting him and throwing him high into the air, while sending part of her sleeve out with him, encircling him with light. The crowd cheered louder at the same time she found the new arrivals. They were moving away from the stage, two of them holding someone by the arms.

"Damn it," Abbey said as Gant came down, momentarily cradled in her arms. "They're making off with my shithead."

18

"Throw me," Gant said, sliding down her arm, holding her hand in his. "I'll slow them down."

She pulled, and he folded back into her, sitting gently with his feet in her hand, ready to be propelled into the crowd. She could feel the Gift pulsing around her and inside her, so pure and bright and giving. Not at all like the corruption of the Nephilim. She pushed out with it, guiding it with her hand as she threw Gant forward, launching him over the crowd below.

She froze as she realized that the Gift wouldn't touch him. It would circle him, it would come near him, but it wouldn't make contact. They had both believed it was his fury that had saved him from Ursan Gall's wrath on Drune, but as Gant fell half a dozen meters short of the target, she realized that wasn't the case.

Somehow, he was immune. Completely immune. The naniates wanted no part of him. How? Why?

It didn't matter right now. Gant landed on top of the crowd behind the escaping targets, placing his feet on their shoulders and springing off them, using the density of the gathering to find purchase and pursue the individuals in the black masks.

Abbey was static on the stage, and the crowd that had been cheering loudly only seconds ago started to boo, complaining because her light show had gone dark. She felt a tingle run through her skin, familiar to her and at the same time fresh. She followed the direction of the warning with her eyes as a second group of individuals in blacksuit and masks made themselves known, pushing through one of the side doors to the main stage of Taggers.

"Frag," she said.

She dropped and rolled while a hail of flechettes whipped through the air where she had just been standing, vectoring in from both sides of the stage and hitting the lights above it, destroying them in a shower of sparks that got the masses cheering again. The music within the building changed to something loud and thumping and alien that covered up the din of the rounds.

"Joker, where the frag are you?" she said, quickly finding Gant approaching the group that was trying to escape with her target.

"Small problem, Queenie," Joker said. "You've attracted your usual crowd of assholes who want to kill us. A group of Children jumped us two blocks from your position."

"I hate these fraggers," Pik said.

"I think we can take them, but they're slowing us down big time."

"Why the frag didn't you tell me sooner?"

"I guess it slipped my mind while I was trying not to have my throat ripped out."

"Shitty excuse."

Abbey bounced to her feet. Gant was almost at the soldiers, and two of them had paused to confront him. He vanished beneath the sea of individuals who still had no clue what was happening, and a moment later the first of the blackmasks sank into it with him. Then he popped up, slamming the other enemy hard in the mask with his foot, the force of it knocking him back.

A dark form landed on the stage beside her, bouncing too far to be anything but Gifted. She turned to face him, staring at the mask.

"Halloween is an Earth holiday," Abbey said. "And we're a long way from Earth."

The Immolent remained still while a stream of metal slivers exploded from his suit. She raised her hand in response, spreading the Gift of the Shard out before her and catching them easily.

A distraction. She realized it immediately but still almost too late. She spun, pulling the slivers with her bringing them around as more rounds screamed at her from the rear. The flechettes hit the sudden wall, but she had to keep spinning, turning back toward the Immolent before he could hit her from behind.

She dove to the ground a second time, barely avoiding the blade as it whistled overhead, nearly removing hers. The Immolent had closed the gap in an instant, moving so fast she barely recovered in time to catch the blade between her hands, turning it aside. She kicked up, hitting him in the side and knocking him away, rolling to her feet again, and again having to evade the attacks from the enemy soldiers.

"Joker, I really need you guys," she said into her comm, bringing her wrists together as the Immolent's blade came down again, stopped by the shardsuit.

"Doing our best, Queenie," Joker replied. "Cherub broke through; she should be on her way."

The Immolent kept at her, and she pushed out with the Gift, the force of it throwing him back and giving her a few seconds of breathing room. She managed to get up, reaching out with her hand and beckoning for the guns she had left behind the bar. The weapons came to her, launching through the air as if by magic. She caught one in each hand, firing on the Immolent as he approached. He evaded them all, seeming to blink in and out of existence as he dodged the rounds, covering the distance back to her in a second. He had almost reached her when something fell from the top of the building, landing between them and causing the Immolent to pull up.

"Queenie," Trin said without looking. "Sorry we're late."

Trin closed on the Immolent, blades extending from her armor, which moved as fast as the enemy did, sparks flying as weapon met weapon.

The crowd beneath them started screaming, finally realizing that something was wrong.

"Why doesn't anyone use their damn communicators?" Abbey said, getting back up.

The patrons were trying to run for the exits, clearing the area around Gant. Four of the enemies were down, including her target. Blood was running from the side of his head and chest.

"Gant, why did you kill him?" Abbey asked.

She jumped toward the shooters on her flank, using the Gift to catch their rounds and throw them back. The flechettes tore into two of the soldiers, the others managing to get back behind cover. She landed in the middle of them a moment later, freezing as she found herself surrounded by Goreshin.

"I didn't, Queenie," Gant replied. "The assholes did."

"Queen of Demons," one of them said, exchanging his gun for razor claws. "Prove it."

Abbey smiled, holding her hands out at her sides. The shardsuit extended beyond her fingers, creating dagger claws of her own. "Tell your boss if you live long enough. I'm not the same Cage he knew before, and he made the second biggest mistake of his miserable life to drag my daughter into this."

"You can tell him yourself," the monster replied. "He'll be here soon."

Abbey felt a sudden burst of fear and anger. Thraven was on his way here? She should have known. Why else would one of his Immolents be planetside? But what the hell was he coming here for?

The questions were forgotten an instant later as the Children charged her in unison, moving in with claws and teeth.

She brought her arms in, closing her eyes and pushing with the Gift. Her entire body flared with brilliant white light, causing them to yelp in sudden pain and confusion. The Light of the Shard vanished almost as quickly as it had come, but it left the Goreshin disoriented. Abbey charged forward, stabbing one of them in the base of the neck and holding it while she brought her other set of claws around and through, removing its head. She turned to the next, stabbing it in the head, backing away as it slashed blindly at her, moving back in and cutting its throat.

"It's fragging time!" Pik shouted, bursting into the building, clearing a path through the escaping civilians.

"Queenie, we're here," Joker said through the comm, at the same time he started sending rounds across the suddenly open floor of Taggers and toward the blacksuits on the other side.

"It's about time," she replied, sweeping in on another Goreshin and cutting off its head. She turned to the next, nearly knocked away as Trin was thrown past, crashing and sliding along the floor.

"Void," she said, returning her attention to the Immolent.

He was charging her again, a second blade in his other hand. She bounced forward to meet him, claws catching the blades, turning them as she twisted and kicked him in the chest. He fell back, rolling to his feet in silence, throwing one of the blades at her. She tried to move aside. Too slow. It dug past the shardsuit and into her shoulder, burying itself deep in her flesh.

"Queenie," Pik shouted.

Bullets started hitting the Immolent, seeming to bounce off his armor. He kept coming at Abbey, not giving her time to remove the blade. She fought one-handed, backing up as she blocked strike after strike, throwing out the Gift to help defend herself. While the Shard's Gift was clean and pure, she could tell it was weaker in some ways than the Nephilim's version. She didn't have the same brute force power as before. She had to fight smarter.

She turned into the Immolent's next attack, allowing the blade to strike her, letting it dig into her side. It hurt, but if she survived the wounds would heal. She twisted, giving her opponent the choice of following the blade or losing it. He chose to follow, stepping in a little closer than he should have.

She lunged forward, slamming her forehead into his mask. It shattered beneath the blow, the pieces digging into the Immolent's face as he was sent reeling away. Abbey ignored the blades in her flesh, bringing up her claws, ready to send them deep into the Immolent's throat.

She froze at the sight of him. Or rather, her. She was just a child.

No more than sixteen. But her eyes. They were black and empty. She stared back at Abbey with no emotion, no submission. No anything.

She was somebody's Hayley or had been once.

The thought caused Abbey to hesitate. Almost for too long. The Immolent's hand lunged forward, a fresh blade springing into it, aimed at the base of her neck.

Trin's hand caught the Immolent's wrist, stopping the blade. She broke it smoothly, the effort not eliciting anything from the Immolent. Then she removed the enemy's head.

Abbey took a step back, glancing at Trinity before tracking the rest of the space. The Goreshin were all dead. Phlenel and Jequn were standing over them, suddenly still as the battle wound down. Further away, Pik and Benhil were kicking soldiers with their feet, making sure they were dead and would stay that way.

Gant was kneeling over their target and looking at her; his expression concerned as his eyes landed on the Immolent's blades. She let the claws sink back into the shardsuit, reaching down, pulling them out of her flesh, and dropping them on the ground. She could feel the naniates move to heal her body, the pain easing as they did.

"They're nothing but servants," Trin said. "Slaves to Thraven. It looks childlike, but there's nothing childlike about it."

"How?" Abbey said, still a little off-balance.

"He trains them as Evolents. If they're strong enough, he may make them Immolents. His personal bodyguards. He takes their identity. Their memories. Everything. That way they have no opportunity to be disloyal. He wanted to make me into one of them after Villanueve was done with me."

"If it's a bodyguard, why would it be here without him?"

"If it's here then Thraven isn't far behind. He probably sent the Immolent because he couldn't send me."

"I can't fight Thraven yet," Abbey said. "I'm not strong enough."

"I know. We have to finish what we came here to do. Locate the factory."

"How? My target is dead."

"I found you after Mamma Oissi was dead," Trin said. "You can do the same."

"Read a dead man's mind?"

"Yes. We need to hurry."

19

"Joker, Okay, Pudding," Abbey said. "Secure the building. We're going to be surrounded by Planetary Defense in about twenty seconds, and I don't want them coming in here."

"You want to start with PD?" Benhil asked.

"Want has nothing to do with it."

"Roger," Pik said. "On it."

"Imp," Abbey said.

Bastion didn't reply.

"Imp," she repeated.

"Shit. I'm here, Queenie," Bastion said.

"Where the hell have you been? Void and Pudding are here, and you never said a fragging word to me about it."

"Yeah, I know. Gant trailed the goons, some scary asshole trailed Gant, and Void and Pudding trailed him. Little did I know they were going to try to get onto the *Faust*. Their ship is like a fragging clown car."

"A what?" she asked, not getting the reference.

"Ancient history," Bastion replied. "I got it from Gant. Anyway, I managed to get the *Faust* in the air but not before they got inside."

"Are you okay?" Abbey said, her anger fading, replaced with a level of concern that surprised her.

"I'm fine now. I'm sorry I let you down, Queenie."

"Forget about it. I need you over Brighton for extraction. Think you can handle it?"

"PD is swarming toward you, but I can make a pass. Is Cherub with you?"

Abbey looked back at Jequn, who was holding up a teleporter.

"She is. Good thinking. Give me two minutes."

"What for?"

"I'm going to read a dead man's mind."

"Are you fragging kidding me?"

"Do I sound like I'm kidding you?"

"Good point. They haven't figured out who you are yet, so I've got clearance at ten-thousand meters. I'll drop down to you on your mark."

"Roger. Standby."

"Roger."

Abbey turned to Trinity. "Tell me what to do."

They walked over to where Gant was standing beside the dead Tridium employee. He looked her over, satisfied that her wounds had healed and the shardsuit had closed back over.

"What's our move?" he asked.

"The Nephilim have a specially designed glove that uses electrical impulses to stimulate the brain and an onboard chip that turns those signals back into a visual memory." Trin knelt beside the man, lifting him so that his head was propped on her knee. "It's the same method of recall he would have used if he were still breathing."

"I don't have a glove," Abbey said.

"You seem to be able to shape them into whatever you need," Trin replied.

"It can't be that simple."

"It might not be. What choice do we have? We were spotted on our way in, and now the only link from Tridium to the Elysium Gate is dead."

Abbey looked into the man's dead eyes. She had to try. "What should I do?"

"You need to get to his brain. It's easier with a Rudin, but not impossible here." She extended one of her blades, sinking it into the man's face. "Cutting away the top of the jaw is the easiest." She wrenched the blade, a wet crack sounding beneath the man's flesh.

"This is one of the least pleasant things I've had to see lately," Gant said. "And that's saying a lot."

Trinity didn't respond. She cut away the man's skin before finishing the job with one of her hands, separating part of the skull and leaving access to his brain.

Abbey felt nauseous at the sight, but she leaned in anyway, reaching into the bloody mess until she felt resistance. She kept her hand there and closed her eyes. She sent the instructions to the Gift, hoping they would understand what to do, like they had with the *Faust*. She needed to see his memories. She needed to know what he knew.

She felt the Gift moving along her skin, a soft warmth growing where she was touching the flesh. Pain in her eye nearly caused her to release him and step away, but she didn't. They needed the intel. Sharp stabbing pains followed in her left eye, followed by quickly accelerating flashes. Her hand was growing warmer, the naniates flowing around the dead man's brain and firing electrical impulses into it.

The man's mouth opened, and he moaned softly.

"Queenie, I'm in position," Bastion announced.

"Shh," she replied. "I'm trying to concentrate."

"Geez, first you give me shit about not calling you, and then you give me shit when I do."

"She's a woman," Gant said. "That's her prerogative."

Abbey spared a glance at Gant for his comment. He chittered in reply.

"Could both of you shut up?" she said.

She returned her attention to the Gift. The pain was increasing, but so was the flow of color. She recognized it as data. A different form, maybe, but she knew that's what it was. She pushed a little harder, and the color began to coalesce and form a scene. It was chaotic and confusing and frightening, and it took her a moment to realize it was what he had seen and felt the moment before he died. It wasn't supposed to end this way. Thraven had betrayed him.

What else was new?

She needed to go back. Earlier. She passed the message along to the naniates, and the image dissolved back into color, reshaping a few seconds later. Now she saw the pod tunnels, right before the lights went out completely. It was the moment she had crashed the system. She hadn't gone back far enough.

Once more, the colors dissolved and reformed. Now she was looking at a terminal with a list of names and times. It vanished all too quickly as her target stood to leave.

"Bring it back," she said out loud. "I need it."

"Need what?" Gant said.

She didn't reply. The terminal returned, frozen in time. She scanned the list. They were starships. All of them had left the planet already.

All of them except for one.

The Termilon.

It was waiting at the spaceport. Launchpad fourteen.

It was leaving in eighteen minutes, headed toward a destination marked only as 'F.' She assumed that meant factory.

She pulled her hand away, the blood and detritus pushed away from her by the naniates as she did.

There was one last ship headed out to the Gate, and she intended to be on it.

20

"THAT'S CRAZY," BENHIL SAID AFTER ABBEY HAD QUICKLY FILLED THEM all in on her idea. "We should stick together."

"We need to get to the Gate," Abbey replied. "This is the easiest and most efficient way. There's nothing crazy about it."

"Except for the part where you make yourself invisible."

"That was Okay's idea."

"Glad I could help, Queenie," Pik said over the comm.

"What about the part where Thraven is on his way here?" Benhil added.

"All the more reason to get there before he does," Abbey replied. She still didn't know why the Gloritant wanted to visit the factory now, but anything he wanted, she wanted to take away.

"Queenie, you need to be careful," Jequn said. "Even if the Gift is pure, it can't support you indefinitely. It will expend its energy and require more of yours."

"My stomach's already grumbling," Abbey said. "But all I need to do is get on board. Then I can stay hidden on my own. When the Termilon reaches its destination, I'll hack the comm array and send you the coordinates. You ride in, we sabotage the Gate, and we're on our way."

"You know it isn't going to be that simple," Benhil said. "It never is."

"I know. But we always manage."

"Queenie," Bastion said. "I'm on my way in. Is everybody ready?"

Pik, Benhil, and Jequn had been firing potshots out at Planetary Defense, keeping them honest. Now that they had what they came for it was time to bug out.

"Standby," Abbey said. "Cherub, Okay, Joker, time to go."

"Roger," Pik said.

"Why do we keep getting split up?" Gant asked, looking at her with big, sad eyes.

She smiled. "It'll only be for a few hours at most. Then you owe me the rest of our dance."

He laughed in response. "Roger that."

Abbey felt a hand on her shoulder. She glanced over, finding Phlenel standing beside her. The Hurshin hadn't brought her bot along, leaving her unable to vocalize easily. She used hand gestures instead, pointing to herself and then to Abbey. A moment later, her gelatinous form shifted, leaving only a faint outline of her form. Apparently, Abbey wasn't the only one who could make themselves disappear.

"Fine. Pudding, you're with me. Imp, we're ready to go."

"Roger," Bastion replied. "Initiating drop now. Count to ten and then step through the teleporter."

"You heard him," Abbey said to the others.

"Be careful out there, Queenie," Pik said.

"You too, Okay," Abbey replied.

She watched as Jequn dropped the teleporter on the ground in front of her and activated it. The light on it was still red, the other end out of range. Benhil and Pik appeared from opposite ends of the room.

"PD is moving in," Benhil said. "Don't let them catch you here."

"Don't worry about us," Abbey said.

She could feel the warmth of the Gift on her skin, and she held up her hand, smiling as the naniates began bending the light, wrapping it around so that it started to blend with the background.

"Cool, it works," Pik said.

"Yes, it is cool," Abbey agreed. "And yes, it does work."

She felt a tickle on her face as the machines moved up and over it, some of them slipping into her nose and ears and mouth, covering every inch of her. She heard boots moving toward them from outside and pointed as the light on the teleporter changed.

"I'm in position," Bastion said.

"They're on their way," Abbey replied. "Get back to orbit, make yourself scarce, and standby."

"Roger. Stay safe out there."

The other Rejects vanished through the teleporter one by one, with Gant taking up the rear. He glanced back as he stepped into the device, a worried look on his face.

Abbey reached down and scooped up the teleporter, sticking it in a tightpack. "We need to move," she said to Phlenel, barely able to see the slight alteration of light as it passed through her nearly transparent form.

A Planetary Defense squad swept into the room before they could move, weapons raised and ready. They scanned the area quickly, moving in and checking first on the headless monsters littering the floor, and then on the Immolent.

"What the frag?" one of them said.

"I've never seen anything like this," another added.

"Sarge, we've got a seriously fragged situation in here," the first said into his comm. He noticed the dead Tridium employee a moment later. "Seriously fragged," he repeated.

Abbey waited for him to look away before moving carefully in the other direction. She could sense Phlenel nearby, surprised when she saw the Hurshin had changed shape, flattening herself and crawling along the floor.

Now that was impressive.

They didn't have time to be too cautious, and Abbey picked up the pace as they reached the side of the room, rushing forward and toward the exit. She could see the street ahead of them, where dozens of bystanders had gathered to see what all the fuss was about, and PD vehicles were ringing the area, bright lights running along the buildings in search of anything suspicious. She could still hear the slight rumble of the *Faust's* thrusters carrying her back into space, and see the fiery trails of the starfighters in pursuit.

She slowed again when she reached the exit, a little nervous about stepping into the open. There were dozens of eyes on her position. Was her cloak sufficient to hide her? She stepped over the threshold, feeling as though she were back on Taggers' stage, except this time she was completely naked.

She looked out at the individuals, trying to meet their eyes with hers. The world was fuzzy in front of her, the thin line of naniates covering her head blurring her vision. She could see well enough to know that they couldn't see her. The cloak was perfect.

It was also draining. She could feel her energy being sapped, her energy fading with the effort. Cloaking a starship used massive amounts of reactor power. Why would cloaking herself be any different? She would be able to keep it up until they boarded the Termilon, but she knew already she would be desperately hungry afterward. Maybe Phlenel could raid their fridge.

She moved away from the crowd, pausing to look back for the Hurshin. She had disappeared, blending in so well Abbey couldn't find her either. She decided not to worry, certain that Phlenel would be able to keep up. She focused on getting herself away, passing within inches of an armored PD vehicle with a squad of soldiers behind it, using it as cover. They didn't turn their heads as she walked by. They didn't know she was there.

She dropped the cloak once she was outside the main defensive perimeter, choosing to take her chances instead of wasting too much energy. She stepped back out into the street dressed in light once more, though she chose a more subtle pattern that wouldn't draw so much attention. The pod terminal was a short distance away, and she headed for it at a brisk walk. The Termilon was leaving in ten minutes.

She was joined by a stranger at the halfway point, a man who didn't speak as he sidled up next to her, winking at her with a single translucent eye. Abbey reached out and took his hand, holding it as though they were a couple as they covered the rest of the distance together, descending into the terminal and waiting only a few seconds for a pod to share.

"Spaceport," Abbey said as they boarded. "Launchpad fourteen."

The pod started to accelerate, zipping into the tunnels.

"There are going to be guards at the launchpad terminal," Abbey said.

Phlenel nodded.

"Do you have a gun hiding in there somewhere?"

She shook her head.

"Okay. There's more than one way to take out a guard."

Abbey shifted herself, moving from her seat and putting herself on Phlenel's lap, wrapping her arms around the Hurshin's shoulders and leaning in close.

"Don't tell Gant about this," she said. "He might get jealous."

Phlenel smiled. They remained in that position until the pod began to slow on approach to the terminal. Then Abbey leaned in further, putting her lips against Phlenel's. It was weird to be kissing a male that she knew identified as female. It was even weirder to be kissing what to her was an alien, another species entirely, and one she knew was almost literally an evolved form of primordial ooze.

The pod came to a stop, the side hatch sliding open. She couldn't see the guards, not with her face pressed to Phlenel's, but she could hear their movements.

"What the?" one of them said.

Abbey pulled back, looking at them. "Oh," she said. "Oh. I'm sorry. This isn't the cruise port. Sweetie, what did you do?"

Phlenel made a surprised face.

"This is a restricted area, miss," the guard said.

"I'm so sorry. Can you help us? We aren't from around here, and I'm having trouble working the controls."

The guard stared at her, slightly suspicious. She did her best to look harmless.

"You can't be here," the guard said. "Get out of the pod. I'm going to have to report this."

"What? It was an honest mistake. I swear. We just want to go to the cruise port. It's our honeymoon. Right sweetie?"

Phlenel nodded in agreement.

"Just help me get this thing pointed in the right direction, and we won't trouble you."

The first guard glanced over at the second, who shrugged.

"Fine," he said. "Let me set it for you." He started leaning in.

Abbey lunged toward him, grabbing him and yanking him hard into the pod, slamming his head against the top. Phlenel grabbed his sidearm at the same time, picking it from his hip and pointing it at the other soldier.

"Don't move," Abbey said while the first man crumpled to the ground. She climbed out of the pod, standing in front of the other guard. She grabbed his sidearm, shifting it in her hand. "This is going to hurt later."

She slammed it against the side of his head, knocking him down, too. Phlenel joined her on the platform, and they hurried up to the pad. A large, square hauler was resting on the launcher, nearly ready to go. Three loading bots were making a final trip up the wide ramp into the back of it, pulling large metal crates behind them. She thought there might have been more soldiers nearby, but it seemed as if they had already made their way on board.

They paused to make themselves invisible again. Then the two of them crossed the tarmac to the starship, joining the loading bots and ascending the ramp. A Trover was directing traffic inside, telling the bots where to leave the cargo. He didn't see either of them as they broke away, peeling off and taking position behind one of hundreds of crates that were already on board.

Abbey released the Gift, feeling a slight tingle as she did. She had used a lot of energy and had no means to replenish it. At least not yet. Phlenel solidified beside her, retaking the male form from the pod. She smiled at Abbey, giving her a thumbs up.

"Nothing to do now but wait," Abbey agreed.

21

THE TRIP IN THE HAULER WAS SHORTER THAN ABBEY EXPECTED. ONLY fifteen minutes had passed in FTL before the cargo ship dropped, the commotion in the hold beginning the second it did. The loading bots reactivated, and an entire crew of workers appeared from the decks above, quickly taking up positions beside the crates and coming to attention.

Abbey peered out from behind one of the crates, remaining visible but tucked away, trying to conserve her energy. She was already a little nervous her growling stomach might betray her, and she kept her hand on it, hoping it would behave. She watched as the Trover moved out from a second hatch to her right, taking big steps to the center of the hold.

"There's been a change in plans," the Trover said. "This shipment isn't going out to the yard. Once we dock, all of the crates will be transferred to the Nautilus."

"Aye, sir!" the workers shouted in unison.

"Once payment has been made we're going to rendezvous with the main fleet for reassignment."

"Aye, sir!"

"This is a glorious day for the Nephilim Empire," the Trover said. "This is a glorious day for Gloritant Thraven. This is a glorious day for the coming of the Great Return!"

"Aye, sir!"

The Trover tapped his communicator, checking the time in the projection. "Two minutes to lock. You know what to do."

"Aye, sir!"

The workers changed position, aligning themselves to move the crates with practiced efficiency.

Joining the master fleet? Was that why Thraven was coming here? For reinforcements? Abbey wasn't convinced. The few remaining ships that were powered by the Gift hardly needed more than a skeleton crew. So why else would Thraven be close?

"We have to ping the *Faust*," she whispered to Phlenel, who responded by altering her transparency.

Abbey considered doing the same but decided against it. She had been in situations like this before she had the Gift. She didn't need to use it for everything.

"See if you can create a slight distraction," Abbey said. "I'll make a break for the exit."

Phlenel nodded again, the slightly shifting air the only indication of the motion. Then she moved away, vanishing around the corner of one of the crates.

Abbey turned her attention back to the hatch the Trover had emerged from. He had moved to the other side of the hold and was speaking with one of the workers there, pointing and making angry faces. Clearly, the worker had done something wrong. Good. She stepped lightly around the crates, pausing to watch the faces of the workers before she crossed the narrow columns. She had gotten across two of them before Phlenel's distraction became apparent.

A loud siren blared from one of the crates. A loud clang followed a moment later as the magnetic seal on the door suddenly failed, causing it to drop open and nearly killing one of the workers in the process.

"What the frag is going on over there?" the Trover yelled, rushing in that direction. The other workers broke rank to follow him.

"Nice work," Abbey said, even though Phlenel couldn't hear her. She sprinted to the edge of the last crate, pausing to look around the corner. A long corridor leading deeper into the cargo ship. She slipped through it, glancing back at the commotion as she did.

The Trover was cursing and shouting, pointing at the mess of smaller boxes that had poured out of the crate when it opened. It had been packed so tightly that the door was the only thing holding some of the contents in, a development that was less than innocent. Something had held the door in place while it had been sealed. Something would hold the smaller packs in place when it was opened.

Something like the Gift.

It was more than that. The rectangular containers that had fallen out of the larger module were instantly familiar to her by the size, shape, and Plixian writing on the sides. The ship was transporting guns. Thousands of guns, at least some portion of which were Emgees. The Trover had said they would be shifted to some other ship named the Nautilus. It was a Republic name, but not one she was familiar with.

If Thraven was giving thousands of weapons to anybody, it was sure to be bad news.

She moved down the corridor, speeding up as she got further from the hold. Most of the crew beyond the officers were probably already in there at their stations. The rest would be closer to the bridge or near engineering, handling the maintenance of the ship and preparing to dock. They had one minute remaining.

She came to a stop as she reached the first viewport in the side of the ship, a small square that gave her a look at the expanse beyond. She could see the corner of the station through it, a small portion of the ring the composed the outer edge of the factory. It looked like any other stardock, except for the number of ships already attached to the docking arms.

They weren't just any ships. They were warships. Republic designs, but not marked with RAS tags, as though the schematics had been used, but the ships had been built somewhere else. They each had a simple emblem on the sides in the form of a flaming sword.

A light tap on the shoulder caused her to spin quickly, throwing her fist out and nearly connecting with Phlenel's head. The Hurshin had anticipated the reaction, standing on the opposite side of the touch. A soft buzz escaped from her, not a vocalization but an emission of sound. Laughter.

"Do you know those symbols?" Abbey asked.

Phlenel shook her head.

"I'm going to assume one of those is the Nautilus. They have an entire armada out there, and I'm willing to bet it's in league with Thraven. We can't let them get all of those guns."

Phlenel nodded. Abbey started down the corridor again, stopping when she heard someone coming their way. She scanned both sides of the corridor, but they were in an open stretch. She looked at the walls. Not enough time to cloak herself. She looked up. The top of the space was a few meters away. She jumped, turning herself flat and gripping the smooth metal, the naniates extending and gripping in. She pulled herself in as much as she could, wishing she were bald again. Hopefully, she was high enough they wouldn't notice her hair.

The two soldiers turned the corner, moving down the hallway. They were looking over a report of some kind and arguing about the numbers. They didn't look up, and they didn't notice Phlenel as they walked right past her.

Abbey dropped behind them, motioning Phlenel to follow. They turned the corner as the ship shuddered and clanged, the impact with the docking arm shaking them slightly. The arm would guide the rear of the hauler to the loading airlock, where the cargo would be quickly moved from one ship to another.

The vibration was a signal that they needed to hurry. Abbey ran down the corridor, reaching an emergency stairwell and vaulting down it six steps at a time. Phlenel kept up easily, her form able to slam into walls and bounce off surfaces without pain or damage. They dropped three decks and spilled out into another long, silver hallway, much closer to engineering and the comm link.

They ducked into a corner as the shuddering subsided and a group of soldiers emerged from their stations, likely headed to the ring station. Abbey and Phlenel swung out behind them, quickly crossing to the comm room and entering. A single tech was still on duty there, and he almost had enough time to open his mouth before Phlenel grabbed him and quickly knocked him out.

"Watch the door," Abbey said, reaching for the terminal.

She activated it, and then reached out with a thin strand of her shardsuit that vanished into the device. The commands appeared ahead of her eyes, and she quickly ran the protocols to hack into the hauler's aged system. The position was trivial to retrieve, and she entered the *Faust's* Galnet subchannel, getting an immediate connection.

"Imp, do you copy?" she said.

"This is Imp, Queenie," Bastion replied. "I copy."

"I'm sending coordinates now. The factory is huge, and there's an entire fleet docked here. Not haulers, either. Warships. Ask Gant if he's ever seen a symbol of a flaming sword before."

"I heard you, Queenie," Gant said. "Let me think." He paused for a few seconds. "No. I'm not familiar with it."

"You mean there's at least one thing you don't know?" Bastion said.

"Do you want me to tell you something I do know?" Gant asked suggestively.

"What's that?" Bastion replied.

"Not the best time for this," Abbey said, cutting them off before they could really get going. "This hauler is toting guns. Advanced weaponry. Emgees at least, and probably some heavier shit. Combine that with a fleet of unidentifiable ships, and it adds up to nothing good."

"Agreed," Gant said.

"I've got the coordinates in," Bastion said. "We'll be there in fifteen. How are we planning to frag up their day?"

"Any way we can," Abbey said. "Watch your six on the ingress. Queenie, out."

22

Abbey left the comm terminal, passing back into the hallway without a word to Phlenel. She knew the Hurshin would follow as she returned to the stairwell and began to ascend, going back up and retracing her steps to the cargo hold. She could hear the activity within from down the corridor, the crates being quickly lifted and moved by the bots and the workers, passed onto the ring and across to the docked warships.

"Whatever's happening here, we need to stop it before Thraven shows up," she said. "There's got to be enough ordnance on this ship to blow the entire factory to stardust. If the Gate is nearby, the impact from the death of the station should be enough to knock it out. If it isn't, we'll have to circle back later. They won't be able to finish the Gate without the station, anyway."

Phlenel didn't respond, but Abbey could feel her presence at her back.

"Are you ready for this?" she said, turning to look at the Hurshin when they neared the hold.

Phlenel had changed form again, taking on Abbey's monster visage. The form that the Shard had helped her to avoid. The sharp, spiked tail swung side to side behind her, while she spread her long claws menacingly.

They had spent the trip to the station in hiding, but they hadn't come to hide.

They had come to fight.

Abbey lifted her Uin from her shardsuit, holding them closed in her fists. She looked through the doorway into the cargo hold, where the workers had already gotten more than half of the crates onto the station. She reminded herself that they were at war and that armed and armored or not, these individuals were still the enemy.

If they ran, she wouldn't chase them. But if they didn't...

She resumed her walk toward the hold, striding confidently over the threshold and into view. The Trover happened to see her first, his eyes narrowing in angry surprise at her sudden presence among them.

"Intruder," he bellowed, a large hand reaching for a large sidearm. "Sound the alarm."

He raised the weapon. Abbey spread the Uin, feeling the Gift tickling the underside of her flesh. The workers had frozen at the Trover's cry, and most of them shifted direction, heading to their commander's side. Meanwhile, a dozen of them rushed to one of the remaining containers, smacking the controls to open the door, eager to reach the arms within.

"Pudding, cover the weapons," Abbey said, flicking her wrist as the Trover fired his hand cannon.

The large rounds hit the Uin, the Gift flowing along it and creating an energy shield that deflected them away one after another.

The Trover's weapon ran dry a few seconds later, and Abbey used the opportunity to charge, rushing right at the large humanoid, her feet skipping along the floor. Phlenel had reached the container to her right and was digging into the workers there, stabbing them with her tail and raking them with her claws. They tried to fight back but they weren't prepared for an attack, and their flailing attacks were easily batted aside by the experienced fighter.

The alarm sirens began to sound, not only in the cargo ship but also in the loading dock beyond, alerting the entire factory to the intruders. Abbey ignored it, continuing her sprint at the Trover commander, who was in the process of reloading his gun.

He had just loaded a new magazine in when Abbey reached him, slapping the weapon away before he could aim, spinning and kicking him in the head. He was six times her weight, but his neck still snapped at the impact, the loud crack echoing across the space.

She landed smoothly, turning and raising her Uin as the sharp report of rounds echoed across the hold, a group of soldiers from the factory moving into the area. They were dressed in dark red light-suits, the flaming sword emblem clear over their chest, their precise aim testament to their training. She slipped the Uin across the path of the projectiles, catching them with the weapon and knocking them away.

A high-pitched whine sounded to her right. She ducked and rolled instinctively, coming up in time to watch the Emgee tear the soldiers in the loading bay to shreds and send the rest of the workers scattering for cover.

Abbey glanced over at Phlenel, who was holding the weapon against her hip, letting it wind down when the targets disappeared.

"Nice," Abbey said. "But try not to puncture the outer hull. I kind of like breathing."

Phlenel dropped the weapon, joining her as they charged toward the bay. A hatch opened at the back of it, soldiers in heavy battlesuits stomping out, opening fire as they entered. Abbey closed one of the Uin and raised her hand, bringing the rounds to a stop as they hit the sudden shield. They hung there for a moment, and then with a flick of her wrist she sent the missiles back in the opposite direction.

She expected the soldiers to move, or for the rounds to strike the armor but not make it through. She was surprised when the projectiles never struck the targets, curving away and hitting the wall beside them instead.

What the hell?

There was only one thing that could do that to a bullet. Abbey scanned the area, but she didn't see an Evolent anywhere. Were they hiding among the already unloaded containers?

Wherever they were, she didn't have time to worry about it now. The soldiers were spreading out, trying to flank and overwhelm her.

She broke to the left, bouncing toward a group of soldiers angling for one of the crates and cutting them off. Her Uin spread wide again as she reached them, sidestepping a punch that would have broken every one of her ribs and slicing into the armor, finding the weapon wasn't up to the task. She folded it as she slipped away from another blow, going up and over the soldier, coming down behind him and punching him hard in the back. The force pushed him into a second soldier, knocking him down and clearing a path to the remaining one. He fired his wrist-mounted cannon, but Abbey managed to twist out of the vector, coming up, grabbing the wrist and breaking it before getting her hand up under the soldier's helmet. She extended the naniates into claws, running them up and through the man's skull.

Something hit her from behind, knocking her to the ground. A weight landed on her back, one of the soldiers pressing down on her with an augmented knee. She cursed as the felt the pain of her bones bending to the pressure, and she pushed back, using the Gift to give her strength, throwing the soldier off with a grunt. He toppled back, replaced with more gunfire that tore through the shardsuit and into her shoulder, knocking her back to the side.

She hit the ground, growing angry. The nature of the Shard's Gift was making her weak. If she still had the Nephilim's Gift, she wouldn't be getting her ass kicked.

She growled as she forced herself back up, charging the nearest soldier, his return assault going wide. She hit him hard, extending the shardsuit into claws and slashing into the grooves of the battlesuit, cutting into flesh. She sliced one of the soldiers, and then grabbed another, throwing him with extra force into the side of a container. It dented at the impact, and he hit the ground and didn't move.

Abbey turned, searching for another target.

She froze when she saw him, a cold chill running from the brand on her shoulder. He was tall and lean and clothed in a white lightsuit with the flaming sword emblem on the chest. He had a Uin in each hand, and he flipped them nonchalantly as she turned to face him.

"You're a Seraphim," she said.

"If you mean a descendant of a dying race, then yes."

"You have the Gift."

"Also, yes. As do you." He cocked his head to the side. "Yours is different. I'm not sure how."

"You're helping Thraven build the Elysium Gate. You're helping him destroy your people."

"My people were destroyed thousands of years ago," he replied. "What's left is a shadow of that. There's no profit in shadows."

"You're a mercenary, then?"

"I prefer the term soldier-for-hire."

"Oh, yeah. That's much better." Abbey rolled her eyes. "I'm not letting Thraven finish the Gate. I'm not letting him use it."

"Then you'll be disappointed to know," the Seraphim said. "The Gate is already finished."

"What?"

"This delivery was payment for services rendered. The Gate is complete. You're too late. It isn't even here anymore. Not that it's a bad thing. Why try to stop the inevitable? It'll be easier for everyone if you simply let the Gloritant keep the Promise and herald the Great Return."

Abbey eyed the other soldiers, still trying to position themselves around her. Phlenel had disappeared, likely trying to get the drop on them getting the drop on her.

"You believe that bullshit?" she asked, trying to stall a little. The Gate was gone? It had been here, but now it wasn't? Fragging hell. But if the Gate wasn't here, why was Thraven on his way?

"I don't care one way or another. I do a job; I get paid. That's all this is to me. Let the universe crumble around me. I'll take care of my own. If you were smart, you would do the same."

Abbey's thoughts turned to Hayley. She hoped her daughter was okay. She wanted to tear Thraven's heart out, but she knew she couldn't. Not yet. Not like this. She would die if she confronted him, and then where would Hayley be?

"I am taking care of my own. I didn't ask for this."

"I think your situation would be better if you had never tried to fight it."

"What the frag do you know?"

He smiled. "I'm five thousand years old. I know quite a lot."

He had been given the Blood of the Shard to regenerate himself? "So you haven't always been an asshole."

"As much as I'm enjoying our back and forth, I have other things to do with my time."

The soldiers had reached their positions, nearly surrounding her, but they had lost track of Phlenel, the Hurshin having vanished in the chaos.

"Come on then," Abbey said, waving him forward with her Uin. "Cherub will probably thank me for killing you."

"Queenie!"

Bastion's voice interrupted the moment, a desperate call out that took her by surprise.

"Queenie, we're here. Where are you? Frag. Thraven's here. We're too late. He's headed for the factory. Oh, shit."

Something hit the factory.

Something large and powerful.

Abbey was knocked off her feet, the ground shaking violently beneath her. She landed on her hands and knees, looking up as the area behind them began to buckle and fold, the station coming apart in reaction to the torpedo that had struck it.

This was bad.

Very bad.

23

GLORITANT THRAVEN STOOD ON THE BRIDGE OF THE *PROMISE*.

He watched as the torpedo launched from the bow of the ship, streaking toward the Tridium factory, slamming it near the outer edge and causing a massive eruption of burning gas and sudden debris.

"Hit it again," he said calmly.

"Yes, Gloritant," Honorant Bashir said, passing the order to his subordinate.

A second projectile streaked away from the ship, hitting the other side of the factory and causing a similar detonation.

Thraven was calm now, but he hadn't been hours earlier. First, he had watched as the bitch Lorenti turned on him, choosing loyalty to the Republic over his promise of glory and a greater future, and the certainty that her dirty secret would never become known. In one moment, with one word, she had ruined his plans for the Council. She had destroyed years of influence, of back-channel deals and deceptions, of carefully orchestrated lies.

Not that it was her fault. The blame for the failure sat with Evolent Ruche, who had not only failed to contain Captain Mann but who had mishandled every one of his interests on Earth. After Olus had managed to steal data from Tridium, Ruche should have taken greater pains to protect the Councilwoman, to keep her out of Killshot's hands. He also should have also done a better job with Hayley Cage. While Thraven had ordered him to take her, he should have led Mann into the trap and removed her from the equation. Instead, he had lingered with her, giving Olus the chance to set her free.

He felt the anger rising within him, and he clenched his hand into a fist. The Watchers were proving more of a problem than he had expected, the so-called Servants of the Ophanim more numerous than he had guessed. He had always been disgusted by the Plixians, as had Lucifer. There was a reason there were no Nephilim who shared that genetic code, that seed of life. They were barely more than mindless drones. The were barely intelligent at all.

He looked back to the viewport. The factory was slowly breaking apart, secondary explosions running through various parts of the structure. At least the Gate was complete, his need to deal with Ismael and his mercenaries finished. The Seraphim traitor was a fool to believe that he would be permitted to survive with the knowledge he held. It would cost him a few hundred of loyal servants, but they were Lessers, and hugely expendable.

He intended to go and see the Gate for himself, right after he finished here. Ruche's failure had made a mess of his original plan for the Republic, but he would have been a fool not to be prepared for the possibility. Lessers always failed in the end. It was the constant that separated them from their superiors. Evolve or die. That was what he had learned all of those years ago. He had evolved from slave to master. Those that couldn't deserved the fate that befell them.

The war had started. He had shut down the Republic's Milnet. He had triggered the overrides built into the Tridium warships and activated the backup communication channels integrated with the most innocuous hardware.

He had called in his orders to those loyal to him. Across the galaxy, soldiers were fighting their former brothers in arms, from fleet against fleet skirmishes to violent conflicts within crews that had been friends and compatriots only hours before. That was the way of war. That was the way it had been for the Nephilim when they had turned on their brothers and sisters who refused to see the One for the false god that he claimed to be.

Let the Lessers have a taste of the pain that had destroyed their kind.

Let the One be responsible for even more death and chaos and destruction.

"Gloritant, we're picking up a craft to starboard," Honorant Bashir said. "It came out of FTL only moments after we did."

Thraven raised his eyebrow. Interesting. "Project it."

The area at the head of the bridge lit up as the projectors turned on, showing the smallest of star hoppers angling toward the factory. He recognized the ship immediately, even if the identifier displayed with it didn't match the truth.

Cage?

There had been no word from his Immolent on Avalon, who had been sent to handle the loose ends there. Now he understood why.

She was here.

He laughed out loud, a rarity which drew the attention of the bridge crew, causing them all to turn and look at him.

"Your Eminence?" Bashir said.

"She came to destroy the factory," Thraven said. "She came to stop the Gate from being completed. And now she's trapped here."

It was perfect.

"Gloritant, two of the mercenary ships have managed to get away from the factory."

"Target them and fire at will. Honorant, I want that star hopper destroyed."

"Yes, Gloritant."

The *Promise* began to come about, turning to line up better with the *Faust*. The station was still crumbling beyond, a slow death that would leave nothing but space junk in its wake.

"They look like they're heading for the station, your Eminence," Bashir said.

He had noticed that already. The station was doomed. Why would they be going that way? Did Cage think she could escape from him by hiding in the debris field?

"Fire," Thraven said, the smile remaining on his face.

He didn't normally let himself feel such pleasure, but this occasion was too serendipitous to ignore. The Father had seen to it that he would have the revenge he sought.

A flash of light signaled the launch of the torpedo. It streaked toward the *Faust*, nearly invisible to the eye.

A secondary flash appeared from the station, a bright flare of light that intercepted the missile, detonating it well short of the target.

What?

"Is there a ship hiding there?" he asked, the smile slowly fading.

"Sensors aren't reading a vessel, your Eminence."

"What about the escaping mercenary ships?"

"Both are reported destroyed, Gloritant."

The *Faust* was nearing the broken station, sweeping across near a large portion of the debris. A cargo hauler was hanging connected to a docking arm and loading dock against the separated platform, which was spinning away from the central spire.

"Target the debris," Thraven said.

"Yes, Gloritant," Bashir replied.

Lasers began lancing out toward the platform, digging into the cargo ship and turning it to slag. The *Faust* angled through the assault, swinging around toward the rear of the structure and trying to match its spin.

"They look like they're trying to dock with it, your Eminence," Bashir said.

Was Cage already on the station? The Gift would protect her in the vacuum of space, but not indefinitely.

"Place a mark on the target," Thraven said.

"Mark placed, Gloritant."

"Order all ships to fire on my mark," Thraven said.

"Yes, Gloritant. All ships, fire on the mark."

With the combined firepower of the remaining Nephilim ships, there was no chance that Cage would escape. There was no chance that she would survive.

Except they never had the chance to fire. The area in front of them flared suddenly, in a bright, piercing light that caused warning tones to sound on the bridge as sensors were thrown offline and eyes were rendered blind.

Thraven drew back at the light, putting his hand up in front of his face and falling into his seat, a chill racing down his spine. It couldn't be possible. How could it be possible?

The light faded seconds later. It took him longer than that to recover, blinking as the Gift worked to bring his senses back. The warning tones continued, and the bridge crew remained stunned as he got back to his feet, stepping forward and looking out the viewport.

The debris was still there, flying away from them as it had before.

Thraven didn't need the ship's sensors to know that the star hopper and Cage were gone.

He remained still and silent as the warning tones faded, the *Promise's* systems returning to normal. He continued staring out in the black beyond, trying to come to terms with what he had witnessed. He knew that Cage had seen the Light of the Shard. She had told him as much back on Anvil.

Now?

Now she had control over it. The Shard had come to her. He had saved her life. He had stopped the change. Thousands of individuals over thousands of years had born witness to the Light, and none had ever been chosen.

That she had was no coincidence. When he considered it, he wasn't even surprised. The Father had always said the path to freedom was not a path easily crossed. There would always be barriers. There would always be challenges.

Besides, the Gift of the Shard was nothing compared to the Gift of the Father. She had been more capable of defeating him before she had accepted the lies of the One and allowed the Light in.

The factory was destroyed. The Gate was complete. The Great

Return was underway. The first worlds would begin to fall, and the first souls would be collected. Soon enough, he would control the entire galaxy. Soon enough, he would be able to power the Elysium Gate and open the portal back to the origin. He would make a war machine unlike anything the universe had ever known, and then he would lead the Nephilim through it to victory and glory.

It was all as the Father had promised. Cage couldn't stop it. The Shard couldn't stop it. She had escaped, but that was no true cause for concern. He was angry with himself for his fear. The Father would be disappointed in the momentary lapse of faith.

"Take me to the Elysium Gate," he said. "I want to see it."

"What about Cage, your Eminence?" Bashir asked.

"She is nothing," he replied.

24

THREE MONTHS AGO, OLUS WOULD HAVE NEVER THOUGHT HE WOULD live to see the day that the center of the Republic, the planet Earth, would be moved to chaos.

Now, he found himself riding in a dropship en route to who the frag knew where, with the daughter of the one person in the universe who could stop it all from going to total hell beside him. A girl who was only eleven years old, who had already killed at least one Nephilim, and who seemed more than comfortable with the thought of killing a few more.

The reports were coming in almost too fast for him to manage, sent from the main pipeline of the Servants of the Ophanim, a command and control center buried deep beneath New York City. Deeper even than he had ever been, in tunnels that were kept secret from the outside world, tunnels where most people assumed Earth's Plixian Queen created her brood.

The Milnet was down. Republic forces had turned against one another. Outworld ships had been seen in Republic space near the Fringe, joining in some of the battles and helping turn the tide over to Gloritant Thraven's side. Planetside, the Council chambers had been put on lockdown, the building defended by those loyal to the Nephilim, holding a good portion of the government hostage. The Prime was safe, taken away and sent off-world to a location only a handful of people would know about, people who were vetted to be beyond reproach.

At least, Olus hoped they were beyond reproach. It seemed these days that nobody was incorruptible. He glanced over at Hayley, who was staring out the window with a tired, angry look on her face. Well, almost nobody.

The RAS forces on the planet were taking sides, and already there had been word of massive attacks in Switzerland and Germany, with the death toll constantly rising and the fear of the citizens of the world steadily growing. Most had been ordered to stay inside. Curfews were being put into place. But was the Law Enforcement enacting those rules for or against Thraven and his goals? It was impossible to know.

Olus could imagine the same scene playing out across the galaxy. It was chaos. Pure chaos, on a scale that boggled his mind. How could anyone orchestrate something like this? How could so many individuals buy into the bullshit that the Gloritant was selling? What had he shown them? What had he promised them?

There was no turning back from this. Even if Abbey managed to destroy Thraven, this was damage that couldn't be immediately undone. It would be a start, but only a start. The galaxy had changed, right now for the worse. He reminded himself that all of this was going to happen one way or another. The Nephilim had been waiting to return for thousands of years. It was just his shitty luck that he had to be alive when they made their move. It was just his shitty luck that he had to be one of the individuals trying to stop it.

There was nothing to do but the best he could. To him, that meant getting Hayley to safety and letting Abbey know that her daughter was alive, well, and with him. Then, he would see what he could do to help the Republic recover from Thraven's assault and start fighting back. With the Milnet down, the Republic was running deaf. Could he help give them back their ears? If anyone were able to solve that problem, it would be Gant. He knew the Gant's history, even if the Republic Research Division had done their best to bury what had been going on. As the Director of the OSI, it had been his job to know as much as he could about everything, and that was no exception. That they had locked him up in Hell was as much of an injustice as he could think of. They had created him and then punished him for being what he was. Gants were loyal to an extreme. They should have never let him bond if they didn't want to risk the consequences.

Olus let that thought slip away, a fresh one coming to the foreground.

Pahaliah.

He had learned only moments after escaping that she hadn't made it. One of the other soldiers had found her body on the north side of the reactor, amidst the remains of a pair of Goreshin that he hadn't been around to help disable. He didn't ask for details, but he could imagine how she had died. Brutally, but also quickly. He lowered his head. She had spent so many years training to be part of this fight, and she had been taken out of it so soon. Too soon. He didn't blame himself for it; he had been in the game way too long for that. It didn't mean the loss was easy to accept.

He dropped the thought, looking over at Hayley again. They had been in the air for nearly three hours, staying in the slim zone between ground and orbital sensors where they would be more challenging to spot. The girl hadn't said a word the entire time.

"How are you holding up?" he asked.

She kept her eyes on the viewport beside her. "I'm fine," she said flatly.

"Are you sure?"

Hayley turned toward him. "You don't need to patronize me, Captain Mann. I'm a child, but I'm not an idiot."

Olus almost laughed. He couldn't stop the smile.

"What's funny?"

"You sound like your mother."

"Good. My father is dead. My mother is out there, and she's in trouble. The whole Republic is in trouble. How am I supposed to process that, Captain? How am I supposed to make sense of it?"

"Those are mature questions to ask. I don't have any answers for you. I can't make sense of it either."

"Then you know the answer to your question. I'm fighting to hold it together, but I want to crawl under my blankets back home and hide. I want to wake up from this nightmare. I want to unsee all of the things that I've seen." A tear rolled down her face. I'm not okay, Captain. Are you?"

Olus shook his head. "No," he replied. "I don't know if anything will ever be okay for me again. Not after the things I've done. But maybe I can make it okay for you. Maybe I can help make it okay for others. I don't know yet. I'll die trying."

Hayley stared at him for a moment, and then she nodded. "Me, too."

"I can't let you be part of this. I'm going to get you somewhere safe, and then I'm going to join this war."

"I don't remember asking you," Hayley said, channeling Abbey again. "There is nowhere safe, Captain. We both know that."

Olus didn't know how to respond, so he didn't. Hayley returned to staring out at the sky. He turned his attention toward the front of the craft, where Xanix had emerged from the cockpit and was scuttling toward him.

"Captain," Xanix said. "We've been trying to find the means to get you off the planet, as you requested."

"And?" Olus said.

Hayley turned her head to follow the conversation.

"Many of the spaceports around the world have been shut down until order is restored."

"That's going to be a while."

"Yes. Our sources have been in contact with a launch site in California. We have come to terms with a freighter captain who is willing to take you on before he leaves."

"Excellent," Olus said, taking note of the position of the Plixian's antennae. "What's the catch?"

"The launch site is currently under contest." He paused, glancing at Hayley. "If you want to leave Earth, we will need to drop you into a war zone."

Olus looked at Hayley, too. She met his eyes. "I want to go back to my mother," she said.

"I know," Olus said. "How bad is the fighting?"

"We weren't able to ascertain. The captain did say he can't guarantee he will survive long enough for us to arrive."

"I don't understand? Why would this captain be willing to wait for us at the cost of his own life? What did you offer him?"

Xanix's head shifted toward Hayley again. "He asked me who I was trying to evacuate."

"And you told him?" Olus said, getting angry.

"Not exactly. He mentioned the incident at the restaurant the other night. He knew Plixians were involved, and that you were there. He correlated that we were Plixian, and suggested that perhaps you might be present. I'm not certain how he made the connection between you and Miss Cage, but he did mention Miss Cage."

"And he's going to risk dying to get her out? To get me out? Why?"

"He told me that his boss wants to speak to you. And that his boss owes Lieutenant Abigail Cage a favor, even if she doesn't know it, which means that he owes her a favor. I imagine getting Miss Cage to safety would be an adequate fulfillment of this debt."

"Do you know who his boss is, that it would make him so bold?"

"Of course. Don Pallimo, President of the Crescent Haulers."

Olus narrowed his eyes. The last he had heard, the Haulers thought the Rejects had slaughtered the crew of the *Devastator*. That wasn't exactly the kind of activity that would lead their President to want to grant any favors.

What the hell was Abbey up to out there?

Whatever it was, it hopefully meant that she had gotten off Azure and rejoined her crew. Maybe she had even tried to contact him? His access to the Galnet had been limited for days, and without his backchannel to Ruby, his ability to reach out was close to nil.

Then again, was it safe to believe Pallimo's offer was legit? If he were pissed at Abbey for killing one of his crews, this would be the perfect opportunity for him to get revenge.

Except the Don didn't work that way. He had morals and a code of honor that would prevent him from relying on deception. If Olus were on his list, he would send a team for him, and that would be that. He wouldn't beat around the bush or drag him into a trap, especially in the middle of the current shitstorm.

"How long until we reach the launch site?" he asked.

"Fifteen minutes."

"And he doesn't think he can last that long?"

The dropship shifted as if in response, nearly knocking Xanix over as it twisted in an evasive maneuver. Warning tones sounded around them, suggesting they were moving into the danger zone.

"Captain, I am unsure if we will last that long."

25

THE DROPSHIP BANKED HARD, LEAVING OLUS PRESSED TO THE SIDE OF his seat, the magnetic clamps on his seraphsuit holding him in place. He glanced over at Hayley, noticing the smile on her face as she shifted against her more conventional harness, still staring out the viewport at the chaos around them.

She seemed unfazed by the thought of dying. She was young. Did she think she was invincible? She was Abbey's daughter, so maybe she was.

"Commander!" the pilot shouted over the comm, loud enough that it hurt Olus' ears. "Drop zone is three klicks that way, but I've never seen fighting like this before."

"We have to get inside," Xanix replied. "Infantry, line up!"

The squads of Plixians unhooked themselves from their seats, gripping metal flooring with their toes as they scrambled toward the rear of the dropship.

"We'll lead you out and keep you covered," Xanix said.

"I don't deserve this," Olus replied.

"It's what we have sworn to do. Get ready to join the back of the line."

Olus didn't argue. He nodded while Xanix headed to the rear of the ship, ready to open the hatch and get them out. He reached out and put his hand on Hayley's shoulder. She glanced over at him.

"We're going to have to jump. Hold onto me, and you'll be fine."

She smiled. "Roger, Captain."

He remembered when his fear had been beaten out of him during HSOC training, all of those years ago. Why didn't Hayley Cage seem to possess any?

"Captain," Xanix said over the comm.

Olus shifted his weight, working to unlatch himself from the chair. He didn't have Plixian feet that were able to cling to nearly anything, and the seraphsuit didn't have the magnetic footpads of a battlesuit. He would have to be careful.

He got to his feet, pivoting toward Hayley. "I'm going to unbuckle you."

The dropship shook, and Olus had to grab onto the back of the chair as they started to dive and bank.

"Hold onto your thoraxes," their human pilot said. "For those of you who have them."

The dropship's thrusters screamed, the vibration of their effort running across the deck. Olus caught sight of the streak out of the viewport, left without enough time to curse as it hit the starboard thruster and detonated, sending debris and flame shooting away from the impact point. He grabbed Hayley, yanking her toward him as a piece of the dropship flew toward them, impaling the side of the ship where she had just been.

If only that had been the end of it.

The dropship began to bank harder, yawing at nearly sixty degrees and knocking him from his feet, throwing him into the damaged side with Hayley on top of him. He protected her from the impact, using the Gift to get his feet under him and planted, rolling in the air as the dropship rolled around him.

Red lights flashed, and a crash warning sounded in the bay. The Plixians were being thrown around the space, crashing into the walls and one another. They were going down, and going down hard.

Hayley screamed beside him, her calm exterior suddenly giving in to the moment. He held onto her, pulling her close and wrapping the Gift around them, using it as a shield. Xanix came crashing toward them, hitting the shield and bouncing away. His abdomen was twisted at a bad angle away from his upper thorax, and he looked like he was in pain.

"Brace for impact," the pilot said.

Olus looked forward to the cockpit, just in time to see a line of heavy projectile rounds cut through it, and the pilot. The whole thing disappeared in one massive burst, exposing them to the air as the remains of the craft fell to the earth, spinning in the air like a flailing leaf.

Hayley was still screaming, but she didn't fight against his grip. He managed to get his feet planted, bracing them momentarily as he gathered his strength. With one heavy push, he launched them away from the ship and through the freshly made hole, out into the open air. The twisted metal at the edge of the craft caught his knee, tearing a deep gash in it and nearly severing his leg, the momentum pushing him into a spin of his own.

He looked down. The ground was closer than he thought. There was no time. He cried out as he used the Gift to slow his descent and straighten himself out, feeling the strain of the energy he was burning to do it. A few seconds later they hit the dirt, Hayley on top of Olus. The dropship reached the surface right before them, an echoing crash and hiss as the remains slid along the ground.

Olus stayed there. His leg hurt. His body was battered. He could feel the Blood below his flesh, working to knit him back together. He was hungry. Worse? He could see a fighter circling and pointing toward them, streaking down to finish what it had started.

"Hayley, run," he said, looking over to her.

She was on her feet, reaching out to help him up.

"Come on, Captain," she said.

"I can't," he replied. He tried to move the foot on his injured leg. He couldn't even feel it. "Not yet, and there's no time." He pointed to the Crescent Hauler freighter, the top of which was visible in the distance, its shields flashing as it defended itself from attack. "Get to the freighter. Get off the planet. If the Don owes your mom a favor, he'll take good care of you."

"We don't leave anyone behind," she said, insistent. "That's the first rule."

Olus felt the twist in his gut. He had left people behind. They were dead because of him. But this young girl was giving up her life to try to save his. The sudden guilt could either break him or give him the incentive he needed to survive.

The fighter leveled off. The first rounds hit the earth right in front of them. Olus grunted as he pushed off, diving to Hayley and tugging her out of the way. The projectiles never reached them. A second fighter that matched the first intercepted, twin missiles hitting the first and knocking it off-course. It exploded a few seconds later.

"Shit," Hayley said, watching the action. "We need to hurry."

"You're telling me," Olus said.

Hayley approached him, getting her body under his shoulder and propping him up. "Let's go."

They moved slowly at first, with Olus limping toward the freighter. His wounds continued to heal, and within a minute he was back on both feet, joining Hayley as she started to run.

A heavy pounding to their left drew his attention, and he spotted a Komodo near one of the launch site's outbuildings, rounding the corner and facing in their direction. The heavy mech was laden with firepower, too much for him to stop even with the Gift.

"Get down," he shouted, diving forward and grabbing Hayley, pulling her to the ground. The mech pilot hadn't spotted them yet, and Olus remained still, hoping that he wouldn't.

The machine stomped toward them, each footfall shaking the earth. Olus could hear gunfire everywhere, and when he thought about who was fighting who, he felt only sadness. Thraven had turned them against one another with empty promises and lies. He had infiltrated so deeply into their psyches that they were killing their friends and comrades.

Did they even know why?

He felt a second vibration join the first, and then the ground began to rumble. He looked to his right. An entire squad of lighter mechs had converged, taking aim at the Komodo and opening fire. Missiles streaked across the open space where they were waiting, slamming into the opponent's shields and drawing its attention.

"I'm going to carry you," Olus said. "Hold on."

He put his arm around Hayley's waist, rising to his feet and lifting her easily in front of him. Then he used the seraphsuit to bounce forward, keeping a long, low arc that brought them away from the mech's battlefield. He landed roughly, stumbling to keep the inertia from hurting Hayley.

"Are you okay?" he asked.

"I think I'm going to puke," she replied.

He took that as a yes, and bounced again, repeating the process a few more times.

The launch site was owned by the Crescent Haulers, and the massive warehouses that surrounded it were behind thick walls that abutted surrounding hillsides, the rear of which overlooked the Pacific Ocean. The freighter was gigantic in the center of it, rising way above the tallest buildings and the control tower, still absorbing attacks from passing fighters while the ground defenses tried to hold them back. The only reason they had kept Thraven's forces from overrunning them was because the loyal Republic soldiers had intervened, disrupting the assault and keeping the front split. Even so, the enemy seemed to have the upper hand, their battlesuited infantry advancing on the walls, trying to jump over them and get inside. Guards were positioned around the perimeter, working to prevent it.

Olus landed again, right next to a soldier that had been shot from the walls nearly a kilometer away. He bent and scooped up the dead man's rifle, checking the ammo before adjusting his grip to use it. Hayley squirmed in his grip and then pointed to a second weapon a few meters away. He let her go, and she scampered to it and grabbed it.

She was returning to him when she dropped to the ground. Olus started turning, his flesh beginning to burn as the fresh round of flechettes dug through the seraphsuit and into him, the impact nearly turning him sideways. He managed to get himself around, putting his eyes on the squad of blacksuits that had appeared out of nowhere, watching as one of them started sprouting holes from Hayley's new weapon.

He called on the Gift, sweeping it up in front of him, deflecting their attack as he charged ahead, shoving the muzzle of his rifle into the nearest soldiers' head and pulling the trigger. The round went right through his helmet and his brain, but Olus barely saw it. He was already moving to the next target, throwing an enhanced punch that knocked the enemy back a dozen meters. He pivoted again, firing another round into another soldier before vectoring for the last. They went down in a hail of bullets, some from Hayley, some from the wall beyond.

Olus looked out to the defenses, finding a line of guards there, weapons lined up on him. He put his hands up, dropping his rifle, not wanting them to mistake him for an enemy. One of them shifted, motioning to him to make a run for it.

Hayley rejoined him, unarmed once more.

"Out of ammo," she said as he scooped her up and resumed their escape.

The soldiers on the wall were covering them now, shooting out beyond them. Olus risked a glance back, finding three dropships had landed nearby, all of them unloading Thraven's forces. He could only imagine what that meant for the planet as a whole if the Nephilim were dropping infantry from orbit. Had Earth been lost already? He wasn't ready to believe that. It was more likely they were making a last-ditch effort to keep him from escaping with Hayley. He could imagine how angry the Gloritant would be once he learned that Ruche had lost her.

They neared the barrier, getting close enough that the soldiers were right above them. One of them dropped a line to him as they approached and he grabbed it, letting them pull him and Hayley up to the top and over.

"Miss Cage?" the lead guard said, his large Curlatin eyes barely visible through his tinted helmet.

"Yes," Hayley replied. "And Captain Olus Mann."

"I'm Sergeant Coxie. The Don wants us to bring you to safety. Allow me."

The Sergeant took Hayley the same way Olus had, and without another word leaped from the side of the wall toward the ground inside. His squad followed him, making a smooth, synchronized bounce that the best Republic platoons would be jealous of. Olus trailed behind them, leaping from the wall at the same time a fighter began strafing where they had just been. A sharp crack sounded from beneath the freighter, and then the fighter started to smoke, unable to pull up and crashing into the nearby hillside.

Olus kept pace with Coxie and his team, rushing toward the small open hatch of the freighter. The fighting was getting more intense, both sides nearing the launch site, each trying to stop the other from succeeding. He was nearly knocked down when the ground shook once more, and a wave of heat blasted him from behind. He stumbled, chunks of debris hitting him in the back, and when he turned, he saw a portion of the wall had been removed. A woman was standing behind it, hands raised and still burning from the energy she had unleashed.

"Another fragging Evolent?" he said out loud. "Great."

She spotted him, one of her hands dropping and unleashing another torrent of flame. He raised his hands, begging the Gift to protect him, feeling the drain on his energy as the barrier formed, blocking the energy. He held it, being pushed backward by the force until Coxie's squad noticed the assault and started firing back. The Evolent couldn't attack him and defend the soldiers at the same time. The flames vanished, freeing him to retreat, bouncing three hundred meters to the freighter's hatch.

"Get in," Coxie said, standing beside it.

"Hayley?"

"She's already on board."

"Thank you."

"Just doing my job."

Olus boarded the freighter. Immediately, the launcher beneath it began to vibrate and hum, a massive sling that would help the ship climb to orbit. Coxie joined him inside the airlock a moment later, his squad entering one by one and the hatch sliding closed.

"We aren't safe yet," Coxie said, brushing past him.

He followed the Sergeant, grabbing onto the side of the corridor. The freighter's velocity was increasing, pushing against him.

"We're going to jump in atmosphere, aren't we?" Olus asked.

"No choice," Coxie replied.

Olus crinkled his face, not looking forward to that, or to Hayley having to go through that. It was the only way to escape.

The ship shuddered, a loud crack audible through the dense hull. A yellow warning light flashed, and they started lilting to the side.

"Frag," Coxie bellowed. "Hold on tight. This is going to be funky."

Olus looked down the corridor, searching for Hayley. Where was she? She shouldn't have to be alone during an atmospheric jump.

Too late.

Olus felt his entire stomach clench, the pressure on him increasing tenfold. Time seemed to slow around him, everything moving like mud for what felt like minutes but was only a few seconds. His head began to throb like it was about to explode, and he wanted to close his eyes and fall on his knees.

He did a second later as his perception of time regained itself and allowed him to move once more. The pain of the jump was still there, but it subsided relatively quickly thanks to the Gift. Hayley. He needed to find Hayley.

He forced himself up, then slowed down, allowing himself to relax.

She was on board. They had made it out. Earth was already millions of kilometers distant.

They were safe.

For now.

26

"Dak, do you copy?" Abbey said, trying the comm again. When nobody answered, she looked back at Gant. "Are you sure you set this thing up right?"

Gant chittered. "Seriously, Queenie? I invented the fragging thing."

"Then why aren't they answering?"

"Maybe Kett isn't as afraid of you as you thought?" Bastion suggested. "It could be that he arrested Dak and seized the *High Noon* the moment they showed up nearby."

"That would be a stupid thing for him to do."

"Pretty much my opinion of that asshole," Benhil said.

"Queenie," Phlenel said, calling her from their limited medical bay. "He's awake."

"Keep trying," Abbey said. "Gant, double-check your work. I'm going to say hello to our new guest."

"Double-check my work?" Gant said.

"I trust you, but we need to be sure. This is important."

"Roger, Queenie. I'm on it."

Abbey reached the ladder, descending it to the lower deck. Her body was still a little sore from their escape from the factory; the naniates pushed into overtime to help her recover. She had nearly died out there. Again. But like before, the Gift of the Shard had protected her when every other option had run out.

The attack on the factory had left her, Phlenel, and everyone else in the loading dock suddenly exposed to the vacuum of space. While the Hurshin was able to survive without an external oxygen supply and her gelatinous form was impervious to temperature changes, Abbey wasn't so lucky. She had been choking and freezing when the Gift of the Shard had wrapped itself around her defending her from the cold of space, and maintaining her systems while she was unable to breathe, mechanically keeping her alive when her organic parts couldn't.

It had also understood the danger she was in, and like on Avalon had cast out a last-ditch burst of energy, this time in the form of a starburst of light that she guessed had completely fragged with the Nephilim fleet's sensors. The flare had left her barely conscious, but she could remember Phlenel enveloping her, yet another skin over the shardsuit and her body, keeping her warm and safe and surrounded in a living cocoon. She recalled the sense of intimacy of the action, a gentle care that she would never forget.

That care had given Bastion time to bring the *Faust* around to pick them up, getting them away from the area before Thraven could recover and start shooting at them again. She had spent the next hour after that slumped against the wall with Gant sitting beside her, holding her hand while her body came back to life. Pik had retrieved enough food bars to keep them all going for a month in the meantime, and she started powering through them, feeling her strength beginning to return. Even with the pure Gift of the Shard, she couldn't help but wonder if she would have recovered faster by drinking blood. Not that she would have asked any of the Rejects to donate any.

It was only after she had gotten back to her feet and started for the bridge that Gant informed her they had picked someone else up from the debris field, finding faint life signs near her position. They had brought him to sick bay to recover.

Phlenel looked up as she entered, a smile forming on her translucent lips.

"Queenie, how are you feeling?" her bot asked.

"Better," Abbey replied. "Thanks to you."

"I was happy to be of service."

She turned her attention to the newcomer. She wasn't sure how to consider him just yet. Prisoner? Guest? It all depended on him.

"Do you have a name?" she asked, standing over him.

He was laying on a gurney, the parts of his body visible beyond the sheet that covered his nakedness pale and unhealthy. There was a thin choker around his neck, one that she knew would have a small container of the Shard's blood stored within. It was the reason he had been able to survive in space. The reason he was here and alive now. But she could tell without looking that the blood had been used up in bringing him back to where he was and that unless he were given more, he wouldn't be alive much longer.

She also knew that she could give him what he needed. But would she?

Again, that depended on him.

"I said, do you have a name?" she repeated when he didn't speak.

"Uriel," he replied.

Abbey turned her head toward Jequn when she gasped.

"You know him?"

Jequn shook her head. "Not personally. But there are stories. Some have even made it into human legend. He's supposed to be dead."

"A hero," Uriel said. He coughed out a laugh. "I'm not what the legends say I am. Not exactly."

"Then what are you?" Abbey asked.

"Imperfect."

"In our legends, Uriel traveled the galaxy and helped the Seraphim being hunted by the Nephilim escape," Jequn said. "Without Uriel, there would be no Ophanim."

"That's the trouble with legend," Uriel said. "It only gets things half-right."

"What's the other half?" Abbey said.

"I didn't ferry Seraphim out of the goodness of my heart. I'm a profiteer. They paid me to bring them to safety." He paused. "Thraven fragged me over. He promised me worlds to protect the Gate. How could I be so stupid to trust a Nephilim? Especially a fragging prophet."

"How could you be so stupid?" Abbey asked. "If you've been around for as long as you say, you should know better. I mean, it only took me a few days to figure it out."

"There's a reason why greed is a deadly sin," Uriel said. "Five thousand years is a long time to be working for others. I wanted something different. I wanted to be in control."

"How's that working out for you now? Your regeneration device is dry. The Blood's run out."

Uriel slowly lifted his hand, putting it to the choker and unclasping it. He looked at the clear vial inside its container. A slight red stain ran along the bottom, but there was no liquid remaining.

"It figures I would die like this. You should have left me out there."

"Probably," Abbey agreed. "But you have something I need."

"I do?" He paused and then smiled. "You want to know where they brought the Gate."

"Thraven wanted you dead for a reason. I imagine that's it?"

"I'm sorry to disappoint you. I don't know where they're taking it. I can show you where it used to be, but it won't be all that helpful."

"You're sure you don't know?" Abbey asked. "Because it's the only reason you're alive right now."

"Thraven wanted me dead because I'm a Seraphim. He wanted me dead because I know how the Gate operates and how to destroy it."

Abbey stared at Uriel. How was it that this one had been so corrupted? Could he be saved the way Trinity had been saved?

"You said there was something different about my Gift," Abbey said. "But you didn't know what it was."

"Yes."

"Tell me how to destroy the Gate, and I'll show you."

"I have a better idea. Find a way to save my life, and if you find the Gate, I'll help you destroy it."

"You aren't in a position to bargain."

"No? I have information you want, but I'm dying. Stop me from dying, get the information. Let me die, get nothing. I think that puts me in a fine position."

"He'd make an excellent Reject," Phlenel said.

"Shut up," Abbey replied. "He doesn't need encouragement." She looked back at Uriel. "You do have a point."

She leaned over him, reaching out and taking his hand.

"What are you doing?" Uriel said.

She lifted his hand, turning her head and pushing her hair aside, leaving the Hell brand visible. The Light of the Shard had entered her, but it had also remained there on the surface, causing the brand to glow.

"What is that?" Uriel asked, suddenly frightened.

"Everything you've turned your back on," she replied.

He tried to pull his hand away. To resist. He was nowhere near strong enough. She brought his palm to the brand, pressing it against the mark. His eyes widened, and he started to moan. When he tried to yank his hand away, she let him.

"What did you do?" he asked, turning his palm over so he could look at it. The brand was etched into the flesh, glowing with a pale light. "What is this?"

He started to shiver, his body quaking beneath the sheets. His eyes closed, but the tears escaped through his eyelids, running down his face.

"You betrayed the Covenant," Abbey said. "The true Covenant. You turned away from the promise you made. You profited from your people's sorrow. Your Gift twisted you. Corrupted you. I saw what the Seraphim did on Avalon. They were trying to change the Blood, to make it more powerful and more capable of helping them commit violence. They failed."

"On Avalon," Uriel said. "Yes. On Jubilation. On Deminoss. The Infected are there, too. That's why I abandoned them. That's why I didn't want to help them. They killed thousands seeking to be more like the Nephilim. They gave me their tainted Gift, and it would have killed me if not for the pure Blood. I'm guilty, Queen of Demons. But not any more guilty than the rest of them. My actions are different, but my motives are no worse than theirs."

"The Shard didn't want me," Abbey said. "He chose me because he was desperate. I'm too violent. Too angry. Sometimes violence is needed. Sometimes it's the only way. Anyone who says otherwise is either too naive to be realistic or is lying to begin with. It doesn't matter. Let the Light show you the truth you hide from yourself."

"What is the truth?" Uriel said. He opened his eyes. "Knowing won't save my life. Removing the corruption won't don't anything for me."

"Swear yourself to me, and I'll save you," Abbey said. "I'll give you a chance to make up for the damage you've done by helping Thraven build the Gate. Billions of innocents are going to die otherwise."

"You won't be able to reach the Gate. You'll die trying."

"Maybe. But at least I'll die for something. How do you want to die?"

He stared up at her. Then he smiled. "Okay. Fine. I pledge my loyalty to you, on my honor."

"Queenie," Jequn said. "He doesn't have any honor."

"I think he does now," she replied. "Phlenel, hand me a laser scalpel."

The bot picked the tool off a nearby counter and walked it over to her.

"What are you going to do with it?" Phlenel asked.

"Uriel, open your mouth."

He did as he was instructed. Abbey took the scalpel, turning it on and running it along the edge of her thumb. It opened up her flesh, allowing blood to pool on the edge. She suspended her thumb over Uriel's mouth until a single drop fell from her finger and entered him.

He swallowed, staring at her. Then his eyes closed, and he was still.

"Did you kill him?" Jequn asked.

"He isn't dead," Phlenel said.

He was better than not dead. His skin began to tighten, his

complexion losing its sick paleness. Abbey could sense the change in him, the pure Gift of the Shard working its way through his system.

"What did you do?" Jequn asked.

"I'm not sure yet, exactly," Abbey replied.

"What? I thought you knew what you were doing?"

"To an extent. He looks better, don't you think?"

"He will survive," Phlenel said.

"Good enough," Abbey replied. "Keep an eye on him, help him get settled in when he wakes up again."

"Aye, Queenie."

"Queenie, are you sure we can trust him?" Jequn asked.

"Yes. If for no other reason than because Thraven fragged him, too."

"What if we can't?"

"Then we'll finish killing him. But not before he tells us how to destroy the Gate."

"Roger that."

"Queenie," Gant said. "I, uh. I'm a little embarrassed to admit, but I did enter one of the keys for the subnet incorrectly. Communications with the *High Noon* have been restored. I'm sorry."

"You made a mistake," Abbey replied. "It happens."

There was a pause on the other end of the comm.

"Not to me," Gant said softly.

Abbey could tell he was distressed by the oversight. Probably more than he should have been. She would deal with that later.

"Imp, find out where the fleet is hiding and set a course."

"Roger, Queenie," Bastion replied.

"General Kett's about to have the worst day of his life."

27

THE *FAUST* DROPPED OUT OF FTL THREE HOURS LATER, APPEARING amidst a disterium plume that formed in the center of what Abbey considered her fleet, and what she was sure General Kett considered his fleet.

She had tried to talk to Gant during the trip, but he had been unusually sullen, excusing himself when she mentioned how hard he was taking his error and vanishing somewhere on the lower deck. She decided after that not to follow him or to push him again, at least not yet. Maybe he would come back to her on his own; maybe she would have to approach him later. It bothered her that they were supposed to be close, but he wouldn't open up to her. At the same time, she didn't know all that much about his past. There was a reason for his distress. She just didn't know what it was.

She couldn't worry about it now. Putting the *Faust* into the middle of the fleet was a bold maneuver, one that had the potential to leave them surrounded and under attack, with only the *High Noon* to try to defend them.

She found the battleship quickly, positioned near the outer rim of the assembled starships, on the opposite side of the *Brimstone*, which was hanging directly below them.

"We're being hailed, Queenie," Bastion said, checking the comm equipment. "The *Brimstone*."

Kett.

"Tell the General I'll only speak to him in private. I expect clearance to dock with the *Brimstone*."

"Aye, Queenie," Bastion replied. "This is the *Faust*."

"Abigail, are you there?" Sylvan said. "I'm glad to hear you made it off Azure. We need to talk."

"Number one, it's Queenie to you," Bastion said. "Number two, we're coming in to dock. Queenie will meet you in your quarters in fifteen."

Sylvan laughed. "That's how you want to play it? Very well. I'll see you there. *Brimstone* out."

"Very well," Baston mimicked. "I'll see you there. Asshole."

"At least he didn't put up a fight."

"Which probably means he has an entire company of soldiers waiting to try to subdue you."

"Good luck with that. Bring us in."

"Roger."

Bastion directed the *Faust* toward the *Brimstone*, staying focused as they made their approach. The ship's laser batteries were barely visible beneath the sleek outline, but they both knew they were present, and could take down the star hopper in one instant blast. Abbey could only hope Erlan would give them a heads-up if Kett were planning something like that, but what if Erlan had been replaced?

It seemed ridiculous to her that she even had to consider it. Sylvan Kett had built an army separate from the Republic, specifically because he and his Seraphim spouse had known how badly things might go. They were on the same side, so why the hell did she have to fight with him or worry about him? She didn't even care if he stayed in control of the fleet. She had other plans, anyway. She just wanted him to start doing something.

And she wanted Ruby back.

The *Faust* closed on the *Brimstone*, reaching the docking clamps on the top side without incident. Bastion brought them into position, locking the smaller ship to the larger while Abbey headed down the ladder to the exit.

"Imp, keep the engines warm, just in case. Gant, Cherub, you're with me. Pudding, is Uriel awake yet?"

"Not yet, Queenie."

"Roger."

"Can I come, Queenie?" Pik asked. "I want to help Ruby."

Abbey considered. "Okay, Okay. You're with me, too."

"Thanks, Queenie!"

They gathered beside the hatch until Bastion signaled that docking was complete. It didn't escape Abbey's notice that her Rejects were all wearing lightsuits instead of standard utilities. They weren't obviously armed, but none of them needed to be obvious about it.

"We've got your back, Queenie," Gant said. "Whatever happens."

"Thank you," Abbey replied. "Imp, open her up."

"Aye, Queenie."

The hatch hissed as the pressure equalized and then it slid aside, revealing a secondary airlock and ladder down into the *Brimstone*. Abbey could see a few pairs of boots from her position. Soldiers in battlesuits. Great.

"I'll take point," she said, descending the ladder. The soldiers came into view as she neared the floor. Eight of them, all armed and ready for trouble.

"Some greeting," Abbey said to them. "Does Sylvan intend to arrest us?"

"Ma'am," the lead soldier said. "Our orders are to escort you to the General's suite, and your companions to a holding area for their protection."

Abbey laughed. "Their protection or yours?"

"We don't want any trouble, ma'am."

"If you try to stop my companions from joining me, you're going to get it. I know you're following orders, but I'm not in the mood for this bullshit."

The soldiers trained their rifles on her. She was feeling much stronger again, though it had taken nearly half of the ship's rations to bring her back up to par. Even so, she wasn't ready to play that card. Not yet. She had another scare tactic in mind.

"Void, why don't you join me, too?" Abbey said.

"On my way, Queenie," Trin replied.

"I think you should point those somewhere else, soldier," Abbey said to the lead guard.

The other Rejects came down one by one behind her. She could sense the change in the soldiers' confidence as they did, especially when Trinity started descending into the *Brimstone*.

"What the hell is that?" she heard one of them whisper.

"Get your squad out of my way, soldier," Abbey said.

The soldier was hesitant for a moment. Then he motioned for the others to lower their weapons. "I don't want to fight an ally," he said. "There's enough of that happening already."

"Well said," Abbey replied.

"We're going to escort you."

"Fine with me."

Abbey started walking ahead of the soldiers. The Rejects trailed behind her, moving past them as well. The guards leveled their rifles at their backs, which was fine with Abbey. If they even tried to shoot, they would be dead before they had a chance to figure out what had gone wrong.

There were other crew members in the corridors leading to the General's quarters, and they moved aside as Abbey and the others approached, watching them pass with a mix of fear and awe. Abbey didn't pay much attention to them, keeping her head straight and her eyes forward, maintaining the composure of a Queen.

The whole entourage came to a stop outside of Sylvan Kett's private suite, the same rooms that Abbey had taken during her short stay on the starship. The lead guard cut in front of her then, blocking her entry.

"Let me announce you," he said, practically begging.

"Fine," Abbey replied, putting a hand impatiently on her hip.

The soldier opened the door and entered, the hatch closing behind him. Abbey counted to ten. When the door didn't open again, she reached out with the Gift, pulling it aside and walking through, cutting the guard off mid-sentence.

"You took too long," she said, her eyes flicking forward to the desk.

Kett was sitting behind it, his expression both angry and slightly amused. She noticed immediately that Ruby was standing next to him. Except she didn't look like Ruby anymore. Not exactly. The synthetic skin was the same. The facial structure, the build. But the clothes had been exchanged for a seraphsuit, and the hair had been cut and altered.

What the hell?

She looked just like Charmeine.

28

"WHAT THE FRAG DID YOU DO TO HER?" ABBEY ASKED.

"Of all the things to lead with, that's your primary concern?" Sylvan replied. "Need I remind you that she was a synth? A pleasure bot, no less?"

"Need I remind you that she was part of my crew, whether you like it or not?" Abbey moved past the guard. "Go wait outside."

The guard looked at Kett, who nodded. He retreated from the room, closing the hatch behind him and leaving them alone.

"He's gonna get it," Abbey could hear Pik say as the door sealed.

Kett stood up. "Abigail, if you give me a chance I-"

Abbey flicked her hand out, the Gift pushing him back against the wall and holding him there. "You went to Kell to help my Rejects, not to imprison them, you son of a bitch."

She stormed toward him. He didn't put up a fight. In fact, he was smiling. That only made her angrier.

"Why are you smiling?"

"I knew you would be angry. I'm glad to see I was right."

"I don't get you," Abbey said, reaching him and putting her face near his. He was taller than her, even after her Gift-fueled growth spurt that had gained her a handful of centimeters. She wanted to drag him to his knees to bring him down to size, but she didn't.

"Give me two minutes, and I can explain."

Abbey released him. He shook his limbs out and then circled past her to Ruby.

"You've been part of this for months, Abigail," he said. "We've been doing this for years."

"We?" Abbey replied.

Ruby smiled. "I'm sorry, Abbey," she said.

Only her voice had been changed. Re-synthesized or something. She even sounded like Charmeine now.

"I know Ruby was important to you, but this is more important than her. More important than all of us."

"What did you do to her?" Abbey repeated.

"Seraphim technology," Sylvan said. "A Configurator. The brain of the target is mapped and digitized, including all of the memories stored within. I've always kept a copy of my Charmeine in the case of an emergency. I was hoping never to need to use it."

"You mean you made a copy of her consciousness?"

"Yes," Charmeine said. "It was done before I met you, but Sylvan told me everything that transpired. I'm happy you're here."

Abbey stared at her. "You can't make a duplicate of a living thing. Maybe you can digitize the brain. You can't copy a soul."

"What is a soul, Abigail?" Charmeine said. "We're all a collection of atoms. DNA. Break it down further, and we're masses of positive and negative. Ones and zeroes. Anything can be copied once you understand the base. But that isn't the point or the purpose."

Abbey shook her head. "Let's back up a step." She looked at Kett. "I stayed behind on Azure to save your life, and to keep Thraven from finding out where the Shardship is hiding. Charmeine. The real Charmeine died to save me from Thraven. Meanwhile, you went to Kell, and when the battle was over, you seized control of my fleet."

"I didn't seize it," Sylvan said. "I thought we had an understanding that I was second in command under you?"

"I never said that."

"The majority of the fleet is composed of my resources. My soldiers. My ships. I thought there was an implicit chain of command. Besides, who would you have preferred take charge? Your Gant?"

Abbey's anger flared. "He's not my Gant. He's his own individual. And yes, he's perfectly capable of managing this fleet."

"Maybe your Rejects would follow him, but my people wouldn't. People, Abigail. It's an important distinction. I told you on Azure that humankind is the chosen race, the species made in the image of the One and closely enough related to the Seraphim to reproduce with them. They would never allow a Gant to lead them. You're smart enough to know that."

"You split them up so they couldn't cause trouble. Then you imprisoned them when they didn't agree with whatever it is you're doing. Oh yeah, nothing. You've been hiding out here while the galaxy has been falling to shit. Your daughter abandoned you because she knew you were making the wrong move."

Kett's eyes narrowed at the last part. "Did you look out of the viewport on your way in?" he asked.

"Yes. Why?"

"Did you bother to count the number of ships?"

"Your fleet has grown. I noticed."

"And yet you claim I've been doing nothing."

"Thraven took the Milnet offline. He created a civil war across the Republic with one move."

"Which is precisely why we were assembling this army in the first place. We knew this would happen one way or another. I appreciate and respect your loyalty to your friends, but don't let it cloud your tactical mind. Gant thought I was sitting here bemoaning the loss of my wife. That was true to an extent, but not to the extent he believed. Why would I, when I had a copy of her? It took me a few days to update the routines to integrate with newer synth technology, but I always knew I could bring her back. We could get out there. We could take on Thraven and his forces. Maybe we could win a few fights. But then what? We'd lose one ship after another, slow attrition until there was nothing left."

"You can't win this fight with brute force, Abbey," Charmeine said.

"I know," Abbey replied. "That's part of why I'm here."

"And it's why I am here," Charmeine replied.

"Not because of love," Sylvan said. "Even if I wish that were the case. I did what I had to do to your Rejects to keep them from fragging everything up. I had a feeling they would take the *High Noon* and go to rescue you before they acted on Captain Mann's intel. How did that turn out, anyway?"

"The Elysium Gate is complete," Abbey said. "We were too late. Thraven made an appearance and nearly killed me while he was destroying the evidence."

"It's finished?" Charmeine said, surprised.

"Yes. It's also been moved from its original location. I don't know where."

"Damn it," Sylvan said. "We can't let him use the gate."

"I know," Abbey agreed. "It wasn't a total waste. We ran into someone you might know." She looked at Charmeine. "He said his name is Uriel."

If Charmeine was surprised, she didn't show it. Or maybe it was because she was in Ruby's body? Either way, her expression was flat.

"You don't need him," she said. "He's a traitor. Useless."

"I'll be the judge of that," Abbey replied. "Since you're here, and alive as it were, I need information."

"What kind of information?"

"Azure. The Seraphim fortress beneath the crater. The experiments. The pool with the crystals inside."

Charmeine stared at her in silence.

"What? You aren't going to tell me? I know you know. I know you were there. I didn't find it by accident, did I?"

"I didn't know you were there," she said. "This configuration predates those events. Why would I send you down there?"

"Because I saw the Light of the Shard."

"You did? And you went to the pool?"

"You led me to the pool."

"Did it activate?"

"Yes."

She leaned forward, looking at Abbey more closely. "Another remains, then. Another Shard. They aren't all gone."

"You knew?" Abbey said, her words coming out as a growl.

"Knew what?" Kett said. "Charlie, what are you two talking about."

Abbey laughed. "And you didn't tell your husband?"

"Tell me what?"

"This isn't an isolated incident. The Seraphim follow the Shard to another universe, and then they turn on him. Sooner or later, they betray him."

"It isn't the same everywhere," Charmeine said. "And it doesn't matter here. Not in the way that you think. They can't reach this universe from theirs, not without going through Elysium. If the One had fallen, they would already be here."

"But for every Shard that's killed, that's one more potential assault on the One."

"Yes. Elysium Gates are not easy to construct. They are even more difficult to power. Even with the Gate finished here, Thraven will need more Blood from the Shard than he can possibly obtain. There isn't enough remaining."

"What if he could make more?"

"He can't. The Focus has the only untainted Blood that remains. That's why he wants it."

Abbey felt a chill wash over her. "You're wrong on two counts. One, the Blood in the Focus isn't untainted. Whatever the frag you and your fellow scientists were trying to do, the spoil made it back to the source. But then, you already know that, don't you? The Blood kills humans as much as it does pure Seraphim, even though it shouldn't. So that means he can use tainted Blood, as long as it's still compatible. Two, there is untainted Blood, and you know where that is too because you set me up to get it."

Charmeine looked at her. Then she smiled. Then she started laughing.

"Charlie?" Sylvan said.

"Perfect. This is too perfect. Syl, this is better than we were hoping for. Forget simply killing Thraven. Everything is falling more perfectly into place than we could have imagined. He purified you, didn't he? He made you his progeny."

"Perfect?" Abbey said. "None of this would be necessary if you hadn't messed with the naniates in the first place. You tried to turn the peaceful technology of the Shard into a weapon, and not only did you kill massive numbers of your own kind, but you also failed to match what Lucifer produced. You pretty much screwed up this universe for everything living in it."

"We did what we thought we had to do to stop the Nephilim from destroying this universe. If we hadn't altered the naniates, they would have taken over thousands of years ago, and you wouldn't be here now. The subjects knew the risks."

"Did their families? Did they know you were going to create naniates that would go out of control and begin seizing them as carriers? It wasn't just Azure, was it? Jubilation. Deminoss. How many others?"

Charmeine's expression shifted. Her hands clenched at her sides. "You weren't there, Abbey. You don't know anything about it."

"But I'm learning. The Shard wanted me to learn. He wanted me to see. To understand that you are to blame for this as much as the Nephilim. To know that he's ashamed of you."

The last sentence stole all of Charmeine's anger. She slouched in sudden defeat, and though her synthetic replacement body was incapable of crying, she looked as though she should be.

"The Nephilim would have destroyed us if we did nothing. The Focus would have never been enough."

"You've forgotten the Covenant," Abbey said, remembering what the other Shard had told her. "All of you. You said the words. You told them to Jequn so she could tell them to me. But you didn't believe in them."

"What do you mean?"

"The One's Covenant was to protect the Seraphim. Did you think because the Shard was dead that the One would abandon you? You survived for millennia without bringing yourselves to their level."

"We used the Focus to destroy most of the life in the galaxy. We couldn't use it again, and we knew the Nephilim would return. What other choice did we have?"

"To prepare with your strengths, not try to duplicate theirs."

"It's funny you should say that. What does the Republic do? What do the Outworlds do? You race one another to be the strongest. To have the best weapons. To protect your kind, as we sought to protect ours."

Abbey paused. She had a point. War was war.

"Where do we go from here?" General Kett asked, looking at them both. "What's done is done and can't be changed. All of it. What Charlie did years ago. What I did days ago. The past is past."

He had a point, too.

"I need Ruby back," Abbey said. "My daughter is in trouble, and I need to reach Captain Mann. He's the only one who might be able to help her."

"I'm sorry, Abbey. Ruby was wiped."

"And you didn't save a copy of her?"

"I did," Sylvan admitted. "But there's only one compatible synth in the fleet."

"Meaning we can't have Ruby and Charmeine at the same time?"

"Yes."

"Hold that thought, then. I need more information first."

"What kind of information?"

"The Keeper of the Covenant."

"Who told you about that?"

"The Shard. I need to find him. If anyone knows where he is, it's one of you."

"We can't tell you," Sylvan said without hesitation.

"Can't or won't?" Abbey replied.

"I'm sorry, Abigail. It's too dangerous for you to know. If Thraven finds out, it will be worse than having him get his hands on the Focus."

"Why?"

"The Covenant is the Truth. Lucifer took it and twisted it, and you saw what happened as a result. If Thraven got the Covenant, he could turn the others against us. The Gant, the Trover, the Atmo. Not individuals, but all of them."

"I don't understand. How?"

"In whatever way his corrupted mind determined. He's already influenced millions, manipulating them to his way of thinking. If he had the Covenant, he would be able to convince them he had irrefutable proof of his words, whether they were truth or not."

Abbey still didn't get what the original Covenant was, or how it could do that. The only part of the Nephilim Covenant she had seen suggested it was filled with details on how to use the Gift for war. But she also knew what Thraven believed in. The Promise and the Great Return. That had to come from somewhere. Another part of the same source that she hadn't seen?

"Dangerous or not, I need to know. If it can help Thraven turn the other species against us, it may be able to help us turn the Nephilim against him."

"That isn't possible," Sylvan said. "We have to think of another way."

"Damn it," Abbey cursed, bringing her fist down on the desk. It crumpled beneath the force of the blow, leaving a large depression on the surface. Abbey turned to Charmeine again. "You left us to fight the Nephilim. You helped make me into what I've become." She held up her hands, facing back so Charmeine could see the ridges. "You fragging owe me!"

"Abigail!" Sylvan shouted. "Enough. Nobody speaks to my wife like that."

"What are you going to do about it?" Abbey asked. "Give me a break. The Seraphim made a mess of this whole thing, and now they won't help me clean it up? Uriel was right. He said you were a shadow. A dying, useless race."

She started for the door.

"Where are you going?" Sylvan asked.

"I'm taking my Rejects and whoever else around her who's loyal to me, and I'm going to find Thraven."

"He'll kill you," Charmeine said.

"Most likely. But at least I'll die trying."

She kept walking. She was angrier than she had ever been before. How could the two of them stand there and let Thraven destroy everything, just to keep the Covenant safe? What good was the fragging Covenant anyway, if they were all dead?

"Abbey, wait," Charmeine said behind her.

She didn't listen. She kept walking. She would have to kill Thraven now when she was certain she couldn't. She was going to die. And she still didn't know if Hayley was safe.

"Abbey," Charmeine repeated. "I'll tell you where to find him."

"Charlie, you can't," Sylvan said.

Abbey stopped, turning slowly.

"Don't tell me what I can do," Charmeine replied. "You brought me back for a reason. Now I believe this is the reason."

"I didn't bring you back for this," Sylvan replied. "I need your tactical feedback. You always said-"

"Forget what I always said. That was before Abbey came along. That was before the Shard chose her."

"Whoa. Hold on," Abbey said. "I'm not some Chosen One. This isn't fragging destiny. I was available, that's it. The Shard said so himself."

"It doesn't matter. You know about the Keeper. That does matter. And you're right. The Seraphim are responsible for this. We didn't do enough to stop the Nephilim when we had the chance, and in the end, we only made things worse. The Seraphim didn't grow the way they did because of the infections. Jubilation and Deminoss are only two of dozens that had to be cleansed."

"Dozens?" Sylvan said. "How many did you lose?"

Charmeine was hesitant to say it. She looked from Abbey to Kett and back. "Eight billion," she said at last. "The bunkers were one thing. But when the naniates turned on us? We lost entire cities. Entire planets. We left them uninhabitable to keep our failure from being discovered."

Abbey paled at the number. Eight billion? That was more than the current population of Earth. It was so many; she could barely imagine it.

"We rebuilt an entire civilization after we used the Focus on the Nephilim," Charmeine said. "And then we destroyed it. I won't do the same thing to all of these species that the Shard brought us here to raise. I will leave the coordinates embedded in your synth's permanent memory banks, so it won't be lost when I am wiped. She'll lead you to the Keeper, but know this: there are defenses in place to keep anyone from reaching him. Defenses we can't control or disable. You'll have to fight your way in."

Abbey nodded. "That's fine with me."

"The defenses were designed to prevent Venerants from entry. Don't underestimate them."

"We're Hell's Rejects, Charlie. We don't back down from a fight."

"Charlie," Sylvan said. "This isn't a good idea, and I don't want to lose you again."

"Then find another synth and bring me back. The Queen of Demons has need of this one. Your Queen and mine, Syl."

General Kett looked at Abbey. Then he bowed his head. "If this is what Charlie wants, then this is what we'll do. I'll follow whatever orders you give me, Abigail."

"Please, General. Call me Queenie."

29

"GEEZ, QUEENIE," PIK SAID AS ABBEY EMERGED FROM KETT'S OFFICE. "You were in there for hours. I was about to start getting rambunctious."

Abbey was amused by the word her translator selected. "Everything's fine. The General and I came to an understanding."

"As in, now Kett understands your fist in his face?" Benhil asked.

"No, but he does recognize what needs to be done, and who's in charge of this army."

"Reeejects!" Pik shouted. "What about Ruby?"

"I'm here, Pik," Ruby said, emerging from the suite behind Abbey.

"Ruby!" the Rejects said, almost all at once.

"It's good to see you again," Bastion said.

"Welcome back," Benhil said.

"Are you okay?" Pik asked.

"No," Ruby replied. "You are." She smiled.

"You tell jokes now?" Bastion said.

"A minor upgrade," Ruby said. "For more accurate emoting."

"Uh. Yeah. Sure."

"So are we going to go kick Thraven's ass or what?" Bastion asked.

"Not yet," Abbey replied. "We have some other work to do first. Cherub, your father wants to speak to you."

"I'm not interested," Jequn replied angrily.

"I think you should."

"For what purpose, Queenie? He made his decision. I made mine. There's nothing to discuss."

"I think there is," Abbey replied. "Trust me?"

Jequn's face softened slightly. "Fine," she said. "But only for you."

She moved past them and into Kett's quarters. The door closed behind her.

"Do we need to be worried?" Bastion asked, motioning to the door.

"No. Sylvan is an asshole, but not as much of an asshole as we thought."

"Joker, go to the bridge and tap Nerd. I want him with us for this one. Imp, Gant, head back to the *Faust* and get her ready for action. I don't just mean travel; I mean serious action."

"Uh, okay, Queenie," Bastion said. "Do you mind telling us where we're going?"

"Not yet. Okay, find Dak and get him to help you put together a supply inventory. Make sure you bring extra rations, I'm probably going to eat most of them."

Pik laughed. "Aye, Queenie."

"Void, I don't know how it works, and I don't think I want to, but if you need a refuel now's the time."

"Thank you, Queenie," Trin replied. "Can you get me access to the reactor?"

"Ruby?" Abbey said.

"It will be done, Queenie."

Trin turned and headed away, the guards behind them hurriedly splitting to make a path for her, obviously still afraid.

"Ruby, we need to try to sync up with Olus. I need his help."

"It might be difficult to communicate. The Milnet is down, and our Galnet backchannel would require that he is actively monitoring for us to make a connection. With the current state of affairs in the Republic, that isn't likely to be occurring."

"Then we'll leave him a message. Thraven went after Hayley. I don't think she's dead, but she may be a prisoner, or she may be running scared. I don't know."

She closed her eyes, struggling to fight through the worry she had been doing her best to bury. She wanted more than anything to abandon this mission and go back to Earth, but she also knew if she did she'd be doing exactly what Thraven wanted her to. He couldn't accelerate her change, not anymore. But he could distract her if she let him.

"I need a terminal to make the connection," Ruby said.

"I'm sure we can find one," Abbey replied.

They checked a few of the rooms, finding an empty one not far from Kett's suite. Ruby activated the terminal, quickly logging in.

"I am connecting to the backchannel now," Ruby said. "Standby."

Abbey found herself pacing as she waited for the connection to be made. Hayley was in trouble, and she was going to be heading off the frag knew where to find the Keeper of the Covenant, whoever or whatever that was.

"Connection established. Captain Mann is not online."

"Damn it," Abbey said. "It figures. Can you record me?"

Ruby swiveled away from the terminal. Her eye changed, illuminating and capturing Abbey. "Go ahead."

"Olus. I don't know where you are, or everything that's happening back on Earth. I do know that Thraven threatened me with Hayley, and she may be in trouble. Whatever you're doing, you need to drop it and find her. You need to keep her safe from the Gloritant." She could feel her emotions fighting their way up, trying to get the best of her. She fought against them, but a tear still found its way to her eye. "I wish I could do it myself, but you know the situation we're in. I have a plan to help stop him, but it's taking me further away from you, not closer. All I want." She paused to keep herself from losing it, waiting a moment and drawing in a few calming breaths. "All I want is for Hayley to be safe. She's a strong girl, but even the strongest are going to suffer these days, and I." She paused again. She had never felt so weak. "I can't bear the thought of losing her. I know if anyone back there can help her, if anyone can take care of her, it's you. When you find her, tell her that I'm sorry I'm not there. That I'm doing my best to be the hero she thinks I am and to save everyone in the galaxy from this asshole. That I'm thinking about her all of the time, every time I think I can't do it anymore. Tell her-"

"Abbey?"

Olus voice was crisp as Ruby's other eye illuminated, casting a projection between them. Olus was standing in what looked like a small but well-appointed officer's quarters.

Hayley was standing beside him.

"Hayley?" Abbey said, unable to contain herself anymore. Both of her eyes began to gush, the tears running freely down her face. "Oh, Hayley."

"Mom," Hayley said, waving to her. "I'm here."

Abbey found herself on her knees, reaching out even though they couldn't touch. "Are you okay? I've been so worried about you."

"I'm okay. Those assholes tried to take me, but Captain Mann saved me."

Abbey looked up at Olus. "Thank you," she said. "Olus. Thank you."

"You know I would never let Thraven hurt a Cage," Olus said. "You're welcome, Abbey."

"Mom, you should know." Hayley paused, hesitant.

"What is it?" she asked.

"Dad is dead. They killed him."

Hayley started to tear up. Abbey could feel her gut wrench at the sight of her daughter's pain, at at the truth of their loss. "I'm sorry, Hal. I'm so sorry."

Hayley nodded. "It isn't your fault. I know you're out there trying to stop this."

"I should be there with you."

"No. You should be where you are. Mom, I'm safe, and the Republic needs you. Everything is falling apart. Earth is falling apart." She wiped at her eyes. "I'll be okay. I'm sad, but I'll be okay."

"I love you," Abbey said.

"I love you, too," Hayley replied. "And I'm proud that you're my mom."

Abbey smiled. "I'm proud that you're my daughter."

"What happened to your hair?"

The simplicity of the question made Abbey laugh. She reached up and took a chunk of it, careful not to cut herself.

"I've changed a bit," she said. "It's a long story. Do you like it?"

"I think it's cool."

"It is pretty cool."

"Abbey, I don't mean to interrupt," Olus said. "The Rejects got you off Azure. Where are you now?"

"With Kett's fleet, but not for long. I have a plan to help us fight Thraven. I don't want to divulge too much, just in case."

"Understood," Olus said. "We're on a Crescent Hauler freighter, headed to a meeting with Don Pallimo. Apparently, he owes you a favor?"

"Another long story," Abbey replied. "I outed Thraven to him. He knows it was the Gloritant's fault the crew of the *Devastator* was slaughtered. Fragging Coli. I'm sure you can imagine, he's not very happy about that."

Olus smiled. "Hayley is officially under the Don's protection, so try not to worry too much about her. She's as safe as anyone can be these days."

"That's good to know," Abbey said, looking at Hayley again. "Gant is setting up a secondary comm link to connect the assets that are still loyal to the Republic. I'll make sure he passes you the intel you need to connect to it. I recommend keeping it close until you're sure Pallimo can be trusted."

"Roger. I was hoping Gant would have some ideas on how to reorganize the Republic. With the Milnet down every fleet and battlegroup is on their own."

"I know. How are you holding up, Olus?"

"Better now that I know you're still fighting." He smiled. "I'm like you now, you know. The Watchers slipped me the Gift. It's going to kill me eventually, but that's okay. I'm an old man."

"You aren't that old," Hayley said.

"I'm older than you think," Olus replied. "How are you feeling, Abbey? Do you have the situation under control?"

Abbey knew what he was referring to. "It isn't an issue anymore." She adjusted her shardsuit, revealing the Hell brand and the Light of the Shard within it. "I've got a new benefactor."

Olus' eyebrows went up, and he smiled. "Excellent. Does Thraven know?"

"He might. We ran into one another near Avalon. Olus, the Gate is finished. All he needs is a power supply, and he'll be able to turn it on and go back to Elysium."

"He has to raise an army first, or there will be no point. That will still take years."

"I'm not completely sure about that. I've learned a lot since the last time we spoke. I think the rest of the Nephilim are just waiting for their so-called Prophet to deliver, and once he does, they'll be joining him in this mess. Since you're getting a direct audience with the head of the Crescent Haulers, you have to do whatever you can to convince him to commit his assets to this war. Every freighter, every cargo ship, every mercenary on his payroll. Have them rendezvous with Kett's fleet and get them ready for a counteroffensive."

"It will be done," Olus said. "Though I think you may wind up owing the Don a favor by the end."

"If it saves the Republic, that's fine with me."

She shifted again, reaching out toward Hayley's projection once more. Hayley raised her hand, bringing it right up to hers as though they were making contact.

"I have to go," Abbey said.

"I know," Hayley replied. "Be careful out there."

"Thanks, kiddo. You be safe, too. Follow Captain Mann's orders. He's a certified badass."

"Aye, mom."

"I'll be in touch as soon as I can. I love you."

"I love you too, mom."

Abbey glanced up at Ruby. She cut the link, both of her eyes fading back to normal. Abbey felt a momentary emptiness in her chest when Hayley's projection vanished, replaced a moment later by a renewed sense of hope and purpose. Her daughter was alive and safe and away from the fighting. It was the best news she could have hoped for.

As for Thraven?

He had no idea how fragged he was.

30

"Your Eminence," Honorant Bashir said, entering the Font Room and falling to his knees. "We have word from Earth."

Gloritant Thraven heard the words despite the fact that his head was submerged in the Blood of the Font. He lifted it from the liquid, letting it run down his head and face as he opened his eyes to look at his Honorant.

"Good word, I hope," he said.

Bashir placed the projector on the floor and activated it.

"Your Eminence," Evolent Carsyn said, bowing her head. "I have news."

Thraven stared at the woman. Shapely, with dark hair and large, blue eyes. She was barely qualified for the role she had been pushed into, but Olus had killed Ruche, and Abbey had killed Elivee. She had killed his Immolent as well. He felt his teeth grind together. He was losing Gifted Nephilim faster than he could produce them.

"Go ahead," he said, waving to Bashir to bring him his robes.

The Honorant ran to where they hung against the wall of the room, next to his remaining Immolent, a neophyte who was also barely ready for the role he had been given.

"Gloritant, Captain Mann and Hayley Cage were identified outside of a Crescent Hauler launch site in California. Honoring Devaille sent me and three dropships to engage but met with heavy resistance from Republic loyalists. They prevented us from reaching them before they made it to a waiting freighter. We gave chase, your Eminence, but were unable to prevent the freighter from entering FTL within Earth's atmosphere." She looked at him, her expression surprisingly calm. It gave him a new respect for her. "Captain Mann and Hayley Cage escaped."

Thraven stood up, letting the Blood run off him while he reached out for his robes. He knew Carsyn could see the lack of manhood at his groin. He could tell that she was looking. He didn't care.

"Where is Honorant Devaille now, Evolent?" he asked, taking the robes from Bashir and unhurriedly wrapping them around himself.

"After Cage escaped, he set about dismantling the Crescent Hauler launch site to prevent other nearby ships from using it to reach orbit. Then he focused on quelling the rebellion."

"Was he successful?"

"Yes, Gloritant. While surface fighting has continued to intensify, we are making positive gains across the planet. We expect to have asserted full control within two weeks, though of course, it will take longer to put down what we expect to be numerous uprisings."

"Until the true power of the Nephilim can be revealed to them," Thraven said. "Why did the Honorant not make this report himself?"

"Your Eminence, he is still in the thick of the fighting."

It was the only answer he would have been willing to accept. The only answer that would have prevented him from ordering the Honorant's death. It was enough that Devaille had failed to capture Mann and Cage. He could accept that perhaps the fighting around the launch site was too intense. Barely.

"Your Eminence, what of Captain Mann and the girl?" Carsyn asked.

Besides, he already knew where they were headed. Don Pallimo believed his alias was a well-kept secret. He believed he was untouchable. Untraceable.

He was wrong.

"Don't concern yourself with them," Thraven replied. "I know where they're headed."

"As you say, your Eminence," Evolent Carsyn said, bowing her head.

"Do you have anything else to report?"

"No, Gloritant."

"Then continue on the path I have set for you, which is the path the Father has set for me. Glory and honor, Evolent Carsyn."

"Glory and honor," Carsyn said.

The link disconnected and the projection vanished.

"Honorant Bashir, how long until we reach the Gate?"

"We will arrive very soon, Gloritant," Bashir replied.

Thraven crossed the room, heading for the exit. His replacement Immolent trailed behind him, a few steps too far. He noticed the error, reaching out with the Gift and taking hold of the Immolent's mind, pulling him forward like a misbehaving animal. He had been a Lesser before, so in a sense he was.

"Connect me with Honorant Freich," he said.

"Yes, Gloritant."

Bashir returned to the projector, using it to open a channel to the *Asmodeus*, one of the remaining Nephilim ships traveling beside the *Promise*.

"Your Eminence," Freich said when Thraven's projection appeared on the bridge of the warship. "How may I honor you?"

"Honorant Freich," Thraven said. "We are nearly at the Gate. When we arrive, I want you to take your ship and set a course for Gamlin."

"Gamlin, Gloritant? I didn't think that world was part of our strategy."

"It wasn't until Olus Mann escaped from Earth with Cage's offspring. He's heading there in a Crescent Hauler freighter to meet with Don Pallimo."

"Are you certain, Gloritant?"

Thraven's face twisted, and he started to raise his hand to choke the Honorant for his question. He stayed himself. There was no need. Not yet.

"Very," he replied. "Are you familiar with Korvin Layle?"

"I've heard the name before, Gloritant. He's an inventor if I'm not mistaken."

"Yes. He's also known as Don Pallimo, though it would be very difficult for anyone else to prove."

Thraven could tell that Freich wanted to ask if he was sure again, but the Lesser smartly held his tongue.

He has an estate near the edge of the city," Thraven continued. "Do I need to say more?"

"No, Gloritant. It will be as you command."

"Good."

He didn't even have to signal Bashir. The Honorant knew when to cut the link.

"Return to the bridge," Thraven said. "I will join you there in time for our arrival."

"Yes, Gloritant," Bashir replied, falling to his knees again before retreating from the room.

Thraven turned to his Immolent, looking at him closely. He was still too mindful. He would need to do more to break him before he would be ready.

But not yet. They would be arriving at the Gate within minutes. He had been waiting millennia for this moment, and he wasn't going to miss it.

He hurried to his quarters, quickly dressing himself in his finest uniform, including the sash he had received when he had been ordained an official Prophet of the Nephilim. He checked his reflection, smiling at himself with a pleasure he rarely felt, adjusting the sash across his chest and then making his way toward the bridge. His Immolent didn't fail him again, following close behind.

The *Promise* was still in FTL when he reached the bridge, the crew standing at attention as Bashir announced him. He didn't grant them their release as he normally did. Instead, he made his way to the command station and then fell to his knees, spreading his arms wide.

"As you have Promised, my Father. So have I delivered."

The fleet fell out of FTL, quickly clearing the disterium cloud it left behind. Thraven's arms shook with excitement as the Elysium Gate came into view ahead.

"Let this Gate be a symbol of our devotion to you, and to your cause. Let this moment be a mark in history as the moment the Nephilim began to fulfill your Promise to free all of our brothers and sisters from the tyranny of the One."

He looked out at the Gate. It was massive. Bigger than he had even imagined. That he had managed to get it made in secret over the last twenty years was a testament to his perseverance and cunning, as well as the loyalty of his true followers. From here, it looked like a smooth ring of golden metal, but he knew it was much, much more complex than that. The ring would soon be inhabited by his acolytes, who would continue to work on finalizing the inner mechanism of the device. When the time came, it would be turned on, and with enough of the Gift's energy it would generate a wormhole across the multiverse that led all the way back to Elysium.

Back to their home.

"Glory and honor to you, Father, who opened our eyes to the truth," he said. "The One shall fall as was foretold in your Covenant, and the loyal will be delivered from slavery to live in power and unity until the ends of all time. So it is written, so it shall be."

31

"Queenie," Phlenel said over the comm. "You said you wanted to know when Uriel was awake. He is awake."

"Thank you," Abbey replied. "Get him comfortable, and I'll be by to check on him soon."

"Aye, Queenie."

Abbey disconnected the link, looking up from the report Dak had given her when Jequn entered the CIC. The *Faust* was nearly ready to go, having been refueled, restocked, and rearmed during their eight-hour stay with the fleet. They were in the best shape they had been in since Olus had handed the star hopper over to them, an event that felt like it had taken place years ago, not weeks.

She had a feeling they would need every last bit of all of it to survive what was coming next.

"Queenie," Jequn said, coming to a stop in front of her.

"Cherub. How did it go?"

Jequn smiled. "We yelled at one another for a bit. Then we embraced and cried together for a bit. We're good now."

"I'm glad to hear it."

"Gant told me you were able to talk to your daughter. I'm glad she's safe."

"So am I. That's one weight off my back. I already feel more focused on the path ahead."

"I can tell. You're looking at an inventory report like it's interesting."

Abbey smiled. "If you spoke to Gant, then you know what he's working on?"

"Reverse engineering the teleporters. Yes. He told me he thinks he can improve the range. How did a Gant get to be so adept at well, pretty much everything?"

"I don't know. He hasn't told me. There's something to it, though, isn't there? He got so upset about making a mistake. Like he doesn't think he should ever not be perfect."

"He isn't the One."

Abbey didn't reply to the statement. She didn't think the One was so perfect, either. "I've been trying to tease it out of him, but you know how he is. Always so guarded, even with me." She put the report down and stood up. "Anyway, I'm glad you showed up when you did. Pudding just let me know that Uriel is awake. Since you're here, I want you to come with me while I talk to him."

"Of course, Queenie."

They made their way down to sick bay, moving aside as Pik entered the *Faust* hefting a large crate over his shoulder.

"Hey, Queenie. Cherub."

"What's in the box?" Abbey asked. "I thought we were finished loading out?"

"Gant asked me to pick up a few more things. I don't know what most of them are. You should have heard him yelling at me through the comm." He waved his free hand and mimicked the high-pitched voice the translator used for the Gant. "Not that one, you behemoth. The condenser to the right. No. Your other right." He laughed. "If he weren't so cute, I would crush his fragging head."

Abbey and Jequn both laughed.

"Is that the rest of it then?" Abbey asked.

"It is for me. If Gant wants anything else, he can get it himself."

He went to the end of the corridor and dropped the crate on the floor, in front of the space Gant had claimed for his workshop.

Abbey turned back to medical, entering the module with Jequn behind her. Phlenel's bot was standing at Uriel's side, handing him some water. Phlenel was further back, facing away from them.

"You're finally awake," Abbey said, approaching Uriel. He looked much better. Younger. Healthier. He kept his eyes on her as she reached the end of the bed.

"I feel a lot better," he said. "Lighter. More clear. How did you do it?"

"A theory."

"What do you mean a theory?"

"I didn't know if my blood would heal you or kill you. My theory is that the altered naniates don't respond to control the way the original version does. They have a limited intelligence of their own, and when you resist them, they fight back, which can lead to some pretty nasty side-effects. In the case of the Nephilim, without the Serum they will eventually turn you into a mindless, violent monster. The Seraphim's Gift simply overpowers the body's ability to sustain it, and the naniates kill the host and themselves in the process. Now, anyway. There was a time when they went completely out of control. You already know about that."

"The Infected," Uriel said. "Yeah. I get it. So you gave me some of your blood?"

"With the hope that the reprogrammed, proper version would subjugate the others."

"I don't think it worked."

"Why not? You're still alive."

He put up his hand. "The Gift is gone."

The answer surprised her. "What do you mean, gone?"

"I don't have it anymore. I can't feel it under my skin. I can't use it. I don't think it converted the rest. I think it destroyed them."

"Interesting," Phlenel said.

"Very," Abbey agreed.

Uriel looked at the bot. "Interesting? I'm fragging normal again. Worse." He looked at Abbey. "I'm going to die someday."

"We're all going to die someday."

"But, I mean soon. Fifty years? Sixty?"

"You would have been dead already if I hadn't helped you."

"I might as well be dead. That's hardly any time at all."

"Maybe for someone used to being immortal," Abbey said. "I've barely lived more than half as long, and sometimes it feels like an eternity."

"Funny," Uriel said. He closed his eyes and sighed deeply. "Frag. I lost my crew. I lost my immortality. I lost my Gift. Is there anything else you want to take from me? Maybe cut my scrotum off?"

"Not unless you piss me off," Abbey replied. "I saved your life; you owe me. I need to know how to destroy the Gate."

Uriel smiled and wagged his finger at her. "Uh-uh, Queenie. You keep me around; I'll show you. I'm not telling. It's the only leverage I have."

"Some legend," Jequn said. "Some hero."

"I already told you I was never a hero. Someone else made up lies about me. Why should I have bothered to correct them?"

"Fine," Abbey said, not wanting to get into that argument. "What do you know about the Keeper of the Covenant?"

He cocked his head at the question. "Why do you want to know about that?" He paused. "Oh, frag. The Shard told you about it?"

"So did Charmeine. She gave us the coordinates, and that's where we're headed."

"Charmeine? Archchancellor Charmeine? She's here?"

"She was. You know her?"

"We have a past. That's all I'm going to say about it. What do you mean was?"

"The original died on Azure," Abbey said. "General Kett had what he called a configuration of her."

"I didn't think there were any of those left," Uriel said. "Do you know how much I could get for one of those things? That's real immortality."

"Forget it," Abbey said. "The Keeper."

"I've never encountered it myself," Uriel said. "There are legends about it, just like there are legends about everything. Like I said, they're probably all half-right. Or half-wrong." He laughed.

"What do the legends say?"

"The usual schlock and bullshit. Only the pure of heart can defeat the challenges and reach the Keeper. Fraught with danger, blah, blah, blah. I don't believe in the pure of heart garbage. I do believe the Keeper has some serious defenses, and if we're going there, we're going to die."

"I don't think we're going to die. I expect you to help me make sure we don't."

"What the frag am I supposed to do? I don't have the Gift anymore."

"You've still got five millennia of experience, and you know how to handle a Uin."

"Which might all turn out to be useless."

"It might. If you remember, you swore allegiance to me in exchange for your life. Your life, Uriel. I didn't promise you continued regeneration."

"I should have bargained harder."

"Probably."

"I'm telling you right now, Queenie. This is a bad idea. A bad, bad idea."

"It might be, but it's the only option we have."

"When do we leave?"

"I think we're just about ready."

"You're sure you won't change your mind?"

"Quite."

"Damn. Well, if I'm going to die, I'd rather not die naked. Do you suppose you could get me some pants?"

3 2

"Well, that's it," Bastion said, looking out of the *Faust's* cockpit viewport to the blank space beyond. "We're on our way."

"ETA?" Abbey asked, glancing to the co-pilot seat where Ruby was sitting.

"Forty-six hours," Ruby replied.

"Forty-six?" Bastion said, whistling. "That's a long way. Are you sure we'll be able to make it back to the fleet?"

"We aren't going back to the fleet," Abbey said.

"Huh? I thought we were going to visit this Keeper, and then circle back. Could you update me on the plan again?"

"Let's make it to the Keeper first, and then we can worry about the rest of the plan. It won't matter if we die on the way."

"Encouraging words. Thanks, Queenie."

"I appreciate the candidness," Ruby said.

"I appreciate the candidness," Bastion mimicked. "Whatever."

"We're on course, and there isn't much else for you to do here," Abbey said. "Why don't you go relax for a while?"

"Yeah, sure," Bastion said. "How can anybody relax around this place? It's getting crowded in here."

He unbuckled himself and stood, swinging around Abbey on the way out of the cockpit.

"He seems uncomfortable," Ruby said.

"He's nervous," Abbey said. "Most of them are. He has a point, though. Our numbers have grown since you and Olus picked us up from Hell. Erlan, Phlenel, Jequn, Trinity, Uriel. At least we haven't lost anyone."

"Airi," Ruby said.

"She lost herself." Abbey paused. She refused to feel guilty for Fury. Airi had made her choice. "I trust you can handle the *Faust* while we're in FTL?"

"Of course, Queenie. You know where to find me if you need anything."

Abbey left the cockpit, heading back to the CIC. Pik, Trinity, and Uriel were there. Pik and Trinity were sitting across from one another, with Pik's replacement hand wrapped around one of Trin's.

"What are you doing?" Abbey asked.

"Arm wrestling," Pik said. His face creased as he pressed against Trin's hand, which remained upright. He relaxed a moment later. "Are you even trying?"

"Yes," Trinity said. "You're doing well."

Uriel laughed. "Your arm hasn't moved yet."

"I'm sweating on the inside."

"Seriously, how are you even possible?" Uriel asked.

"Cut someone's head off. Preserve their brain. Integrate it with powered armor that is fueled by naniates. Simple, really."

"I doubt that. Was cutting your head off an intentional step?"

"No," Trinity replied. "I got into a fight. I lost."

"You lost? Somehow I find that hard to believe. Who was the asshole?"

"I was," Abbey said.

Uriel looked at her. "You seem to have a habit of turning enemies into friends."

"And friends into enemies, unfortunately," Abbey replied, thinking of Airi again. "Are you suggesting we're friends?"

"I was ready to kill you, and here I am. I suppose that makes us something."

"Considering where we're going, perhaps it makes you an idiot?" Trin said.

"That's a given," Uriel replied. "I think the same can be said for any of us."

"Speak for yourself," Pik said. "I'm here because I think it's fun."

"You just reinforced my sentiment."

"No, I didn't, I... hey!"

"You seem to be getting more comfortable with your situation," Abbey said, looking at Trinity.

"I'm trying," she said. "I would rather have my original self back, but there are some benefits to this form."

"Why don't you take a turn?" Pik said, motioning for her to sit. "I haven't been able to move her at all, even with this." He wiggled the fingers on his metal hand.

"I think I'll pass," Abbey replied. "I wouldn't be able to win without using the Gift."

"So?"

"So, that's cheating."

"It's okay, Queenie," Trinity said. "You can't cheat that much, I'm resistant to the Gift, remember?"

Abbey put up her hand in the same position as Pik's. She could feel the Gift responding to her, flowing from her to where Trinity was sitting. She rotated her arm on her elbow, bringing it down. At the same time, Trinity's hand was shoved in the same direction, pinned to the table a moment later.

"I win," Abbey said, smiling.

"You cheated," Pik complained.

"Void agreed to the rules. Have any of you seen Gant recently?"

"I believe he's still hiding in his mad scientist laboratory," Uriel said.

"He hasn't come out in hours," Pik added. "I think something's bothering the little furball."

"I'm sure something's bothering him," Abbey said. "I'm going to try again to find out what it is. I need him operating with a clear head. I need all of you operating with a clear head. If you have something you want to say, come to me and say it. Remember, we're family?"

"Even me?" Uriel asked.

"You're like the annoying cousin that nobody likes because he's always asking for money for selfish indulgences," Abbey replied. "But yes."

"You have me pegged already, do you, Queenie?" Uriel said, smirking. "Maybe I'll surprise you in the end."

"I hope so."

Abbey slid down the ladder to the lower deck, making the short walk to Gant's workshop. She wasn't surprised to find him in there, hunched over one of Jequn's teleporters. It was in pieces around him, and from the few parts on the ground, it didn't seem all that complex.

"Gant," she said, getting his attention.

"It looks simple, doesn't it?" he replied, pointing at the device. "I think most of the design is subatomic. Unless you can get me some fancy goggles, I don't think I'll be able to do much more than slap an amplifier on it and hope it doesn't get our body parts all mixed up."

He chittered softly. "Though I would pay to see Bastion react to having one of Pik's legs."

"I take it the *Brimstone* didn't have any fancy goggles?"

"Unfortunately, no. One of the Seedships might have, but we were in a hurry."

"Gant, we should talk."

"Not this again."

"You've been sulking since you entered the wrong code for the subnet. It's pretty much the most basic mistake anyone can make, and you're treating it like the end of the world."

Gant stared at her, reminding her how adorable his face was. He looked away.

"Gant, we're supposed to be friends. Best friends."

"Damn it, Queenie. I don't want to burden you with this. Why won't you let me deal with it on my own?"

"You typed a key wrong. Why is that a burden?"

"It's not about the typo, Queenie."

"Well, duh. We're in this together, Gant. All of us, but especially you and me. We can't run away from this, but maybe we can fight it together."

"You can't help me," he said. He still wouldn't look at her.

"Maybe I can?" she replied, putting a hand on his shoulder.

He spun around, pulling himself away. "I'm dying, okay?" he growled.

"What? How can you know that?"

He stared at her, backing up a few steps. "I'm sorry, Queenie." He looked at the ground. Then he looked back at her. "There's a reason most Gant don't leave our homeworld. We're simple creatures." He tapped his head. "Simple minded. Most of us have no sense of adventure, no desire to do very much with our lives."

"You're not like that."

"Not completely. I had some spirit for adventure, but otherwise, I wasn't all that bright. Maybe leaving was proof." He forced a laugh. "I joined the Republic Navy as an Engineer. I wasn't a particularly good Engineer, either. Some stuff happened, blah, blah, blah. I wound up getting transferred to a research facility somewhere in the Fringe, along with a few hundred Gant who had been taken off Ganemant. I found out later they were sold to the Republic Armed Services."

"Sold? That's illegal."

"Simple-minded," Gant repeated. "Easy to trick. Easy to manipulate. Anyway, the Republic was trying to make us smarter. To what end, I'm not sure. I was in a separate group with the Gant they considered more advanced, I guess because we left home base. Not that it mattered. They started experimenting on us. All of us. Injections, mostly."

"The Gift?" Abbey said.

Gant shook his head. "It would fit nicely with our current narrative, wouldn't it? I don't think so. The liquid definitely wasn't blood."

"That doesn't mean it didn't have to do with the Gift. You're immune to it. Like, completely immune. It won't even touch you."

"Oh, that. We have stories about the Gift on Ganemant. Legends. I always thought they were bullshit until Trinity showed up on Drune to kill you. It's not anger that makes me immune, though it certainly seems to come with dealing with those assholes. I suppose all Gant are immune to the Gift. Kind of the opposite of the Trover, I guess."

"That's amazing if it's true," Abbey said.

Gant shrugged. "It's come in handy a couple of times, that's for sure."

He paused a second before getting back to his story.

"Anyway, one of the scientists was a Terran woman named Eliza. She was kind. Compassionate. A lot like you. She befriended me, and you know how that goes for Gants. She managed to get me passed over for some of the trials. Trials that killed. Then she got me put on one round in particular. The one that worked. After the injection, she gave me access to the Galnet and set me loose. I found I could absorb anything and everything with one viewing. The shit they gave me turned me into a living computer. I went from being a near idiot to having an unparalleled absorption rate and intellect.

"Eliza and I got closer because of it. Much closer. I helped her improve the sequencing, with a goal to make it compatible with humans. We wanted to become the smartest creatures in the galaxy, and use our intelligence to solve everything."

He sat down. His eyes were sad. The fur on his face was frazzled.

"Then the RAS got cold feet on the program. They didn't just pull the plug. They sent special forces to snuff it out. No witnesses. No survivors. They killed Eliza. You know what happens to a Gant when their alpha dies. Only I wasn't a regular Gant. I killed them. All of them. When it was done, I didn't know what else to do. They came for me later, shot me with tranqs and shipped me to Hell. I don't know why they didn't kill me. Maybe there's a connection to Thraven there, somewhere? Maybe he wanted me to kill for him? Or maybe they wanted me to wake up and know Eliza was dead, and that I wasn't, and wouldn't be. Maybe they wanted me to suffer."

"I'm sorry for what you went through," Abbey said, moving toward him. He put up his hand to keep her back. "I didn't know."

"I know. That's why I'm telling you. But that's not the most important part. The effects of the sequencing, we never knew if they would be permanent. But now I know. I can feel it, Queenie. I can sense the intellect slipping away. The knowledge slipping away. I'm not physically dying, but I'm dying all the same. I don't want to be the Gant I was before. I don't want to live like that."

"I'm sure you won't forget everything. Maybe you won't be over-competent at everything you do, but I'm sure there will still be things you're good at."

"That's easy for you to say. I don't know if I can live with knowing what I lost. If I look at a device like this and can't figure it out, but know that there was a time when I could have."

"You can. And you will. I need you, Gant. The Rejects need you."

"I won't be the same."

"No, maybe you won't. But how do you know that you won't be better in some ways? None of us are perfect."

"I'm supposed to be. I don't want to go back to what I was before. I just don't want to."

"How long do you think you have?"

"I don't know. A few months?"

"Anything is possible in a few months. Maybe you can create another injection? Who knows? Even if you can't, you'll still be a valuable member of this team. The one thing I know for sure is that if you give up and give in, we all lose."

Gant looked up, staring at her. His expression changed, lightening somewhat.

"You're right, Queenie. It helped just to tell you about all of this. And it helps to know you've got my back."

"Will you be okay?"

"I need some time, but I think I will." He held up a piece of the teleporter. "I'll do what I can with this. How long until we reach the Keeper?"

"Forty-six hours."

"That's a long haul."

"I know. If you need me, I'll be easy to find. The ship isn't that big."

"Me, too, Queenie. If you need me."

Abbey moved forward, reaching out. Gant reached out, too, accepting the embrace. They hugged for a moment, and then Abbey pulled back.

"I'll check in on you later."

"Roger, Queenie. Thank you again."

33

"THIRTY SECONDS, QUEENIE," BASTION SAID, GLANCING BACK AT ABBEY.

He was obviously nervous, his eyes wider than usual, his eyebrows up, his forehead beaded with sweat. He had been uncomfortable almost the entire trip, even more of a pain in the ass to deal with than usual, and that was saying a lot. Before Azure, Abbey had found herself growing a fondness for the pilot that went beyond casual. Now? She wasn't sure she could handle him if he couldn't handle the stress.

But what the hell was stressing him out so much, anyway? He was an accomplished drop jockey. He had flown into the shit dozens of times. Even as a Reject, they had been in deep on multiple occasions. Why had he picked this time to be the time he started to crack? Why was he so damn worried that they might not survive?

She had been tempted to ask him if it had anything to do with her. If he had anything he wanted to get off his chest. He joked about being into her, but she could also see past that facade to the honest emotions beneath. He cared about her. That was fine. She cared about him, too. She cared about all of her Rejects, as any good Queen should. But like Gant, there was a part of him that was still distant. A piece that wouldn't commit and seemed to be causing a problem.

There was nothing she could do about it. She had put out enough fires already, and had used the long period in FTL to do as much as she could to build her strength. The naniates were multiplying inside of her, increasing her power slowly and steadily. It was a rate that would never be enough to take on Thraven single-handedly, but she had no intention of doing that right now, anyway. The Republic had to hold out. Kett had to hold out. If Don Pallimo was on their side, there was a much better chance that they could.

There was nothing she could do about that, either. The Rejects were committed here and now, to finding the Keeper of the Covenant. She had a feeling she knew what she was going to find. A Seraphim like Charmeine, with the Blood of the Shard giving them near-eternal life, charged with protecting the promise the One had made to their race. The Shard had told her to retrieve it and to use it, and she could only think of one way to do that.

The Rejects weren't going to like it.

Neither was Kett.

She didn't care.

"This is your Queen speaking," Abbey said, opening a company-wide comm channel. "We're about to drop out of FTL. You're all suited up, and you had damned well better be secured. Nerd, Pudding, are you active?"

"Ready and waiting, Queenie," Erlan said.

"Aye, Queenie," Phlenel replied.

They were manning the *Faust's* gun batteries, allowing Bastion to focus on the flying. The rest of the Rejects were outfitted in lightsuit or battlesuit, full helmeted gear with external life support just in case, strapped into the hull near the exit and ready to drop wherever they found themselves. Charmeine had warned her the Keeper wouldn't be kind to any visitors regardless of allegiance, and she was trying to be prepared for the worst when she had no idea what the worst might be.

She stood in the cockpit between Bastion and Ruby, her hands clasped together in front of her, the Gift flowing across her body, her feet planted on the floor. Bullets weren't the only offensive weapon on the star hopper. She just wished they had a starfighter or two to help them with the ingress.

"I'm going to start yapping right about now, Queenie," Bastion said. "Because I can't handle flying into this any other way."

"Do what you need to do," Abbey replied. "Just get us there alive."

"Wherever there is. Ten seconds."

Abbey pushed the Gift out, spreading it around her. Her skin tingled from its presence, her shardsuit alive with motion.

"Bennett," Bastion said.

"What?" Abbey asked.

"The fourth oldest tree on Earth. It's in California. A western juniper. Something like four thousand years old. My father brought me to see it once."

"Oh frag," Pik said. "Not the damn trees again."

"Shut up," Bastion said. "At least I have an appreciation for my father and his interests."

"I appreciate my father," Pik replied. "Well, I appreciate that I don't have to ever see him again."

"As I was saying. I remember when my old man brought me to see Bennett. It was a warm day. The sun was shining..."

The *Faust* came out of FTL in a flare of disterium, cutting through the mist and out into space.

"Oh frag," Bastion said, forgetting about his story. "What the hell?"

Abbey stared out at the space ahead of them. It was split by what appeared at first to be a small planet, but on second thought wasn't a planet at all. It had clearly been built by an intelligent race, not made from dust and time.

A space station? A starship? Something else?

"Queenie, I'm getting a massive surge of readings on medium-range sensors," Ruby said calmly. "They appear to be spacecraft of some kind."

"Yeah, fragging thousands of them," Bastion said, staring at the same grid. "And they're coming this way." He looked back at Abbey. "What did we just get ourselves into?"

Abbey could see the ships ahead, moving out from across the face of the massive structure, merging in front of it and vectoring their way.

"Nerd, Pudding, standby for my signal," Abbey said. "Imp, quit whining, start flying."

"Maybe they're friendly," Pik said.

The *Faust's* shields flared as the first of the lasers struck it. It was followed by a dozen more.

"I don't think so," Bastion said.

"Imp, get us to that station," Abbey said. "Nerd, Pudding, fire at will."

"Queenie, you might want to hold onto something," Bastion said, his hands tightening on the *Faust's* control yoke.

"I am holding on," she replied, glued to the floor by the Gift.

"Well then, here we go."

The *Faust* rocked to the side, making a hard vector that caused the entire ship to shiver and Abbey to grimace at the sudden force. At the same time, the batteries on the ship began to come alive, rotating and firing on the quickly closing targets.

She could see them a little better now. They were small and wedge shaped, with a pair of lasers mounted on either side of what appeared to be a thick forward spike. It was hard to tell as Bastion flipped the *Faust* over and dove away from the mass, but she didn't see any sign of a cockpit, and by the size she had a feeling the things were unmanned.

She also had a feeling she knew what the spike was for.

The *Faust's* shields continued to flare around them as the swarm began to break apart, swirling out ahead of the ship to cut them off. Abbey glanced over Ruby's shoulder, noting the shield levels as they continually readjusted. Power wasn't dropping all that fast for the number of hits they were taking.

"They're weak lasers," Ruby said. "I do not believe they were intended for combat."

"Well, that's great fragging news," Bastion said, his hands in constant motion as he guided the *Faust*. "Maybe-"

The *Faust* rocked hard to the side, the force shoving him against his restraints and causing his hands to slip on the yoke. They slipped for a moment before Bastion recovered, getting them back under control.

"What was that?" he said.

"They're trying to ram us," Abbey said. "Don't let them."

"Don't let them? Have you noticed we're outnumbered a thousand to one?"

"Have you noticed you complain too much?"

"Don't let them," Bastion muttered, refocusing on his flying.

One of the ships ahead of them vanished in a flash of light, hit by the plasma being spewed from the rotating cannons. Another vanished near it. Then a third.

It was nowhere near enough.

"This isn't looking good for us, Queenie," Bastion said.

"We're fine," Abbey replied, watching the enemy ships break apart and come back together, trying to get a better vector on the *Faust*. "You're doing great."

The *Faust* shook hard again, a warning light blinking on the control panel.

"Fine?" Bastion said. "This is not my definition of fine."

"How far to the station?" Abbey asked.

"Forty thousand kilometers," Ruby replied. "ETA seventy-four seconds."

"We aren't going to survive another seventy-four seconds," Bastion said, sending the *Faust* skipping away from a set of ships trying to collide with them. The ships were destroyed a moment later, hit by successive rounds from the cannons.

"Don't be ridiculous," Abbey said. "I haven't even started helping yet."

34

"Well, whenever you're ready to jump in, Queenie, I'm sure none of the rest of us would mind."

Bastion rolled the *Faust* away from a dozen of the ships as they altered their vectors to try to ram the star hopper. He adjusted their path again, putting enough pressure on the craft that it shook like it was going to break apart. More of the targets were exploding around them, hit by the waves of plasma fire unleashed by Erlan and Phlenel.

"It may be worth noting that if we expend too much energy on the targets, we will not have the necessary resources to travel back to the fleet," Ruby said.

"Gee, thanks for bringing that up, Ruby," Bastion said. "How very helpful of you."

Abbey breathed in, gathering the Gift, concentrating on her connection to it. She could sense it reaching throughout and across her body, but also into the space beyond, spreading out around the *Faust* in preparation. Through them, she could almost feel the enemy around them, hundreds and hundreds strong, flowing like water along different attack vectors, spreading like the roots of a tree. She observed the sensation for a few more seconds, absorbing the activity in her subconscious and gaining an understanding of their opponent's maneuvers. They were trying to surround the *Faust*, getting ready to launch an assault that Bastion couldn't wriggle them away from and that Erlan and Phlenel couldn't break apart with plasma.

She wasn't going to let that happen.

A sweep of her hand and the Gift flowed away from the ship, hitting into one of the lines of enemy craft, pushing back against them and forcing them to go off-course, smashing into one another due to the density of their clusters. An entire line of ships started piling up, crashing one after another and clearing a lane through the mass.

"Got it," Bastion said, noticing the new space and adjusting his vectors to get through it.

Two branches of ships peeled away, stabbing toward them. Plasma bolts started digging in, but they weren't enough. Abbey changed her attention, sweeping her hand back, slapping at the air inside the *Faust* while the Gift smacked the vacuum outside, knocking craft into one another in a fresh tangle.

The *Faust* shook, more warning tones sounding as they were hit from the rear. Bastion cursed, and Abbey nearly fell over as the ship tumbled end over end, righted a moment later by the pilot.

"How the frag do I get off this ride?" Benhil said.

"You haven't convinced me we aren't going to die yet, Queenie," Bastion said.

"Fraggers," Abbey cursed, gripping the side of the cockpit to keep herself steady and doubling down on her effort.

She used her free hand to direct the Gift, sending it forward, bringing it amidst the enemy ships, silently ordering them to attack. The space around the craft lit up in blue flame, millions of tiny fingers that reached out into the horde, a single light touch of massed energy that was almost harmless by itself but caused severe damage as a combined whole. Dozens of enemy craft burned away or fell dark, colliding with even more of the ships and creating a new lane through.

Bastion didn't miss a beat, adjusting vectors and sticking to the path, even as the enemy worked to fill it in and block it.

"They're still coming," Ruby reported.

"How many of those things does this asshole have?" Bastion said.

Abbey risked a glance to the station. A dark line of ships was still forming from it, though she could see the spaces in the surface where they had been launching from, the outermost edge of the sphere becoming more jagged as they emerged. It didn't have an infinite supply of the craft, but it had enough.

"Shields at twenty percent," Ruby said.

The shields were still flaring, the enemy lasers still picking at them. Death by a thousand cuts. Ten-thousand cuts in this case. Abbey let go of the bulkhead and used both hands to help her direct the Gift. A line of flame formed along the port side of the *Faust*, sweeping back and into one tendril of drones. A second on the starboard side did the same, holding back a sudden incoming swell. The *Faust* banked and dropped, barely avoiding a third and fourth stream, splitting the difference and narrowly escaping destruction.

"Thirty-eight seconds to arrival," Ruby said.

"We aren't going to last another thirty-eight seconds like this," Bastion replied.

Abbey sent another flare of energy out from the Gift, destroying fifty more of the drones in the process. Another flare. Another. She cut into the swarm, taking huge bites with each release, but getting the sense that it would never be enough.

"We can't take much more of this Queenie," Bastion said a moment later, confirming with his eyes what she could sense through the Gift. "If you've got a better trick up your sleeve, I suggest using it."

Abbey knocked more of the enemy aside before drawing the Gift back in, surrounding the *Faust* with it. A tendril of enemy ships reached out for them, hitting the sudden blockade and falling apart in a flare of energy, unable to pierce the shields. Another part of the swarm reached for them, and against was cast back.

"De-fense!" Bastion shouted, watching the drones being turned aside.

He thought they were winning again.

Abbey knew they weren't.

The naniates were being destroyed with each impact, thousands of them succumbing to the blows and weakening the overall structure of the wall. She didn't have a computer readout like the *Faust*, but she could feel the change in their overall strength through her connection to them. They couldn't last forever like this.

She needed another plan. Another way to stem the tide, or they were all going to die, and the galaxy was going to die with them. She glanced at Ruby on her right and Bastion on her left. The synth was calm, unimpressed by their impending demise. The pilot was grinning ear-to-ear, thinking they were safe as they zoomed toward the station.

Think, damn it.

"Queenie," Gant said, his voice nearly as calm as Ruby's. "They're unpiloted. Drones. What does that mean to you?"

She was surprised he had recognized their situation, even without being able to feel the Gift. He had been thinking about a solution and was giving her the answer she was looking for. Losing his intellect? It sure didn't seem that way.

"They're being controlled by a central command system," she said. "Or they're part of a mesh network, or they're using onboard deterministic algorithms."

"So we need to figure out which it is."

"Right. Do you have a plan for that?"

"I started scanning for wireless communications as soon as we got here as a matter of course. So, yes I have a plan because I already did it."

"The fragging suspense is killing me, Gant," Abbey said. "Results?"

"Best guess is that they've got onboard directives. The swarm behavior is individually programmed, like a school of fish."

"Oh shit," Bastion said, the *Faust* shifting as one of the drones broke through the naniate shield. It nearly hit the cockpit, his quick reaction causing it to strike the upper deck instead. The ship vibrated sharply, a loud rending sound making its way through the structure.

"Level one hull breach," Ruby reported. "Sealing the area."

"My bed was up there," Pik said. "I liked my bed."

Bastion's face had paled again, his smile gone. "We aren't safe, are we Queenie?"

"Not yet," Abbey replied, using the Gift to reseal the gap, buying them a few more seconds.

"Twenty seconds to target," Ruby said.

"I don't want to die," Bastion stated.

"Me neither," Abbey said. "Give me a second."

She reached out with the Gift, the shield losing a small section as the naniates latched onto one of the drones, sticking to the outer hull. It was flowing along with the rest of them, trying to break through the barrier, far enough back that she hoped she could break it in time.

She sent the Gift below the surface, through the metal hull to the electronic brain. She needed a way to shut them down. Not one at a time. All at once. An override of some kind. But how the frag was she supposed to hack a system she had never encountered before?

The drones swirled around them, so numerous that space beyond was no longer visible through shrinking gaps. They had adjusted their tactic, no longer trying to stab but instead enveloping them with the intention of squeezing them to nothing.

"Fifteen seconds," Ruby said.

"Queenie?" Bastion said, pleading with her to figure it out.

She closed her eyes, concentrating on the single drone. The naniates were trying to connect to it, to give her a link to the onboard systems.

It was taking too damn long.

"Gant," Abbey said. "You've been studying the Seraphim teleporters. I don't suppose you found any weaknesses in them that we can try against these things?"

"Such as?"

"I don't know; you're the fragging super-genius. EMP, RF interference, something."

"Hmm, let me think."

"You don't have time to think."

Gant growled. "You should have asked me this before we got here."

"Because I knew we were going to to get attacked by a hive of killer drones?"

The drones were condensing, compressing tighter and tighter around them, pushing up against the Gift and pressing against it, forcing Abbey to press back. Her muscles tensed, her body rigid as she forced the Gift to stay intact, to continue fighting against the increasing mass.

"Ten seconds," Ruby said.

"How can you even know that?" Bastion asked. "We can't see shit past these things."

"Come on, Gant," Abbey said.

"Vibration," Gant said. "Try vibration. Resonance."

"Try? Do you have something you're a little more confident in?"

"Just do it, Queenie."

"Imp, bring us to a dead stop."

"What?"

"You heard me."

The reverse thrusters fired, vectoring thrusters stabilizing them motionless in space.

"Either this is going to work, or we're all going to be crushed into our base atomic components," Abbey said. Then she pulled the Gift beyond the *Faust* back in toward it. At the same time, she expelled the naniates from herself, spreading them out along the inner frame of the ship.

She raised her hands, placing her fingers wide apart, pushing out against the tips with muscles tense, telling the Gift to shake the *Faust* apart. Resonance. Of course. The crystals in the pool on Azure had been vibrating, creating ripples in the liquid. The Seraphim tech used vibration in some way she didn't understand, so countering that vibration should disrupt it.

Should.

It all happened in an instant. The shell protecting them collapsed inward, the swarm collapsing inward with it. The hull of the *Faust* started to vibrate, quickly enough that a soft, high-pitched buzz was cast inside.

The mass of drones hit the surface of the *Faust*, capturing the vibration as they made contact with it and passed it out to the others as they all collapsed together. The ship creaked and groaned at the increasing pressure against it, and all of the Rejects were silent while they waited for something good to happen.

Would it? Abbey continued to reach out with the Gift, altering the resonance in rapid succession, creating a dissonance that spread across the *Faust* and extended into the enemy. There were drones right on top of them, pressing toward the cockpit viewport, and she could see when the glow of life vanished from them, indicating that the system had been knocked offline.

"Pick my nose and call it breakfast," Bastion said, watching with her as the field around them started going dark.

The creaking stopped a moment later.

"It's working," Ruby said.

They sat in silence, waiting as the vibration crossed from one drone to the next, passed on by contact across the entire fleet. Finally, with one small push Abbey shoved the closest drones away, ejecting them from the surface of the *Faust* and into their lifeless counterparts. Slowly the field began to open up around them, the dead husks cast off and left to drift in the vacuum. Slowly, the station was revealed once more, sitting massive in front of them, only the smallest portion even visible.

"You did it," Bastion said, turning toward her, his face flushing when he saw that she was naked, her shardsuit disseminated to add power to the resonance. He quickly turned his head away.

"We did it," Abbey replied, taking a deep breath and bringing the Gift back to her. The shardsuit reassembled, covering her once more. "Nerd, Pudding, nice shooting. Gant, good thinking. Imp, amazing flying."

"Thanks, Queenie," Erlan said.

"Yeah, thanks," Bastion said.

"Pick my nose and call it breakfast?" Gant said. "That's disgusting."

"You never heard that expression before, freak-monkey?" Bastion replied.

"No. I think you just made it up, and the fact that it's the first thing that came to your mind is a little disturbing."

"I didn't make it up," Bastion said defensively. "It's an expression. Seriously. Just because you never heard it before doesn't make it not so."

"I've never heard it either," Benhil said.

"Me neither," Pik said.

"Shut up, all of you," Bastion said.

"I never heard that expression," Abbey said. "It is kind of gross."

"Maybe if you were a dropship pilot you would have heard it before. We use it all the time."

"I call bullshit," Benhil said.

"Seconded," Erlan said.

"Thirded," Pik said.

"Whatever," Bastion replied. "Frag you all. Anyway, it looks like we beat the defenses."

"Not to interrupt this enriching conversation with bad news," Uriel said. "But I doubt that was all there is."

"Why do you say that?" Abbey asked.

"It didn't matter while we were fighting to survive, but do you know what you're looking at, Queenie?" he asked.

"A Seraphim space station of some kind," Abbey replied.

Uriel laughed. "Space station? No, Queenie. That's the Shardship."

35

"WHAT?" JEQUN SAID.

"How do you know?" Abbey asked.

"I'm old," Uriel replied, as though that would settle it. "So this is where it's been hiding all of this time? Amazing."

"You're sure this is the Shardship?" Abbey said. "The Focus is on there somewhere?"

"I'm certain," Uriel said. "Now I understand why the Charmeine config didn't want to share. Do you know what it means to have control over the Shardship and the Focus?"

Abbey stared at the sphere with a new fascination. "Yes. I do."

It would give them control over the most powerful weapon in the galaxy. The one weapon that had single-handedly beat back the Nephilim in the past.

"Wait," Bastion said. "This Keeper guy is on the Shardship?"

"It would seem that way," Uriel said.

"You don't know?" Abbey asked.

"Yeah, I thought you were old and wise?" Pik said.

"No one knows the full truth of these things anymore," Uriel replied. "All I have are bits and pieces. That's the Shardship; I'd stake my bank account on it. Whether or not the Keeper is on it? Charmeine sent you here to find him, so this must be where he is."

"Imp, get us moving again," Abbey said. "See if you can find somewhere for us to land."

"Aye, Queenie," Bastion said, adjusting the throttle and getting the *Faust* moving toward the Shardship.

"Cherub, Uriel, I want to know everything that you know about the Shardship."

"It isn't much, Queenie," Jequn replied. "You know it is the ship that traveled through the Gate from Elysium to this universe, carrying the Shard and fifty-thousand Seraphim. You know that it was hidden after Lucifer's betrayal to keep the Nephilim from gaining control over it and the focus. You also know the location is a closely held secret, passed down by the Seraphim across the millennia to protect it. Besides my parents, there are only three others who know it is out here, and their identities are secret."

"Is there anything you know about it that I don't?" Abbey asked.

"The Archchancellors used to make regular visits here," Uriel said. "They came to replenish their supply of Blood from the Focus, and to pay homage to the Shard. They came alone, to keep the secret. I heard they stopped visiting about eight thousand years ago."

"Why?"

"I don't know. Maybe the well ran dry?"

"The Focus is still active," Jequn said. "We can still channel through the Seedships."

"Then I don't know," Uriel replied. "Maybe they thought it was too dangerous? That the Nephilim would follow them?"

"Or maybe they lost the ability to get past the defenses?" Gant suggested. "We can ask false Charmeine the next time we see her."

"So this place has been abandoned for eight thousand years?" Bastion asked.

"Yes," Uriel replied.

"Hmm. Is it just me that has a bad feeling about this?"

"It isn't just you," Abbey said. "Something tainted the Focus. For as powerful as it still is, it isn't anywhere near as powerful as it used to

DAMNED IF YOU DON'T

be because of it. If only a limited number of Seraphim could even reach this place, then what happened?"

"The trillion credit question," Uriel said. "I'm pretty sure we aren't going to like the answer."

"Charmeine must have known about this," Ruby said. "She chose not to provide you guidance."

"Good observation," Abbey said. "She already did that to me once on Azure. Whatever is wrong with the Shardship, I think she decided to tell me where it is because she thinks I, or rather we, can fix it."

"Not because she gives a shit about us peons," Bastion said. "Frag that."

"Yeah," Pik said. "Frag that."

"In other circumstances, I might agree," Abbey said. "But we need the Keeper. Besides, I did ask for this, and she did warn me that it was dangerous."

"She still could have given you the whole story," Benhil said.

"Good old Charlie," Uriel said. "I'm not surprised. At least she's helping me to prove my point."

"What point is that?" Jequn asked.

"The Seraphim aren't and never have been the perfect angels some of us would like you to think we are."

"We are the Chosen of the One," Jequn said.

Uriel laughed. "And who says the One is perfect? Besides, if we're so great, then why did he want to make humans?"

"You dishonor the One?" Jequn said, getting angry. "How could you?"

"I'm old," Uriel said again. "And not caught up in dogma and legends."

"Cherub, cool it," Abbey said. "It doesn't matter. Thraven is our problem now, and this is part of the solution."

"Aye, Queenie," Jequn said.

"Keep it simple," Uriel agreed.

"I believe I have located a landing area," Ruby said. "Imp, I am passing you coordinates."

"Got them," Bastion said, adjusting the *Faust's* vector. "Going in."

The ship crossed the Shardship, swooping in low and running close to the surface. The outer portion of the ship was much more jagged than it had appeared from further away, with numerous dark towers extending from the main sphere. Empty channels filled the space between them, littered with now-vacant docking hooks where the drones had once been held. Threads of dim blue energy crossed the entire thing, reminding Abbey of similar veins that surrounded the Seedships.

"It looks like shit," Bastion said.

Abbey couldn't disagree. The Shardship was in bad shape, both from the deterioration of time and a violent history. The closer they came to the towers, the more obvious the damage became. Some of the structures were missing large panels of metal, others were torn from explosions, and others were simply frayed and dirty, subjected to thousands of years in the midst of space, collecting space dust and minerals that ate away at the surface. There was no part of it that appeared fresh, clean, or unscathed.

"It may all be external," Ruby said. "Sensor readings suggest at least part of the hull contains breathable atmosphere."

"I can't wait," Bastion said.

"You won't have to," Abbey replied.

The landing bay was approaching, its presence obvious now that they were close. The opening was massive, easily large enough to allow entry to a Republic battleship or three. A glowing green energy shield sat on top of it, preventing the internal atmosphere from bleeding out into space.

"Do you think it'll let us in?" Bastion asked.

"Only one way to find out."

"Roger."

The *Faust* dipped a little more, angling toward the center of the opening. They could see the bay beyond the shield as they approached, cavernous and dark, with signs of decay and distress marring the space. Piles of debris lined the corners, while dirt and grime had settled on a scuffed floor.

"It isn't just external," Bastion said, noting the damage.

"I suppose not," Ruby agreed.

The *Faust* approached the shield. Bastion cut the thrust, reducing them to a crawl. If the energy field didn't allow them to pass they would need to react quickly to reverse course before the impact crushed them.

"Slow and steady," Bastion said.

The nose of the *Faust* reached the curtain of energy. The moment it did the green glow faded, allowing them to continue drifting in.

"Whew," Bastion said, smiling. "It doesn't want to kill us after all."

"Imp, bring us down."

"Roger, Queenie."

"Ruby, I want you to stay with the *Faust*. The rest of you meet me outside."

"Roger," the Rejects replied.

Abbey looked out the viewport, scanning the bay.

What had happened here?

Was it still happening?

She spread her fingers, the Gift flowing beneath her skin, a constant tingling tickle of anticipation. The Shard had led her here. The Keeper was waiting. She was expecting trouble, but then she and her Rejects were bringing plenty of trouble of their own.

"Let's do this."

36

"It smells," Pik said.

"You said that already," Bastion said.

"At least a hundred times," Benhil added.

"Well, it does. It stinks like a bad fart."

"Sulfur," Gant said. "The air is full of it. Probably a malfunction of the atmospheric processing unit. If the Seraphim APU is anything like ours, the filters are probably decayed."

"A-pee-eww?" Pik said, laughing.

"How do you manage to spend any extended period of time around these individuals?" Uriel asked.

"I tell them to shut up a lot," Abbey replied, drawing a huff of laughter from Trinity.

They had traveled away from the landing bay, through a set of large doors which were stuck in the open position, their mechanism crumbling and dirty. They had followed a long corridor deeper into the station on foot, making good progress but barely scratching the surface of the Shardship. Ruby had estimated the circumference of the sphere at nearly two hundred kilometers, meaning they couldn't possibly walk it in a day. In fact, it was probably going to take weeks for them to do anything useful here.

Weeks they couldn't spare.

They had been walking for three hours, coming across smaller intersections along the way but not discovering anything of significance during the time. The layout of the Shardship seemed to be an aggregation of the underground facility on Azure, and the interior of a modern Republic starship. There were plenty of long corridors, plenty of hatches leading to other sections of the craft, and plenty of rooms. The landing bay they had entered through was surrounded by storage units, most of which were either empty or in total disarray, their contents thrown around as if something even bigger than the ship had been playing catch with it.

Other than that, the ship was dim and deserted. There were no signs of life. No signs that anything had walked any of the corridors for thousands of years. It might have been easier to find what they were looking for if they knew where they were going, but while Uriel could read the Seraphim labels spread along their path, most of them were faded or damaged.

Damaged. That was the part that was keeping Abbey on edge. While they had yet to come across any bodies or any signs of life at all, the corridors were scuffed and marked as though something violent had gone down in them. It wasn't just laser and plasma blast marks, but also deep scratches in the metal that suggested claws. Goreshin maybe? Or Evolents using the Gift to transform themselves the way she could? But if the Nephilim knew the Shardship was here, why hadn't they claimed it, kept it, and either used or destroyed the Focus?

And if it wasn't the Nephilim that attacked the ship, then what had?

"I'm surprised there aren't any cars or anything in here," Bastion said. "It must have taken you guys forever to get anywhere."

"Why rely on vehicles when you can teleport?" Uriel replied. He paused a moment. "Then again, we haven't come across any so far."

"They've been removed," Jequn said. "Taken for use beyond the Shardship."

"Hold on," Gant said. He reached into a pack on his hip and withdrew his teleportation device. "I amplified the signal on this one." He withdrew an extender and connected it to the device with a thin wire. "And now I can use it to scan for others."

The Rejects gathered around him while he scanned.

"If this thing's right, there are eight of them still on board," he said. "The signal is fairly weak, which means they aren't close."

"Can you get a general idea of location?" Abbey asked.

"No, Queenie. It's a rudimentary system." He unplugged the extender and put everything away. "And I don't think we should use this one to get to them. We don't know where they're positioned. You could come out on the outside of the ship."

"My bot can go through," Phlenel said.

"What if it gets beyond signal range?" Abbey said. "It won't help us if you lose it. And it won't be able to report back."

"True."

"We should stay together," Abbey decided. "I know it sucks to walk, but for now we walk."

"Roger."

"Why do you think they left the life support running?" Benhil said as they continued moving. "Not to mention, what do you think is powering this thing that it's kept going all this time?"

"Stories of Elysium suggest the One's power source is infinite," Jequn said. "As is the reactor on the Shardship."

"Another reason for Thraven to want it," Abbey said.

They kept walking, with two more hours passing before Abbey called for them to pause.

"Ruby, how are things looking back your way?" she asked, thankful the comm link was still strong.

"No activity to speak of, Queenie," Ruby replied. "Sensor readings haven't changed since we arrived."

"No news is good news, right? Keep me posted."

"Aye, Queenie."

"Hey, Queenie." Pik's voice echoed along the corridor. "Come check this out."

Abbey looked down the hallway. Where the hell had he gone?

The Trover appeared a moment later, leaning out of a doorway a hundred meters distant. "Over here."

Abbey walked over to him, the others trailing dutifully behind her. She hadn't explicitly ordered them not to touch anything, which she realized now was a mistake.

"Check this shit out," Pik said, moving back into the room.

Abbey entered, scanning it quickly. It appeared to be another storage area. There were hundreds of cabinets lining the walls, many of them hanging open, their contents distributed across the floor.

Crystals. Hundreds and hundreds of crystals. They ranged across the spectrum of colors, shapes, and sizes, from pure white to purple to red and green. Some were cracked. Others had been pulverized, their dust underlying the larger shards.

Shards. The word didn't pass Abbey's thoughts unnoticed. But what did it mean?

"Isn't it pretty?" Pik asked. "I thought you'd like it."

"This place looks like somebody ransacked it," Benhil said, peeking in.

"I saw similar crystals on Azure," Abbey said. "Submerged in a liquid of some kind and set to vibrate. They opened a portal to another universe. That's where I spoke to the living Shard."

"Do you think someone came looking for the supplies they needed to make their own portal?" Trinity asked.

"I don't know," Abbey replied. "If the Seraphim had these already, why would they need to rip this place apart? They appear to have been organized at some point."

"Somebody got into a fight with somebody," Uriel said. "The evidence is everywhere. I'm willing to guess whoever the aggressor was, they were looking for something in here and didn't have access to the catalog."

"I wonder if they found what they were looking for?" Jequn said.

"We haven't found what we're looking for," Abbey replied. She had a feeling this mess meant something, but she didn't know what. "Let's keep moving."

"Queenie," Bastion said. "I have to tell you. This place is huge, and we're looking for one guy who, judging by the evidence, may already be dead. Are you sure we're doing the right thing being here?"

"As sure as I can be," Abbey replied. "But you're right. We can't keep walking indefinitely. New plan. Gant, break out the teleporter again."

"I thought you didn't want us to split up?" Gant said as he began unpacking it.

"I changed my mind. I'm allowed. I'll go through and take a look around, and come right back."

"One of us should go," Pik said. "It could be dangerous, and we need you alive."

"I have the best chance of survival," Abbey said. "I'm not risking any of you on this."

Gant placed the teleporter on the floor and pressed the button to activate it. A moment later, the light on it turned green.

"Link established," he said.

Abbey took a step toward it.

"Queenie, wait," Trinity said. "I should go. I can survive more easily in a vacuum than you, and I'm more expendable."

"I won't ask you to do that," Abbey said. "This is my idea. I'll take the risk."

"You aren't asking," Trin replied. "I'm volunteering."

Abbey looked at Trinity. She knew her former enemy was eager to help, and she was just as capable of surviving extreme environments. More so, because she didn't need to expend extra energy to do it.

"Okay," Abbey said. "Go in, look around, get out, report. I'm counting to ten, and you had better be-"

She didn't get to finish her sentence.

Trinity didn't get to go through the teleporter.

Something came through to them.

37

IT WAS ONLY SLIGHTLY LARGER THAN GANT. IT WAS MOTTLED AND GRAY, hairless, naked but lacking in genitalia, with large hands that ended in long claws and a bow-legged posture that kept it low to the ground. It stepped through the teleporter almost calmly, but when it saw the Rejects in front of it, it shrieked and jumped at Trinity.

The blades sprang from her wrists, and she slashed the creature as it tried to slash at her, its claws digging at her faceplate and somehow leaving a deep gouge along the armor. It toppled to the ground, its head rolling away from its body, blood pooling around it.

"What the frag?" Bastion said, bringing his rifle up and pointing it at the teleporter. The other Rejects did the same.

"Gant, shut it down," Abbey said.

Another creature came through, moving faster than the first, bouncing away as they opened fire. It landed beside them, turning and springing at Benhil. He cursed, swinging his rifle and catching it in the face, knocking it to the side. It got up, taken out by a series of rounds that tore its body in half.

The teleporter switched off. Gant picked it up.

"Shit," Bastion said. "That was not funny."

Trinity had her hand up to the faceplate, feeling the damage. Abbey could tell that it matched the marks from the corridor.

"It shouldn't have been able to get through this," she said.

"What are those things?" Erlan asked.

"Nothing I've ever seen or read about," Gant said.

"They came through the teleporter like they were just waiting for it to activate," Uriel said.

"You're right," Abbey agreed. "And I hate that you're right."

Something made a noise somewhere in the ship. A sharp echo that reverberated through the corridor until it reached them. It was repeated a moment later.

"They know we're here," Jequn said.

"Queenie," Ruby said.

"Let me guess," Abbey replied. "Sensors are picking something up?"

"Yes, Queenie. Many somethings."

"This place was overrun," Bastion said. "There's no way the Keeper is still alive. We should get the hell out of here while we can."

"We aren't leaving," Abbey said. "Keeper or not. If this is the Shard-ship, the Focus is in here somewhere."

"So?"

"Have you been paying attention at all?"

Bastion shrugged.

"Let's move, Rejects," Abbey said, turning in the direction of the noise.

"Wait," Benhil said. "We're going to them?"

"Something's been keeping them alive in here," Abbey said. "Possibly for thousands of years, and it isn't fresh meat. The reactor? The Focus? Whatever it is, I want to see it."

"You're the boss," Pik said, hefting his rifle. "It's fragging time!"

"Ruby, pass the data across," Abbey said. "Give us as much as you can."

"Transferring now," Ruby replied.

Abbey's eyes filled with a red splotch of color as the *Faust's* sensor data was passed over their network to the entire team's Tactical Command Units. Without a map of the area, the threat display was vague, but it at least provided some indication of the enemy's position. The system would refine the results once they made visual contact.

They moved down the corridor at a light run, heading toward the oncoming mass, which began to tighten up as it entered the same hallway. The noises grew louder ahead, scraping and howling and behind it a more rhythmic cadence. It was that secondary noise that caught Abbey's attention. Two different patterns suggested two different types of targets. The first creatures they had seen were simple, but they had no idea what kind of technology this enemy might possess.

On second thought, maybe they shouldn't be running headlong into them?

It was too late to change tactics. The first of the targets came into view of her TCU a moment later, painted with a red outline by the naniates that had replaced her human-made SoC. That target fell as a single burst of rounds met it.

Two more targets were outlined. Two more targets fell. The Rejects fired with precision, cutting the creatures down as they charged toward one another, killing them by the dozen within the first ten seconds of the encounter.

"Too easy," Pik said, shifting his aim and firing another burst the dropped three more of the creatures.

There were so many of them, and they continued pouring into the corridor, bottlenecked by the smaller space and apparently unconcerned with throwing their lives away. They pushed over their fallen counterparts, drawing closer and trying to spring at the Rejects, knocked away and killed by return fire they couldn't match.

The Rejects' advance slowed as the corridor ahead became littered with the dead creatures. Still more of them came, climbing over corpses and trying to attack, drawing fire and collapsing.

"I'm dry," Benhil announced, throwing his rifle to the ground.

"Shit, me too," Bastion said a moment later.

Abbey looked ahead. The only enemies attacking them were these frog-like things. But what about that other noise she had heard?

"Dry," Phlenel reported.

"Dry," Erlan said.

The volume of fire was slowing as each of the Rejects started running out of ammo. Fortunately, the volume of the enemy was finally decreasing as well.

Almost in direct proportion to the amount of firepower they were producing.

Abbey felt a chill run down her spine. Could it be?

"Cease fire," she said. "Cease fire."

Uriel, Jequn, Phlenel, and Pik stopped shooting immediately. The front line of creatures continued toward them, and Abbey moved forward to meet them, extending her seraphsuit into claws of her own and quickly dispatching the targets.

No others followed, leaving them standing ahead of a corridor filled with corpses on either side, the floor slick with their blood.

"Disgusting," Bastion said.

"At least we won," Pik replied.

Abbey glanced back at them. They hadn't won a damn thing.

"It was a trap," she said.

"Come again?" Benhil replied.

"A trap," she repeated. "Okay, how many rounds do you have left?"

"Thirty-two, Queenie," Pik replied.

"Queenie, are you suggesting these things were intended to absorb our bullets?" Gant asked.

"Frag me," Bastion said.

The secondary cadence Abbey had recognized resumed.

"Let's go," she said, rushing forward, navigating the bodies.

"We're still running toward them," Bastion said. "I can't believe we're still running toward them."

Abbey gathered the Gift as she ran, spreading it out ahead of her, creating a shield that filled the entire corridor. At first, she moved on without incident, the hallway in front of her clear.

Then the Gift flared, and for an instant something invisible became visible. It was dark and ugly, wearing armor of some kind and carrying a jagged blade. It pulled back for a moment from the impact with the Gift, and then impossibly passed through.

"What?" she said as the creature vanished from sight. It reappeared again, directly in front of her, blade raised to strike.

She barely moved out of the way, slipping aside and bringing her claws around, catching it in the neck and cutting it deep. It howled and vanished again, reappearing a moment later on the ground, dead.

"Retreat?" Bastion suggested.

Abbey looked back the other way, throwing her hand out and sending the Gift to the rear of their line. As it extended back, it hit two more of the new creatures, causing them to become visible.

"Shit," she said, watching as the targets passed through the shield and vanished again. "Watch your asses."

The first of them reappeared beside Trinity. It tried to stab her in the side, its blade skipping off her armor. She returned the attack, slashing at it, but it vanished again, leaving her to strike the air.

The second came into view beside Uriel. It nearly skewered the Seraphim, but Jequn managed to get her Uin in front of its blade before it could. She spun, quickly cutting it with her other blade before it could disappear again.

The end of the corridor was right in front of them, leading to a larger room. Abbey swept the Gift out toward it, revealing an entire army of the invisible targets as she did.

She froze, momentarily unable to breathe. This was bad. Very bad.

What the hell were these things?

"I mean, we were in Hell," Bastion said, his eyes darting back and forth, trying to spot the enemy. "But that wasn't hell. This is."

The target appeared in front of him, its blade coming down on his shoulder. He tried to duck aside, but the weapon bit into his arm, sinking through his lightsuit. He cried out, falling backward onto his rear as the creature moved in for the kill.

A bullet caught the creature in the head, knocking it back.

"Why am I the one who always gets stabbed?" Bastion said, clutching at his shoulder.

She heard Pik grunt, and when she looked, he was holding one of the creatures stuck to the claws of his mechanical arm.

"Ugly fraggers," he said, dropping it.

"We can't fight what we can't see," Trinity said.

Abbey pulled the Gift back, momentarily revealing the creatures as they moved in. There were at least sixty of them, and they weren't advancing like bloodthirsty monsters. They were marching in an organized formation.

Soldiers.

If the Gift didn't disrupt their cloaking mechanism, the Rejects would have been dead already.

"Back up," Abbey said, sending the Gift out to their rear again.

They were clear to retreat, but would be slowed by the corpses they had already left behind, a tactic that she was sure had been intentional. But what kind of monster would let so many of their own be wantonly killed?

"Get behind me."

The Rejects did as she ordered, starting to retreat as she moved the Gift forward and back, momentarily revealing the oncoming soldiers as she did. The Rejects fired at them as they became visible, and a handful of the targets fell.

"Keep shooting," Abbey said. "Cover fire. Single shots only."

They did, each of the armed Rejects taking turns sending single rounds at the enemy, hoping to slow their advance. The bullets sparked when they hit the sides of the corridor, leaving them all stunned again.

Whatever these things were, they weren't cloaked. If they were cloaked, the bullets would have hit them. Somehow, impossibly, they were simply gone.

"Frag, it's like they aren't even there," Benhil said, right before he tripped over one of the dead creatures, falling on top of it. He scrambled to get back to his feet, helped up by Uriel.

"Now we know why the Seraphim never came back here," Uriel said.

The enemy was catching up, drawing close as the Rejects tried to escape. Abbey swept the Gift around them, revealing them only a few meters away. She tried to use it to attack, sending a wave of blue flame out from her hands, but by the time she did they were gone, invisible and impervious to harm.

"I don't believe this," she said, whipping the Gift through them again, causing them to appear.

"We need to force them to stay visible," Trinity said.

"I'm open to suggestions."

"The Gift is doing it. How?"

It was a good question. One she didn't know the answer to. A mystery she needed to solve, or they were all going to die.

Or maybe she was thinking about it all wrong. Maybe she couldn't affect the enemy with the Gift, but there were other ways to use it. The soldiers were closing in. She wasn't sure if she could save herself, but at the very least she could save her family.

"Get them out of here," she said to Trinity, turning her back on the enemy.

"What?" Trin replied. "Queenie, wait. You can't."

"I have to. Do it."

She thrust out her hands, the Gift rocketing forward around her. Trinity was resistant and barely moved, while Gant wasn't touched at all. The others behind her were swept up by the power, lifted and thrown down the corridor.

"Sorry, Gant," Abbey said, grabbing his arm.

"What are you doing?" Gant said.

"Protecting my family."

She physically threw him back, watching as he hit the ground and tumbled back to where the others had landed.

"Void, go," she said, finding Trinity still beside her.

"No," Trinity replied, standing pat. "You aren't doing this alone. And you can't throw me like a Gant."

"Fine," Abbey said. "I can't stop you."

She pulled her hand down, the metal frame of the corridor making a sharp wrenching sound as it was pulled inward, folding and collapsing, creating a passage too small for the enemy to squeeze through. Hopefully, they couldn't walk through walls.

"Queenie?" she heard Gant say from the other side. She saw him out of the corner of her eye as she turned back to the enemy, running up to the small opening in the frame and looking through. "Damn it, Queenie. Not again."

"Please, Gant," Abbey said. "Go back to Kett. Help him fight. Save Hayley."

"This is bullshit," Pik bellowed, his fist slamming into the twisted wall. It dented inward but didn't give way.

Abbey faced the soldiers, sweeping the Gift through them. One of them appeared directly in front of her, and she barely got out of the way in time to avoid being stabbed, slipping to the side as Trinity skewered the attacker.

"We can't go back," Abbey said.

"Then we go forward," Trin replied.

They bounced ahead at the same time, carried by the strength of their suits and the power of the Gift, leaping fifty meters in a fast, low arc that put them in the center of the army. Soldiers appeared around them as they landed, flashing in and out of existence, making quick strikes as they did. Abbey managed to block two of them, getting her fresh claws up in time, pushing them aside and leaping forward again. Trinity took three strikes against her armor, the blades creating deep marks in the metal but not breaking through. She stabbed one of them before jumping, catching up to Abbey.

They repeated the process twice more before reaching the larger, open space beyond the corridor, a space that turned out to be an observation deck or some kind. Debris was piled up in the corners, burned and bent and decayed. The floor was stained dark. Blood? To their left, a large, transparent pane revealed space beyond the Shard-ship, empty and black and lonely. The wall on the opposite side had a large hole in it, jagged and rough with torn wires and conduits.

Abbey landed, ducking low as the enemy became visible around her. She was ready to defend herself against their attack once more, but this time, curiously, the attack didn't come. As Trinity landed beside her, the entire army became visible at once, filling the room. Not sixty soldiers but nearly two hundred, all of them holding their blades ready, baring their teeth and hissing.

"What the frag?" she whispered, holding her claws out, ready to fight.

"They must have come through that hole," Trinity said. "It probably leads deeper into the ship."

"Then that's where we're going."

"Through this?"

"Over it."

She tried to jump, to lift herself above the army in the direction of the hole.

She failed.

"What the hell?" she said, trying again, and again unable to leave the ground. "Can you jump?"

"No," Trinity replied.

"This isn't the Gift then?"

"Not any that I have encountered before."

The enemy around them began to move, shifting to the side, creating an aisle from their position to the hole she was trying to reach. Then they all dropped to a knee, placing their blades across their knees and bowing their heads.

"It appears you aren't the only royalty on this ship," Trinity said.

Abbey faced the hole, switching her posture to one of defiance, joined by Trinity as they waited for whatever was coming to meet them to appear.

It did a moment later, coming into existence already halfway down the aisle, its form causing Abbey to flinch slightly. It had a massive head, bony and rigid, that angled forward into a smaller face. Long, crooked limbs and oversized hands fed into a narrow torso covered in heavy robes, while its lower half seemed too slight to support it. It was as if someone had taken an Atmo and crossed it with a Plixel.

It looked down at them with small, black eyes, silent as it approached. The Gift began to tingle beneath Abbey's skin when it neared, drawing back in fear at the presence of the thing, and at the power that she could suddenly sense surrounding it and them. It reminded her of the Gift, but at the same time it wasn't the Gift.

"You are a Queen?" it said, it's voice entering her head in crisp, clear English.

Why had it asked her that?

"Yes," she replied.

The creature made a satisfied humming sound. "It has been so long. We are trapped here. We are hungry. You will help us."

"Why would I do that?" Abbey asked.

The creature lifted its hand. Immediately she was in pain so intense that she fell to the ground, leaning over and clutching at her head. A high-pitched whine filled her senses, her shardsuit falling apart around her, the trillions of naniates scattering along the ground at her side.

"I am your King," it said, its voice booming in her mind. "You will obey me."

Abbey's body shivered, and she raised her head to the creature, naked and bowed before it.

Trinity took a step forward, and the thing turned its hand to her, expecting the same results. It drew back slightly when she continued to move, but then the soldiers were around her, a dozen blades pressed against her armor.

"Interesting," it said, unconcerned. It looked back to Abbey. "You will help us."

"Help you how?"

The pain subsided, her control of the Gift returning, the shardsuit reassembling around her flesh. The creature motioned for her to stand, and she did.

"Follow me," it said.

38

"Frag, frag, frag, frag, frag," Bastion shouted, kicking at the wall of the Shardship, leaving small dents with the force of the lightsuit.

"Queenie?" Gant said, trying to get her to respond on the comm. "Queenie, come in." There was no answer. Gant clenched his teeth, resisting the urge to bark in frustration. "She's not responding."

"What are we supposed to do now?" Pik asked.

"You heard the lady," Uriel replied. "Get out of here, go back to the fight."

"Not an option," Gant said, cutting through the middle of the group. "Queenie needs us."

"Nobody's arguing that," Bastion said. "But what the hell are we supposed to do?"

"I'm arguing that," Uriel said. "There's nothing you can do. We can't fight those things, whatever they are."

"I'm with him," Benhil said. "As much as I hate to say it. Trying to rescue Queenie is going to get us all killed. She knew it would, or she wouldn't have kicked us back here."

"Of course she sacrificed herself for us," Jequn said. "That's who she is. That doesn't mean we should just accept it."

"It's just like you to take the first chance to run," Bastion said. "As soon as I think you're ready to stop being a coward, you go right back to it."

"Coward?" Benhil said, getting angry. "I'll give you a fragging coward." He advanced toward Bastion, fists up.

"Can you both cut the shit?" Gant said. "This isn't about either one of you; this is about helping Queenie. Whoever wants to go back to the *Faust* is welcome to, but I'm staying. I'd rather die here than live knowing I abandoned her."

"Me too," Pik said. "I'm staying."

"So am I," Erlan and Phlenel said at the same time.

"And me," Jequn said.

Benhil backed down. "I guess I'm outnumbered again? Okay, I'll stay. What the hell. Galaxy's going to be shitty to live in when the Republic loses, anyway."

"That's the spirit," Bastion said sarcastically.

"Uriel?" Gant said, looking back at the Seraphim. "You're the only holdout."

"I know Queenie wants me to be part of this motley crew, but this is suicide. They aren't cloaked. They aren't invisible. It's like they're phase shifted or something."

"Phase shifted?" Gant said. He paused and then chittered softly. "You may have something there."

"Did I miss something?" Pik asked.

"You always miss something," Bastion replied. "Phase shifted?"

"I don't have time to describe multiverse theory to you," Gant said. "The short version is that one of the theories holds that universes are stacked on top of one another. Parallel universes. But they aren't really stacked, they're kind of intermingled, but matter, as in us, can only occupy one space at any given time."

"Not following," Bastion said.

Gant sighed. "You know how if you blink your eyes in alternation quickly, your vision shifts slightly because your perspective changes?"

Bastion blinked in rapid succession, alternating eyes. "Okay. Yeah?"

"Now imagine the left eye is one dimension, and the right eye is another."

"Okay."

"Now, we're standing here, but only in your left eye. And those things are standing in the same place, but only in your right eye."

"Fragging creepy," Pik said, copying the instructions.

"Phase shifted," Uriel said.

"So what does it mean?" Erlan asked.

"Somehow these things can move between dimensions. Or maybe they're already between dimensions? I'm not clear which it is, or how it would be scientifically possible, but I have a feeling the Shard has something to do with it."

"Which is great to know," Uriel said. "But we still can't fight them."

"Not if they can stabby stabby poof," Bastion said.

"Queenie was able to force them back into our phase with the Gift," Jequn said.

"Only for a second," Benhil said.

"When it passed through them," Gant said. "It's all starting to make more sense."

"It is?" Bastion said.

"Yes. As long as we can accept a theory that the naniates are phased, too."

"They are?" Jequn said.

"Think about it. You said the Seraphim used the Focus to wreck the galaxy and deny the Nephilim. How else could something material, no matter how small, be distributed instantly across potentially infinite distances?"

"Teleportation," Jequn replied, as though the answer was obvious.

"Possible, but I don't think so," Gant said. "Not at that scale. I'm leaning more toward time dilation."

"Time dilation?" Phlenel said. "You mean time isn't relative across universes?"

"Exactly. The naniates shift into an accelerated parallel universe.

They cross the distance between point A and point B, and then they shift back. To us, it seems instant. Who knows how much time has passed to them?"

"That sounds impossible," Bastion said.

"Like magic," Pik agreed.

"I thought we weren't going there anymore?" Gant said. "It isn't magic. It's science. Technology based on an understanding of the universe around us that we're nowhere near achieving."

"Okay, I'll buy in," Benhil said. "Let's say you're right. Let's say everything is phase shitting around us."

"Phase shifting," Gant corrected.

"Yup," Benhil said. "The Gift, these assholes. We can't touch them because they're in a parallel dimension. Our right eye instead of our left eye."

"Correct."

"How do we force them into our left eye?"

"I'm going to stretch a little further," Gant said. "The reason the Gift forces the assholes to come into view is because when it's phased it collides with them and that collision causes both to shift."

"Uh. Yeah. Sure. Makes sense, I guess." Benhil shrugged.

"So to make them phase into our reality, all we would need to do is force a particle collision across parallel dimensions." Gant looked at them. "Right?"

There was a moment of silence as the Rejects absorbed the statement. Then Pik started to laugh.

"Is that all, freak-monkey?" Bastion said. "No problem. I happen to have just the thing right here up my ass. Let me pull it out."

"We're screwed," Benhil said. "And so is Queenie."

"Should we take another vote on whether to stay or go?" Uriel asked.

"No votes," Gant said. "We're staying."

"You're the brains of this outfit," Bastion said. "Do you have any idea how to make a thingie that can do what you just said?"

Gant bared his teeth in what passed as a smile. "Actually, I do."

39

"WHAT ARE WE DOING HERE?" BASTION ASKED AS GANT LED THEM INTO the storage room filled with the crystals.

"Collecting supplies," Gant replied.

"Here?"

"The Seraphim used these for something, right? Queenie told me about her experience with the other Shard. These crystals were in a pool of liquid, the vibrations opening a link from one universe to another."

"Okay," Bastion said. "So?"

"The drones protecting the Shardship were also affected by resonance. Vibrations. It stands to reason that the Seraphim tech is related."

"But the Gift isn't Seraphim tech," Jequn said. "It came from the One."

"And the Shard gave you schematics on how to integrate the naniates into the teleporters. A marriage of One tech and Seraphim tech."

"The teleporters don't phase," Uriel said.

"No, but thanks to the Shard they do output energy in a highly controlled manner. I was able to amplify the strength of that output to increase the transport distance. What if we can use that same control to cause the crystals to resonate? If that resonance can open channels to other universes, maybe it can also bring them into matching phase."

"There have to be fifty different kinds here. How do we know which ones are for what?"

"We don't. We'll have to use all of them and see what happens."

"Are you kidding?"

"Do I look like I'm kidding?"

"You always look like that," Bastion said. "How do we know we aren't going to make things worse?"

"Again, we don't. But it might be our only shot at helping Queenie."

"Assuming she's still alive," Uriel said. "She won't respond to the comm. Do you think she escaped from those things?"

"Ruby," Gant said, calling on the synth.

"Yes, Gant?" Ruby replied.

"We got split up from Queenie and Void. Are you able to track their TCUs?"

"Negative."

The word felt like a fresh punch in his gut. He balled his hand into a fist, fighting to keep his emotions in check.

"They may have moved further into the ship, beyond our reach," Ruby offered.

"I hope so," Gant replied. He wouldn't be able to stay in control any other way. "Help me collect samples," he said to the Rejects. "One of each of the crystals."

"Does size matter?" Phlenel asked.

"Size always matters," Pik said.

"No," Gant replied. "Smaller is better. It's easier to carry."

The Rejects started going through the compartments, locating the different colored crystals and placing them in a line on the floor. It felt to Gant as though it was taking forever.

Everything felt like it was taking forever. It seemed to be his destiny to keep getting separated from his alpha, to keep having to worry that she was dead, knowing what the consequences would be for him, and likely for them all.

He told himself she had escaped and was still alive. She was no easy kill, and she had Trinity with her.

"Hey, Gant," Pik said. "I think we have a problem." He was standing next to one of the compartments.

"What do you mean?" Gant said.

"This one's empty."

"Empty?"

"Yeah. I guess they used it all up?"

"You know that's the one we need then, right?" Bastion said. "That's just how our luck is going."

"I don't believe in luck," Gant said. "Forget it, just gather the rest."

Gant leaned over the teleporter, nimble fingers adjusting the wires he had added. He had to stop a few times, finding himself sitting and staring at the device in confusion, momentarily forgetting what he was doing. He knew he was losing his mind. He just hoped he could hold out until Abbey was safe.

He gathered the crystals, using the utility belt around his lightsuit to cinch them all together, splicing the wires from the teleporter and using extra wiring from the extenders he was carrying so that he could use them to push an electrical charge to each of the stones. When he was done, he turned the device on.

The crystals began to vibrate immediately, the pitch so high it burned his ears forcing him to turn the device off again.

"What the frag?" Pik said.

"I think I'm deaf," Bastion said.

"It needs a little adjustment," Gant said. "Standby."

He took a few minutes removing the amplifier and then tried again. This time the resonance was inaudible, though he could see the crystals vibrating rapidly within their tether.

"Is it working?" Pik asked.

"I think we need to find some invisible bad guys to find out," Benhil replied.

"It's a logical fallacy to assume that they're bad," Pik said. "We don't know enough about them to make that determination."

"It's a logical fallacy," Bastion said, mimicking Pik. "Where the frag did that just come from?"

Pik shrugged. "It's true."

"They were trying to kill Queenie the last time we saw them, that's all I need to know to decide that they're bad."

"Works for me," Benhil agreed.

"What do we do now?" Jequn asked. "We can't follow them, and Queenie shut us out. We can't use the teleporter either, since we just hacked it to make the..."

"Shift shitter?" Benhil said.

"Phase fragger?" Bastion suggested.

"Rainbow bomb," Pik said.

"Rainbow bomb?" Bastion said.

"It looks more like a bomb than a gun, and it's got all different colors in it."

"Can you pretend someone melted your mouth closed or something?" Bastion asked.

"Is this really important right now?" Gant asked. "Let's go with Phase Blaster. As for the teleporter, don't you have another one?"

"You said the signal wouldn't reach."

"I disconnected the amplifier from this one. Give me yours."

Jequn handed him another teleporter. He quickly opened it, exposing the dense circuitry within. He deftly added the amp back to it.

"You know, the minute you turn that thing back on we're going to be attacked again," Bastion said.

"Not if we attack first," Gant replied.

"I'm ready," Pik said, holding up his mechanical fist.

"How do we know this thing's going to take us to the right place?" Benhil asked.

"I'm connecting it to the same teleporter that thing came through. At the very least, we'll get to test the Phase Blaster." He hefted the bundle of crystals. "Worst case, it won't work, and we'll all die."

"Oh, okay," Bastion said. "Because I thought it might get really bad. Silly me."

"Okay, take point and cover me. Joker, you still have rounds, so bring up the rear. The rest of you, stay close."

"Roger," the Rejects replied.

Gant placed the teleporter on the ground and switched it on. It remained red, and for a second he was afraid that it wouldn't connect and they would never make it to Abbey.

Then the light turned green.

"Once more into the fragging time!" Pik shouted, his voice fading as he stepped through.

Gant entered right behind him.

40

"It smells," Pik said, the moment he came out through the teleporter.

Gant was about to tell him to shut up about the smell again when he breathed in, noticing how strong the stench of sulfur had become. He wrinkled his nose at the same time he hit the switch to activate the Phase Blaster, not taking any chances that they were alone.

Something screeched and jumped at them from the shadows. Pik turned and caught it with his metal hand, crushing it and throwing it down. Another of the reptilian creatures. An entire group of them peeled away from the walls, moving in response to the suddenly active teleporter.

"I don't see any of those other ones," Pik said, stepping out of the way so the rest of the Rejects could get through the teleporter. He walked toward the creatures, a big smile on his face. They hissed and pounced, and he knocked them aside, battering them into quick submission.

"Either they aren't home, or that thing doesn't work," Bastion said, coming through. "But I feel like I'm about to get jumped."

"It may need some adjustment," Gant said, kneeling in front of the

Blaster. He quickly removed the cover while the rest of the Rejects filed in.

"I'll tell you one thing," Benhil said, turning the teleporter off. "I've never seen anything like this before."

Gant wasn't paying attention to their surroundings. He glanced up now, momentarily freezing in place.

"What the heck?" Erlan said.

The room they were in was unlike anything Gant had ever seen. It was large and round, with hundreds of metallic tendrils that stretched along the walls and ceiling and vanished into regularly spaced holes, carrying pulses of light with them out beyond the chamber. He traced one of them back to a tightly wound bundle in the center of the space. It was composed of thousands of similar but smaller branches, arranged in a pattern that reminded him of a nervous system.

"The reactor," Jequn said. "The Seedships are similar, though this one is many times the size."

"See, size does matter," Pik said.

Gant shook off his amazement, returning his attention to the Blaster. If it wasn't working the way he had hoped they could be standing in the center of an army and not even know it.

"Queenie, can you hear me?" he said as he adjusted the power outputs. "Queenie, come in."

They had moved much further into the ship, but she still didn't or couldn't respond.

"Gant, I'm not feeling very comfy in here," Bastion said.

"Form up around me," Gant said. "Defensive circle. Nothing gets through."

The Rejects did as he said, going shoulder-to-shoulder with him in the center. There was no sign of any more of the smaller creatures, and no indication they weren't alone, but none of them trusted it.

He adjusted the outputs and turned the device back on. The pitch of the hum grew louder, and he could see the blur through the translucent crystals confirming their oscillation. For all he knew he was creating high-frequency sound waves and nothing more. Maybe the whole idea was stupid, and he was stupid to have tried it?

The crystals had been raided for a reason, and he was certain they were able to affect spacetime. On their own? What was he doing? What was he thinking?

His heart beat faster, and he looked up at the backs of the other Rejects. He had taken their lives into his hands and confidently assembled the device as though it might actually work. Nevermind that he had frozen multiple times because he forgot what he was doing. Nevermind that he could feel his intellect degrading. In a few weeks, he would be plain, ordinary Gant, no better than the most simple-minded of Terrans. The idea infuriated and terrified him. There had to be a way to stop it. There had to -

"Gant," Bastion said, shaking his shoulder. "Gant, you with us?"

Gant snapped out of his thoughts, looking up at Bastion. "Huh?"

"Whatever the frag is going on, this isn't a great time," Bastion said.

"I. I don't know if this is going to work,' he admitted. "I may have led you here to die."

Bastion's brow wrinkled. "You always come through, freak-monkey. That's the only reason I can stand you."

"Not this time," Gant said. "I'm wrong. This is wrong."

Something appeared in front of Uriel, slashing at the Seraphim's throat. He reacted immediately, bringing his hand up and catching the blade with his seraphsuit, grunting as he was cut. Jequn was beside him, and she slashed her Uin through the attacker, leaving a deep gash in the side of its head.

Ten more of the creatures appeared around them, putting the Rejects into motion. Uin and knives flashed against jagged alien blades, defending against the initial onslaught and managing to kill three of the enemy. The others blinked out and blinked in, one of them sweeping Erlan's legs out from under him and knocking him down, vanishing and then reappearing positioned over him, blade sinking toward his chest.

Benhil shot the creature in the head, knocking him off the younger pilot. Another target swung its blade at him, the edge slamming into his helmet, digging in deep but not making it through. Uriel brought his Uin through its arm, removing it.

More of the creatures blinked in and out around them, making a coordinated effort to approach the defensive circle.

"Gant, keep trying," Bastion said. "Pull some of the crystals or something. Whatever you can think of. I know you can do it. I believe in you."

Gant looked down at the Blaster. His hands were shaking. His body was weak. For the first time in years, he didn't believe in himself.

41

KING LED THEM INTO THE HOLE IN THE WALL, INTO A SMALLER ROOM and through another hole and into what appeared to be a wide access shaft of some kind, maybe for airflow from the source pumps to the outer portions of the Shardship. The strangest thing about it was that these walls were still smooth, with no obvious means to climb without a great deal of effort. And yet, as they reached it, the King stepped out onto nothing and remained without tumbling to his death. He motioned for Abbey and Trinity to do the same.

Abbey followed the creature, trusting that if he had wanted to kill her, he would have already. She put her feet out onto the invisible platform, looking down at the drop beneath as she stepped forward. Trinity was more hesitant, but the army of soldiers cajoled her out onto the shelf, herding her forward.

"Who are you?" Abbey asked, looking back to the alien. "Where did you come from?"

King looked at her, his beady black eyes unblinking. "We are the Asura," he said, his voice always entering her mind directly. "We are carried from beyond the Veil. Called by the lure of the Dark. We hate this place, but we are trapped. You will set us free."

"You attacked us. Why?"

"We are hungry. The Dark has sustained us for many shifts, and yet we cannot be sustained eternally by the Dark alone."

They began to drop, descending slowly on a hidden platform. "I don't understand. What's the Veil?"

King put his hand out. The platform shimmered beneath them, coming into view. It was round and metallic, a technology more advanced than their own.

"The Veil binds everything. All places. All times. Once, we sought only to live in peace. But the call of the Dark is a call that cannot be denied. We want it. We need it. We cannot ignore it. The Dark lifts the Veil." He paused. "I can sense the Dark out there, beyond this prison. I can hear its whispers, even if it does not sing."

"Prison? You mean this ship?"

"I mean this place. I mean this time. You will set us free. You will deliver us to the Dark. I can feel the power inside you. You will be my Queen. You will help me seek the Dark. You will be Mother to the Asura, and we will claim this place and time as our own. That is the fate of all worlds that sing to us through the Dark. That will be the fate of yours as well."

Abbey still wasn't completely sure what King meant, but she didn't like the way it sounded. Free the Asura to do what? Try to conquer the universe? They would have to get in line.

The platform continued to drop, another twelve hundred meters at least. Finally, it slowed to a stop. Not at the bottom. Somewhere near the center above a metallic sphere where thousands of pulsing tendrils extended out, escaping the chamber and spreading like spokes into the rest of the Shardship. A power supply of some kind. Perhaps the reactor was inside?

King approached them, getting close to Abbey. She tried to move away, finding her feet planted beneath her and unable to back up. The creature leaned down, its eyes examining her. It raised a large, narrow hand to her face, stroking her hair. He drew back when it cut, turning the hand over and examining it.

"You will make a good Queen," he said, stepping past. Once he was out of range of her fists, she was able to move once more.

"How is he doing that?" she asked. "It's like I have no Gift at all."

"I know. How do we kill him like that?"

"I don't know yet. For now, we just have to play along."

King had reached the edge of the platform, and now the soldiers prodded them forward, forcing them to follow. They passed through another hole that had been slashed in the wall and into a long corridor. A larger open archway waited a few hundred meters ahead of them, a golden light flickering inside. Abbey noticed that she could hear a hum from the room, a rhythmic throbbing that she remembered from another place.

But how could that be?

Sexless gray creatures swarmed out of holes in the sides of the corridors, arranging themselves in a line and bowing as King approached. He ignored them, walking ahead of his entourage, carrying himself as the ruler he was. Abbey and Trinity followed, the other soldiers at their backs.

"How do you expect me to free you?" Abbey asked.

"There is only one thing here that I cannot touch. But you can. I can sense it in you."

Something that required the Gift. Her Gift?

"What about the others that came before?"

"There was only one other. The one who made the Dark sing. She escaped from us."

"She? What did she look like?"

"So much time has cycled. I do not remember her face. Only her name."

"Charmeine," Abbey said.

King stopped, turning around. "You know her?"

"Right now, I want to wring her fragging neck."

"I do not know what that means."

"But you can speak Terran Standard in my head?"

"I send the meanings. You create the words."

Abbey smiled. She knew what this was about. Charmeine had

come here to visit the Focus. She had decided to use one of the pools like she had seen on Azure to attempt to reach another Shard. Apparently, she had heeded the Shard's warning and set up a containment field. These individuals had been drawn to the energy of the pool, and now they were stuck.

It was a dirty secret Charmeine hadn't bothered to share when she sent them here. For some reason, the Seraphim Archchancellor thought Abbey could do something about the Asura.

Yeah, right. King could hold her in place with zero effort, and she was surrounded by hundreds of the damn things. Which also raised the question: why the frag was the field containing them the size of the damned Shardship?

King started walking again, leading them to the archway and through. Abbey's breath caught in her throat as she realized where they were.

A large, simple room. A metal block in the center, ringed in flame. A torch rested behind it. A round transparency at the front, a small volume of blood visible through it. A dozen thick cables pulsing with energy rose into the ceiling from the edges. A tube ran out into a small font ahead of the flames. There was an inscription on the floor ahead of it, written in a language she couldn't read. Seraphim, she was sure.

The Focus.

"Thraven would kill every soul in the galaxy to be here," Trinity said beside her.

"I just want to get the frag out of here," Abbey replied. She hoped the Rejects already had.

"This is the key to the prison," King said. "As long as the fire is lit, we cannot escape. You will snuff out the flame. You will turn off the containment field. Then you will be my Queen, and you will help us seek the Dark wherever in this place and time it may be found."

That explained why the Focus had been active all of these years, even when none of the Seraphim could get near it. Charmeine had at least been smart enough to make it untouchable to these assholes.

"No," Abbey said. "I don't think I will."

King lifted his hand. Abbey's head immediately felt as though it would explode. She cried out, falling to the ground and clutching at it.

"You son of a bitch," Trinity said, trying to approach. Again, his other hand went up, and she was frozen in place.

The pain subsided. Abbey rested on her knees, looking at the Asura leader. His Gift, or whatever it was, dwarfed hers. Perhaps it even dwarfed Thraven's. How had Charmeine escaped from this?

"You will do what I command," King said. "Or I will do much worse than kill you."

Abbey pushed herself to her feet. What choices did she have? Suffer excruciating pain for who knew how long, or turn off the containment field and let the Asura loose on the galaxy? With her as their Queen. Who could forget that part? She had a feeling there would be pain involved in that one, too.

Charmeine had delivered her here. She hadn't mentioned the Asura. Why? How would knowing about them ahead of time have changed things? How was she different than anyone else? What made her special?

Of course, she knew what made her special. The Light of the Shard had cleansed her. Her Gift was pure.

And now King wanted her to approach the Focus.

He wanted her to turn it off.

He knew she could touch it. Did he know what she could do with it?

Obviously not.

She forced herself to stay calm, to appear reluctant. She considered denying him again, to be sure he wouldn't suspect. She didn't want to go through that pain again. Instead, she bowed her head, moving slowly toward the Focus.

"Yes. Step through the inferno. Shut down the field. The Dark is calling to us, and we to it."

Had Charmeine known this would happen? Had the Seraphim set her up? Had she set King up?

Maybe she wasn't as much of a bitch as Abbey had been starting to think.

She reached the flames, looking down into them. She could see the red line of blood at the bottom of the fire, blood that had come directly from the Shard. The naniates within produced the flame in an endless fountain of regeneration. The Focus had lost much of its power over the years. At least, that's what Charmeine had said. Because of this?

"Step through," King said. "It can't harm you."

Not can't. Won't. Abbey reached her hand into the fire, watching as it shifted to avoid her. She smiled, her back to King, crossing the threshold of the inferno and reaching the Focus. She stood in front of it and looked down. The body of the Shard was visible beneath a transparent plate. Tubes ran in and out of his corpse, carrying his blood, recycling it within him. His chest rose and fell, shocking her. Was he alive? That couldn't be. She could see the stab wound in his side, a constant trickle of blood draining out, collected and re-inserted. Something was making the Shard's body move for him, keeping the blood fresh. Keeping the naniates alive.

"Turn it off," King said. She could tell he had moved closer, as close as he dared to approach.

She continued looking at the Shard. He was indistinguishable from a human. Handsome, with brown hair and a chiseled jaw. He seemed peaceful. He had been peaceful, refusing violence even after violence had been done to him. His Light still shined across this galaxy he had helped develop, and when it had joined with her and cleansed her, it had expressed its disappointment in the Seraphim for trying to change what he had made.

"Do it," King said. "Now."

And she could tell they had. The Blood of the Shard was impure. Corrupted, just as the Seraphim had been corrupted. That was another reason it was weak. Had it been required to keep the Asura at bay? Or had the Asura been invited because of Charmeine's indiscretion?

"Now, my Queen," King said. "Please. Set your Asura free."

Please? King had turned from demanding to pleading in a matter of seconds. There was only one obvious reason why.

He couldn't harm her beyond the flames. He hadn't known before she had entered.

She examined the Focus, searching for a terminal. When she didn't see one, she put her hands on top of the tomb. Immediately, the transparency displayed a series of controls, all of them labeled in Seraphim. She bit her lip to keep from laughing. She had no idea how to turn the power off. Not that she would have, anyway.

"Turn it off," King shouted. "Do it, or I will kill her."

The pleading had shifted away almost as quickly as it had arrived. Abbey turned around, finding Trinity held in place by the Asura, surrounded by soldiers. A dozen blades pressed against her armor, ready to cut her to pieces.

"Let them kill me, Queenie," Trinity said through her comm. "Then they have no power over you."

Abbey didn't respond. She moved to the small fountain in front of the Focus. The Blood was running through it, ready to be taken into vials, ready to be brought out of the Shardship.

"I will not ask again. Shut it down, or she will die."

"Then I will die," Trinity said.

Abbey reached out to the fountain. She could feel the energy of the naniates inside it. She could feel her Gift responding in kind. She let her fingers sink into the thick, red liquid. As she did, her shardsuit began to shift around her, pulling away and entering the Focus, joining with it in its endless cycle.

Within seconds, she was naked, the shardsuit vanishing from her, the rest of her Gift abandoning her as well. She no longer had a comm to hear when Trinity cried out, one of the soldiers stabbing her in the chest. It didn't matter. Trinity wasn't going to die. Neither was she.

The King and his minions, on the other hand?

She reached down with her other hand, placing it in the fountain. Then she stiffened, her eyes widening as everything changed.

The Light of the Shard had cleansed her, and now she was cleansing the Blood of the Shard, the perfect naniates drawn into the Focus, merging with the others and altering their structure, fixing the damage the Seraphim had done. The red Blood began to change, shifting to a milky white as it passed through the Shard himself, out into the system and back to her hands. Once it did, it was drawn back into her, trillions and trillions of naniates running along her flesh, circling and then settling over her, crossing through her skin and beneath.

Her eyes began to glow, bright light spreading away from them as the Gift of the Shard filled her, draining from the Focus and settling into their new host. Her entire body tingled, alive in a new way.

She glanced down at the Shard. His body was pale. The wound was no longer bleeding. His chest no longer rose and fell.

The naniates were gone from him. The Focus was empty.

The flames around it vanished, the containment field falling away.

Abbey could hear King's laughter behind her.

She turned to face him, the glow of her eyes fading while the Gift of the Shard remained. Both he and his soldiers vanished, all except the gray-skinned creatures.

It didn't matter.

He wouldn't be laughing for long.

42

"Anything?" Bastion said, glancing back at Gant.

Gant pulled another crystal from the Blaster, throwing it at one of the enemy soldiers. It hit the creature in the chest, not even hard enough to get its attention as it swung its blade at Phlenel. The Hurshin's form solidified, becoming dense enough to deflect the blow. A second soldier stabbed at her at the same time, his blade sinking into her. She didn't make a sound, grabbing the blade in her hand and holding her attacker in place while her bot punched it hard enough to break its neck.

"How do you kill a Hurshin anyway?" Benhil said, backing up behind Phlenel.

"Our main cortex is extremely vulnerable," Phlenel replied. "But also difficult to locate."

Gant turned the Blaster on again. Again, nothing happened. It was his seventh attempt, and all of them had failed.

He couldn't do it. He was sure of that. He was going to get everyone killed. Bastion was wounded already. So was Benhil. Erlan had almost lost his hand. Pik, Phlenel, Uriel, and Jequn were holding their own, but even they were struggling to damage their attackers.

The creatures slipped in and out of phase, materializing to attack, vanishing before they could get hit. They were also patient, taking a measured approach in their assault.

"It isn't working," he barked, failing to swallow his frustration.

When was the last time he had failed at anything? Before the lab. Before Eliza. He didn't want to try to make this thing work anymore. He wanted to take his knives and start stabbing those fraggers. He could kill them. He would be more useful killing them.

"Pull another one," Bastion said. "Do your best, Gant. That's all any of us can ever do."

Gant was surprised by Bastion's calm, and his support. In Hell, he had always hated the pilot. Out of Hell, they spent most of their time arguing and bickering and calling one another names. But when the stakes were up, and the pressure was on, Bastion had his back. He appreciated it more than he would ever let anyone know, and it was the only reason he tried removing another crystal from the device.

It was still resonating as he pulled it out. A red one, large and sharp. He tossed it angrily aside, over their heads and into the distance, where a number of enemy soldiers were waiting for their turn. There was no need for them to be phased where they stood.

Gant wasn't expecting what happened next. None of them were. The crystal hit the ground, sounding an echoing crackle as it did and breaking apart. Instantly, a massive wall of flame rose from it, spreading out and away along the fissure line and swallowing the nearby enemy. They screamed as it engulfed them, burning them away in the few seconds it was active.

"Oh, shit," Benhil said, turning his face away from the heat.

"Damn," Uriel said, doing the same.

"Whatever you just did, freak-monkey," Bastion said. "Do it again."

Gant looked at the bundle of crystals. That was the only red one they had taken. What would the others do?

He reached for a blue one at the same time the enemy creatures all materialized at once, over one hundred strong. They cried out, not in anger but in a suddenly joyful tone.

What the frag? Why were they so happy?

They chanted as they refreshed their assault, coming toward the Rejects with renewed vigor and energy.

What the hell had just happened.

Uriel grunted, taking a blade across his arm, his seraphsuit allowing the weapon through. Blood splattered from the wound, and his Uin fell from his hand as he stepped back, saved by Jequn, who blocked the follow-up thrust with her Uin and then drove her other weapon through the soldier's neck.

"I think we're in trouble," Pik said, kicking one enemy away before slamming another with his metal hand. He was doing the most damage, his size and strength allowing him to keep their opponents back.

"Deposit that shit," Benhil said. "We're going to die."

Gant growled and dropped what was left of the Blaster on the ground. He drew his knives from his lightsuit and bounced past the other Rejects, using Phlenel's bot as a springboard to land deeper into the fray.

"Gant?" Jequn said. "What are you doing? Don't."

It was too late. He already had. He landed in an open area, quickly packed by phasing soldiers, who appeared around him ready to attack. He jumped up, dancing along one of their blades, climbing it to the creature's face and stabbing it in the eye. He flipped backward, rotating in the air, spreading his legs to avoid a second blade and hitting another soldier's chest. He jabbed his knife into it, hanging from it and pulling himself up, wrenching it free as he arced into the air, coming down toward two more of the enemy. They swiped up at him, but he twisted around the blades, landing between them and removing their hands on the way.

Maybe his mind was failing, but his body was still able, and he had always loved a good fight.

The enemy cried out, their joy suddenly turning to surprise. They all vanished at once, leaving the Rejects apparently alone.

"Okay," Pik said. "Now I'm really confused."

Gant turned his head, knives up and ready for them to reappear.

He stopped pivoting when he saw that the Shardship's reactor had come to life, the dim blue exchanged for a heavy, pulsing wave of energy that passed along the neurons, sparking through the central mass. Dim lights grew brighter, distant mechanisms humming and echoing.

A soldier appeared behind him, blade ready to strike. He didn't see it. He only saw Phlenel, who threw her blade at him.

He ducked his head aside, turning around when he heard the soft hiss of the creature as it nearly toppled onto him.

The fight reset, the enemy washing toward them. Gant rejoined the battle with the other Rejects, desperate to stay alive. The soldiers were different now. They seemed desperate, too. They had lost some of their cohesion and replaced it with pure fury, enough that Erlan cried out as a blade pierced his gut.

"Nerd, no," Bastion said, seeing him get hit.

It wasn't enough. The Rejects were too overpowered, and they couldn't even see what they were fighting until it was almost too late. It was a fragging miracle they had survived this long.

They didn't give up. They didn't quit. They doubled-down, working harder to defend themselves and one another. Gant rejoined them, picking up Erlan's spot in the circle, helping to keep his brothers and sisters alive for as long as he could.

He didn't notice the tendril that dropped behind them, into the center of their defenses.

He didn't see it pick up the Phase Blaster, carrying it up to the ceiling and passing it along and back to the reactor.

He didn't witness the one hundred smaller tendrils shifting the arrangement of crystals, reprogramming the teleporter, amplifying the power output, and turning the device back on.

What he did see was the army shift back into their phase.

What he did see was a figure step around the reactor, cloaked in black, with metallic skin that resembled Trinity.

At first, he thought it was Trinity.

The figure tore into the enemy, Uin flashing as it danced among

257

them. The creatures howled in fear, looking surprised when they couldn't disappear. They fell apart, then, drifting into chaos as the battle suddenly gained a much more even footing.

"It's fragging time!" Pik bellowed, diving into the masses with new, reckless abandon.

"Is it just me, or is he totally overusing that?" Benhil said.

"Whatever," Bastion replied. "Let's kick some ass."

The other Rejects followed him, pressing the attack. The enemy was nothing without their tricks. They weren't even particularly good soldiers. They tried to defend themselves, and they died.

Gant tore through the lines almost as efficiently as the newcomer, blades spinning and twirling as he flew from one target to the next, his feet never hitting the ground. He drove a knife through the neck of one, swung from the handle to the next, slashed its throat, bounced off its shoulders, and came down on a third target's head, sinking his knife into the top of it and through a thick skull. He ripped it out with the strength of the lightsuit, flipping off and reaching out with his blade, bringing it back and landing as he came face to face with the strange figure. He looked up at them; a silvery, sexless humanoid.

"Who the frag are you?" he asked, looking for another enemy to kill.

"I am the Keeper," it replied.

"Where the hell have you been?"

"Sleeping."

"Thanks for waking up."

"You are welcome."

"We came with others. A woman and a living suit of armor. We need to find them. We need to help them."

"I know who you speak of."

The Keeper turned as an enemy approached it, swiftly removing its head. It turned back, scanning behind Gant. Gant spun around. The Rejects were approaching. All of the assholes were dead.

"This hurts so bad," Erlan said, clutching at his side, managing to stand with Jequn's help.

"You will survive," the Keeper said. It pointed at Bastion, and then at Benhil and Uriel. "You and you and you are injured. You will wait here." It pointed at Phlenel. "You will protect them. Wait here." It turned its attention back to Gant. "You will follow me."

"Where are we going?" Gant asked.

"To see the Queen."

43

ABBEY LOOKED OUT AT THE GRAY CREATURES. THEY HISSED AT HER, gathering into a mass and charging.

She put up her hand, spreading her fingers wide. Energy lanced away from her, a beam of crackling light that arced across the room, striking the front line of creatures, passing through them to the next, passing through until all of them were hit, over one hundred in all. She closed her hand into a fist, and the energy vanished.

Every one of the creatures died.

Abbey could feel the power of the Shard coursing through her. He was so rich in naniates it was unbelievable. He had so much ability to destroy she could barely believe it. How had he maintained his peacefulness in the face of this kind of strength? Why had he let himself die? He could have healed himself from Lucifer's blow. She knew that now. He could have lived on, fought back, and snuffed out the Nephilim before they ever escaped the Shardship.

And yet he hadn't. He had refused violence, even with the power to command it. He had turned his back on war, even though it had cost billions their lives over these thousands of years. He had held onto a belief that love would triumph over hate.

Or something like that. As far as Abbey was concerned, the Shard was an idiot, and his ideals were bullshit.

She had seen too many innocent people die in her lifetime to ever think every problem could be solved peacefully. Maybe in his death the Shard had realized that too? Maybe that was why it had chosen her? The Light had been reluctant to cleanse someone like her. A warrior. A soldier. But in the end, it had.

In the end, she was going to try to do what he couldn't.

King appeared at the back of the room, his hand up. She felt something tickling at her, the Asura General's Gift trying to affect her. It couldn't now, just like it couldn't touch the Focus. In essence, she had become the Focus.

She started walking toward him. Soldiers appeared beside her, blades vectoring toward her in a coordinated attack. Her fingers extended into claws, and she moved with unmatched speed, slicing through them, killing two before they vanished.

She breathed in, the Gift of the Shard resonating across her entire body. The world changed around her, bringing her somewhere that was the Shardship and at the same time wasn't the Shardship.

A place outside of their galaxy.

A place slightly off-center.

A place slightly askew.

This had to be the Veil.

The Asura soldiers drew back at the sight of her. They hesitated in their assault, unsure of how she had joined them. Abbey wasn't completely sure, either. The naniates had known what to do. Clearly, they had encountered this race before.

She continued her attack, ripping through the soldiers like a tempest, cutting and slashing, breaking through their lines. They scrambled to get away from her, acting only in fear, turning back toward King only to have him push them to rejoin the fight.

They turned back toward her. She pushed with her hands, throwing them aside. They tried to return to the Shardship, and she returned with them, tracking them across phase.

"No," King shouted, the laughter gone, the joyful triumph erased.

He raised his hands, and a burst of fiery missiles poured from his fingertips, arcing toward her from every angle. She wrapped herself in the Gift, drawing it in and then thrusting it out in matching bursts of light that intercepted the attack, canceling it out.

Soldiers charged her, and she wreathed herself in a white flame that flared around her, bathing them in energy and reducing them to ash. They phased back to the Veil, the Asura General attacking again, doubling his efforts to reach her. Fire and lightning exploded from him, but she phased away, bouncing toward him from within the Shardship.

She phased back, finding him only a few meters away. His eyes were intense, and he turned his hands, pulling at the walls, tearing away jagged strips of metal and directing them toward her. She struggled to keep it away, her Gift meeting his. He was stronger, and her body burned as she fought to hold the maelstrom at bay, the naniate's needs overwhelming to her human form. She cried out in pain, phasing back to the Shardship, the Asura General phasing with her.

She continued to struggle, trying to push the daggers back. All the power of the Focus and she couldn't defeat this thing? How the frag would she ever beat Thraven?

She noticed motion out of the corner of her eye. Trinity was there, her arms and legs gone, her body still trying to move. She was badly damaged, but somehow still alive. She wasn't giving up. She had no way to fight, but she was trying to distract the enemy.

Abbey watched her for a few seconds, tracking her as though her own battle barely mattered. A new sensation wormed its way into her. Admiration. Love. Loyalty. Trinity was an enemy who the Light helped turn to an ally. One that would give her dying breath to save their galaxy from the Nephilim and the Asura.

How could she ever consider not doing the same?

She looked back at King. He had sensed his victory, and his expression had changed accordingly.

"Not today, asshole," Abbey said.

She let the emotions spread across her, into the Gift that surrounded her and out toward the slivers of metal threatening to tear her into ribbons. The world changed again, phasing in and out, shifting back and forth fast enough to make her dizzy. She didn't have time for dizzy. She gathered the Gift against the pressure, holding it there while King opened his mouth to claim victory.

With one last exhale, she pushed, shattering his Gift, breaking it to nothing. The slivers changed direction, launching back at him and spearing him one after another after another, twirling and spinning through space, lifting him and throwing him back.

It was over in an instant. Abbey released the Gift, slumping to her knees. King was on the ground a dozen meters away, his body unrecognizable from the damage she had done. She looked at him and smiled.

"That'll teach you to frag with the Rejects."

44

ABBEY RESTED FOR A MOMENT BEFORE RISING AND RETURNING TO Trinity.

"I'm sorry," Trinity said, as though she had done something wrong.

"Don't be. We won."

"I'm glad."

"Don't say goodbye, either. You aren't dead yet."

"I've lost too much blood."

Abbey smiled. "I'm almost a Shard. Watch this."

She raised her hands. The Gift swirled around her and then spread away, seeking out Trinity's armor. It gathered it, carrying it to her and then lifting Trinity into the air, bringing the pieces back and reassembling them.

"It worked for the *Faust*," Abbey said. "There's no reason it shouldn't work for you."

The naniates did their work, piecing her back together and then gently setting her down on her feet.

"I've still lost too much blood," Trinity said.

"Follow me," Abbey said.

They walked to the Focus together. Trinity leaned over it, looking in at the Shard.

"He reminds me of Ursan," she said.

Abbey didn't see it, but that was okay.

"How is this going to help?" Trinity asked. "The Focus is empty."

Abbey put her hand over the dry fountain. She was still burning, a raging fire that she wasn't able to contain. This was more power than her body was ever meant to hold. She extended one finger on her opposite hand into a claw and then used it to cut her wrist.

Blood dripped from it, thick and milky white, dense with the Gift. She cut herself again, opening the wound further, increasing the flow. It poured out of her and into the fountain, from the fountain and into the tubes to the dead Shard. Within seconds, his chest began to rise and fall again, the Focus gaining power once more. Abbey could feel her Gift diminishing, but she was fine with that. It would kill her otherwise. She let it run out until the burning sensation was gone and it began dripping red.

"Take it," Abbey said, withdrawing from the fountain. "As much as you need. It will sustain you."

Trinity's head tilted toward the Blood of the Focus. "I don't deserve this," she said.

"Yes, you do," Abbey replied.

"I'm not a good person."

"Yes, you are."

Trinity's head tilted toward Abbey. "Thank you, Queenie."

"No," Abbey said. "Thank you."

"Ahem," someone said behind them.

Abbey turned around. She smiled when she saw Gant there, along with Pik and Jequn and a new figure she had never seen before.

"You're late," she said.

Gant chittered in laughter. "You're a hard woman to rescue, Queenie." He looked around. "I assume you have everything under control?"

"Just about. Where are the others?" She held her breath, afraid to find out who hadn't made it.

"Safe," the newcomer said. "They will survive."

"Yeah, they're a little beat up, but no casualties," Gant said.

"Thanks to this guy over here," Pik said. "Wait. Are you a guy or a girl?"

"Neither."

"Of course," Gant said. "We seem to be collecting gender neutrals."

"Pudding identifies as a girl," Pik said. "That isn't gender neutral. So does Trinity."

"Yeah, but they don't have parts, male or female," Gant argued. "Well, Pudding can make them, but that's a technicality. A bit of a gray area."

"It's not the plumbing that matters," Pik said. "Do you identify as male or female?"

"Neither," the newcomer replied.

"Oh," Pik said.

"I hate to interrupt this scintillating conversation," Abbey said. "But can we get synced on current events? Maybe introduce your new friend?"

"Right," Gant said. "This is-"

"I am the Keeper," the figure said.

Abbey nodded. "That's what I thought. You're the individual I'm here to see."

"And you are the individual I have been waiting for."

"You knew I was coming?"

"Not you, specifically. I knew someone would come one day. The Chosen of the Shard." The Keeper looked around the room, at all of the Asura corpses there. "I am satisfied it was not too late, and that you were able to defeat the Asura. You are more... capable, than I was expecting."

"I'll take that as a compliment. If you knew I was coming, then you know what I'm looking for."

"The Covenant. Yes."

"Where is it?"

"Of course, my Queen," the Keeper said. "You are standing in it."

"Whoa," Pik said. "The Shardship is the Covenant? Mind. Blown."

Abbey smiled. She knew there was more to it than that. A lot more. But it was a start.

"The Focus is recharged," Gant said. "The Shardship is back in business. I assume that means we're ready to go kick Thraven's ass and save the Republic?"

"No," Abbey replied. "The Focus is cleansed. It can't be used the way it was before." She looked at the Keeper. "I don't want the Seed-ships using it at all. The Seraphim fragged everything up once already; they're not doing it again."

"As you command," the Keeper replied. "So it will be done."

"Wait," Pik said. "If we can't use the Focus against Thraven, what are we supposed to do with it?"

"Raise an army of our own," Abbey said.

"How? From where?"

"The Extant," Abbey replied.

"Thraven's backyard?" Gant said.

"The Nephilim have been holding slaves for years. He wants an uprising? I'll give him a fragging uprising. It'll be our version of the Great Return."

"Right up his ass," Pik said. "I like it."

"Me too, Queenie," Gant said.

"Keeper," Abbey said. "Do it."

"As you command, so it will be done."

* * *

Made in the USA
Middletown, DE
25 March 2021

36234172R00156